DREAM CHASER

THE BAILEY SPADE SERIES: BOOK 3

DIMA ZALES

♠ MOZAIKA PUBLICATIONS ♠

This is a work of fiction. Names, characters, places, and incidents are either the product of the author's imagination or are used fictitiously, and any resemblance to actual persons, living or dead, business establishments, events, or locales is purely coincidental.

Copyright © 2021 Dima Zales and Anna Zaires
www.dimazales.com

All rights reserved.

Except for use in a review, no part of this book may be reproduced, scanned, or distributed in any printed or electronic form without permission.

Published by Mozaika Publications, an imprint of Mozaika LLC.
www.mozaikallc.com

Cover by Orina Kafe
www.orinakafe.design

e-ISBN: 978-1-63142-615-5
Print ISBN: 978-1-63142-616-2

CHAPTER ONE

I STUMBLE out of the bathroom in Mom's hospital room and nearly collide with Dr. Xipil.

"Are you okay?" the gnome doctor asks.

I'm far from okay, but if I tell him why, he might want to have me talk to a shrink. The injuries I suffered during the fight with Icelus are healed, but mentally and emotionally, I'm a wreck.

Case in point: I'm seriously considering the existence of Phobetor, the god of nightmares Icelus worship. Worse yet, I'm wondering if said deity made my mom kill my sister.

What little blood had returned to my face rushes away again.

I had a sister. A twin.

It's as hard to wrap my mind around that fact as it is to fathom my mom killing her.

Her name was Asha, and I watched her die before I'd even accepted the fact that she'd existed.

What I wouldn't give for a chance to have met her, or to at least remember her.

"Do you want to lie down?" Dr. Xipil asks, sounding more worried. "You look like you're about to pass out."

I give him a forced smile. "I'm fine. Just disappointed I failed to rouse Mom."

Dr. Xipil glances at the bed where Mom lies and sighs. "You'll try again. You're bound to succeed eventually."

Not ready to discuss an evil deity that might be waiting for me in Mom's dreams, I simply nod.

Mom looks serene in her comatose state. Calm, even. But that has to be a lie. Her dreams are of killing a daughter—because that's what she'd done in the waking world.

In a very real way, I don't know my own mother. Makes me wonder if you can know anyone, or trust them.

The doctor clears his throat. "You have loyal friends."

Puck. I have to snap out of this, or the good doctor will insist I go back to my hospital bed.

I head for the door, and as casually as I can, ask, "What makes you say that?"

"They all recovered much faster than you did, but they wouldn't leave your side until your husband chased them away." He opens the door for me.

"My husband?" I'm too shocked to walk through.

Dr. Xipil gestures at my room across the hall. "Boyfriend?"

"Oh, you mean Valerian." I step out into the hallway. "He's neither my husband nor my boyfriend."

Not yet—but fingers crossed.

The corners of Dr. Xipil's eyes crinkle. "Are you sure he knows that? Because he definitely acted like a significant other while you were under. The nursing staff and I had to walk on eggshells."

Really? Aww. "Sounds like I should check on him."

"Good idea. If he wakes up and you're not there, he'll freak."

"Oh, come on, that doesn't sound like him."

"You didn't see what I saw," the doctor says. "If you need anything else, let me know tomorrow afternoon. My shift is now officially over."

I thank him, and he hurries away as I head over to my room.

Sticking my head in, I see Valerian slumped in a chair, his dark, thick hair disheveled around his beautifully symmetrical face. His intense ocean-blue eyes are closed, his kissable lips slightly parted.

Quietly, I tiptoe in. He's in REM sleep, according to my newfound REM-sensing ability and the fact that his eyes are moving behind his eyelids.

Hmm. Maybe I don't need to wake him. The fact that he's dreaming is an opportunity. I could, for example, talk to him in his sleep… or snoop in those black windows he's got.

Yep. I'm going for it.

Resisting the temptation to walk over and touch his

chiseled face, I initiate the dreamwalk remotely. Might as well practice the new power.

Just as I did with Itzel's grandfather, I imagine standing next to Valerian, close enough to breathe in his clean pine scent. I imagine touching his carved jaw and picture how that hint of stubble would feel under my fingers. I imagine how my heart would beat faster and heat would spread—

To my disappointment, I don't need to imagine this further, because with the familiar whiff of ozone and the sensation of falling, I drop into his dream.

———

AS SOON AS I appear in the surreally colored, manna-scented lobby of my dream palace, Pom shows up—and between the expression on the looft's furry face and his deep black coloring, I can tell he knows a lot of what I've learned in Mom's black window.

Taking the scenic route to the tower of sleepers, I fill in any details Pom doesn't know and reassure him that I don't magically have the answers to his million questions—and that I'd like to know the why and how of Phobetor and my twin as much as he does.

"Ah," Pom says sagely when he spots Valerian sleeping on his bed. "You're here looking for a distraction."

I brush my fingers over Valerian's dimpled chin without willing myself to go in yet. "I guess you could say that."

Pom's triangular ears take on a light orange hue. "And how are things going between the two of you?"

"What?"

The pupils in his lavender eyes morph into red hearts. "Are you in love?"

I jerk my hand away from Valerian's face. "Are you crazy? I don't even know what that would feel like. We barely know each other. Plus—"

"You might be overthinking it." Pom perches on my shoulder. "Is it because you've never had a boyfriend?"

I shoo him off. "I'm thinking just the right amount. You should give that a try someday."

He lands on the edge of Valerian's bed. "Just don't go looking for reasons not to love him. We both know you want to."

It's official. I'm getting love-life advice from a looft, a creature that reproduces by asexual budding.

Shaking my head, I dive into Valerian's dream.

CHAPTER TWO

VALERIAN IS SITTING on the floor in a dingy room with paint peeling off the walls. There are folding chairs and a strong aroma of stale coffee. One of the windows is black, but I don't go for it yet. This dream is a memory, and I'm curious to learn about Valerian's past.

Making myself invisible, I let the dream progress.

All the chairs except one are occupied by teenagers, and everyone is unaware of Valerian, which means he's making himself invisible with his illusionist powers. The only adult in the room is a person I've met—Princess Peach, Felix and Ariel's roommate.

Speaking of Felix, his girlfriend, Maya, is here too, sitting next to Princess Peach.

Then another familiar person shows up, someone I never wanted to see again.

Hekima, the illusionist murderer who nearly cost me my life, walks in.

He doesn't notice Valerian either, so an illusionist can fool another illusionist. Good to know.

"Today we continue the subject of the Otherlands," Hekima says as a way of introduction. "Let's begin with a quick review of last week."

He then goes over what everyone should already know—that there's such a thing as Otherlands and that they are what Earth humans would call "universes." He explains that these worlds have different stars and galaxies, and even the flow of time can vary among them. There's an infinite number of them as far as anyone knows, but the gates Cognizant use lead to only an insignificant subset.

This must be Orientation, a kind of school where Earth Cognizant teens learn about secret Cognizant stuff. On Gomorrah, we just call that school, but I can see why they'd need a special class on Earth, what with the Mandate and all.

"I alluded to the dangers of the Otherlands the last time we met," Hekima says when he's finished with the basics. "Today I really want to drive home that point."

He raises his arms, and pulsing red energy streams from his fingers into everyone's heads—including Valerian's.

The room goes away, replaced with what looks like a radioactive wasteland.

Everyone except me starts gasping for nonexistent air. Hekima snaps his fingers once again, causing the world to change to that of a lush forest.

"There are Otherlands where the environment itself

will kill you," he says. "But even seemingly friendly ones like this world can have creatures so dangerous no Cognizant would dare to live or even travel within it."

A cute deer-like creature runs out of the forest, followed by one of the worst monsters in existence.

"That's a drekavac," Hekima explains, but what he says next is lost on everyone because the drekavac catches up with the deer and touches it with one of its pustule-infested limbs.

The deer screams and collapses to the ground.

The drekavac looms over its victim, but Hekima snaps his fingers again, and the classroom comes back.

Why show these children such horror? And why is Valerian here?

"Getting killed by a drekavac is the worst fate that can befall anyone," Hekima says. "Their mere touch brings about such debilitating pain that weaker victims die from it." He looks over the horrified faces. "The environment, the flora, and the fauna are just a few of the many ways you can perish in the Otherlands. Some gates are one way only—so no one knows what happens there—and other gates lead to worlds that we, the Cognizant, turned into deathtraps."

He snaps his fingers again. The classroom morphs into a deserted landscape, where two scary-looking men are chasing someone.

"This is what's left of the world where Tartarus last ruled," Hekima says just as the two men catch their prey.

Tartarus? Now there's a figure you bring up if you want to give people nightmares.

"The humans on this world know about the Cognizant and rightfully blame us for the desolation," Hekima continues, pointing at the endless dunes. "They wait by the gates to catch one of our kind, and if they succeed, they do horrific things to them."

Right on cue, the two men start to cannibalize their catch.

That's just great. The nightmares are guaranteed now. At school, we also learned to be careful traveling in the Otherlands, but it didn't require such theatrics.

Hekima keeps on talking about the doom and gloom of the Otherlands as I walk over to where Valerian is sitting.

"The point I'm trying to make is really simple," Hekima is saying when I pay attention to him again. "Be very careful when traveling to the Otherlands, and do not enter any gates unless you're absolutely sure where they lead." The horrific scenes repeat in quick succession. "Even if you think you know the gate is safe, I strongly advise you think twice before entering, and definitely wait until—"

I ignore the rest.

There's a folder next to Valerian I hadn't noticed before.

Icelus Suspects, the label says.

When Valerian opens the folder, a picture of Hekima is on top of the papers inside. Looking between the picture and the real man, Valerian writes on the paper below, "Eighty percent sure."

Wow. Hekima was Icelus? It would explain why he made this lesson so scary—and is consistent with his murdering personality.

"We're almost out of time." Hekima looks at his watch. "Does anyone have any questions?"

Valerian leaps to his feet.

Princess Peach raises her hand, nearly jumping out of her seat in excitement. Hekima calls on her.

Someone whispers something like "teacher's pet," but she ignores them as she rattles out, "Who made the gates? Who discovered the Otherlands? When? How? Could—"

In reply, Hekima goes into the same theory we learned on Gomorrah—that the gates were made by legendary, powerful teleporters dubbed *the gate makers*. He then suggests the obvious—that there are probably worlds without the Cognizant, left as sanctuaries, or worlds where Cognizant exist but don't have gates that allow them to leave.

Finally, he gets up and walks to the door without waiting for any follow-up questions. Princess Peach raises her hand again but puts it down when Hekima leaves the class, with Valerian following.

Outside the classroom, Valerian stalks Hekima to his destination, a small apartment.

Checking his watch again, Hekima plops into his bed.

Wait, what? Why was he in such a rush to take a nap?

Valerian shakes his head, takes out his folder, and changes the probability to ninety percent.

I almost reveal myself so I can ask Valerian why sleeping on a tight schedule might make someone more likely to be a part of Icelus, but I resist.

And it's a good thing I do.

The Orientation dream stops, but another one begins, again a memory.

———

A NEARLY NAKED Valerian is sitting on a wooden slab in a large windowless room, with sweat beading on his hard-muscled body.

Yum. I like where this is going. Not that I have many options but to keep observing what happens next —the black window is missing. Then again, it might be around, but I can't see it. It's so steamy in the room—in the literal sense—that it's barely possible to see a foot away. This is clearly a sauna, a nightmare invention for those of us who care about proper hygiene.

"Illusionist," says the vapor around the room in a melodious, Russian-accented masculine voice.

"Seer," Valerian replies, looking around. "You might want to show yourself."

With a *whoosh*, the vapor gathers in a single spot a few yards away from Valerian.

Valerian wipes a stream of sweat from his eyes, and by the time he completes the gesture, the vapor is gone, replaced by a man covered only by a small towel.

Tangled blond hair and wild beard aside, this man is almost as impressive as Valerian himself. If I hadn't heard him be referred to as a seer, I'd guess him to be an uber.

Wait a sec. *A seer.* There are a couple of different varieties of them, but all are among the rarest Cognizant types—up there with dragons and healers.

The seer tugs on his beard. "You're wise to heed my summons. I have to repay the favor I owe you today."

Valerian wipes a rivulet of sweat from his brow. "You do?"

"After this conversation, you and I will never meet again," the seer says solemnly.

"Right." Valerian shakes his head. "And I take it you already know what I'm going to ask?"

"I know all the things you considered asking." The seer grabs a nearby ladle, dips it into a water bucket, and pours water into a stove-like contraption nearby. With a hiss, more vapor fills the room. "You want to know how to get rid of Hekima, the newest Icelus agent you've found," the seer continues. "And you want to do it in such a way that it can never be linked back to you—which is difficult due to your obvious ambition to take Hekima's place on the New York Council."

"I can see why your kind has the reputation it does."

Valerian pushes back his sweat-soaked hair. "You know my questions. Do you have an answer?"

"Send an anonymous email to Kain, the new head of the New York Enforcers," the seer says. "Tell him you know of the murder investigation Kain is leading, and that you have a perfect candidate for him."

Despite the room's heat, I feel cold.

It can't be.

He wouldn't.

He didn't.

Valerian frowns. "Who?"

"The dreamwalker who's done a few jobs for you," the seer says. "Suggest her, and you'll get what you want."

"You've got to be pucking kidding me," I mutter.

Valerian looks right at me.

Puck. I didn't mean to say that out loud.

Valerian's frown deepens, and he must assert the reality of his dream the way Hekima once did, because I become visible against my will.

He squints at me. "Bailey? How are you here?"

My disbelief transforms into fury. "You threw me under the bus, didn't you?" I advance on him. "Kain and his vampires kidnapped me and forced me to work for the Council because *you* suggested it. How could you do that to me?"

He blanches. "I'm sorry." He stands up, sweat dripping everywhere. "I didn't know you when I spoke to Yaroslav. We'd only emailed each other."

"And you think you know me now? Because I certainly don't know you."

And before I do something I'll later regret, I jolt myself out of his dream.

CHAPTER THREE

I EMERGE from the sleepwalking trance in utter fury. It's a good thing I did my dreamwalking from a distance. I don't want to be touching him right now.

Valerian's eyes pop open.

I narrow mine.

He jackknifes to his feet.

I turn and sprint to the door.

There's a sound of footsteps behind me, so I slam the door in his face and run down the corridor.

"I have as much right to be angry with you as you do with me," he shouts from behind me.

Reaching the elevator, I stab the button and glance back.

He's twenty feet away but gaining on me quickly.

"Why were you in my dreams?" he yells. "Were you hoping to find something about Soma? You know how I feel about that!"

The elevator doors open, and I leap inside,

smashing the button for the ground floor. "Your whole 'I didn't know you' excuse is weak," I yell back as the doors slide closed. "The first time we met face to face was in that castle."

He lunges at the doors, hand extended, but doesn't make it.

Whew.

The last thing I want is to continue that conversation—or look at his gorgeous, traitorous face.

He's mad at me? Our crimes can't even compare. True, he was cagey when I asked him about Soma—the place where his and my kind seem to live—but I didn't even know his black windows and Soma had anything to do with each other. He, on the other hand, was directly responsible for that whole mess with the New York Council.

The elevator doors open, and I dart out and grab a car, directing it to take me home. Settling comfortably into the seat, I touch Pom's furry body on my wrist.

The dream world is where I have the best chance of calming myself.

———

POM GREETS ME, his fur black and his expression worried. "What's wrong?"

Pacing between the impossible shapes populating the lobby of my palace, I fill him in on Valerian's betrayal.

As I speak, Pom's fur lightens to a mixture of blue

and light orange. "Well," he says when I'm done, "it *is* true. He didn't know you yet."

My hair turns fiery without my willing it to. "If you like him so much, why don't you attach yourself to *his* wrist. Or ass. Or—"

Pom disappears in his signature Cheshire cat style. When only his mouth is left, he says, "You might want to visit your memory gallery to calm down."

"Coward," I mumble when he's gone.

I contemplate creating a version of Valerian I could scream at, but I decide against it. Going to the memory gallery might actually be a good idea, since it's a bit like opening a photo album but on steroids. It's bound to distract me from my crazy thoughts, but I know Pom is still watching and I feel like being contrary, so I teleport to the tower of sleepers.

Aha. I'm in luck.

Ariel, Kit, Itzel, and Felix are all dreaming at the same time.

I pull them all into one dream, take us to my cloud office, and fill them in on everything, from my discovery about my twin sister and the encounter with Phobetor to Valerian throwing me under the bus with the New York Council.

"Wow," Felix says, his unibrow bunching on his forehead. "You've been busy."

I sigh. "Understatement."

Kit shakes her head. "I can't believe Valerian was after Hekima's Council seat. When we offered it to him, he seemed so genuine when he pretended not to want it."

"The Council offered him a seat?" I exclaim. "Already?"

Kit bites her lip. "He was the natural choice. Hekima showed us how useful an illusionist can be and —" She stops. "Never mind that. I can't believe you had a twin. Must be hard learning that you lost her, and in such a way." As she speaks, she morphs into a copy of me.

Ariel gives me a worried glance. "How about we talk about something else?"

"It's okay. I didn't really know her." As I look at my face on Kit, all I feel is a peculiar type of numbness. "Hard to grieve someone you didn't know existed."

What I *am* mourning is my perception of my mom as someone who'd be unable to kill her daughter, even under the potential influence of an evil deity.

Seeming to understand, Ariel squeezes my shoulder.

Itzel looks uncomfortable with all this. Adjusting her breathing mask, she asks, "What did that world look like? The one you saw in your mom's memories?"

Glad to have something to do, I recreate the clearing where I saw my sister killed. I place the tall forest around us just like it was in Mom's memory, with the blue-green trees shaped alternately like baobabs and coral reefs, and I even add in the odd skies that imply the planet is an odd pretzel shape instead of a sphere.

Everyone looks around, mouths agape.

"That sky…" Felix exhales in awe. "So cool."

Ariel turns to Itzel. "Is this a ring world? Built by your kind, maybe?"

Itzel shakes her head. "It could be gnome built, but the structure isn't a ring. It must be two counter-rotating cylinders. Reminds me of a spaceship design I've read about on Earth—O'Neill colony."

She clears the grass at our feet and draws a rough sketch of the design in the dirt.

Everyone stares at it blankly.

Itzel huffs in frustration and gives Felix a defeated look. "You need an Earth pop-culture reference, don't you?"

"No," Felix says.

"Yes," Ariel says at the same time.

"*Interstellar,*" Itzel says. "Cooper Station, at the very end."

"Oh, yeah," Felix says, looking up with even greater wonder. "So you think this is a spaceship?"

"That's a philosophical question," Itzel says. "Any planet can be said to be a spaceship, especially if the planet was artificially created the way this one must've been."

Kit loudly yawns. "I'm dreaming, yet you're about to put me to sleep."

"Guys." I snap my fingers to get their attention. "There's one thing we haven't touched on yet—the most worrisome aspect of what I've learned." I look at each of them in turn. "Do any of you know how a god of nightmares could be a real thing?"

"Maybe he isn't a god, per se," Felix says. "Not in the way humans think of them. Maybe he's just a powerful dreamwalker or something similar who was worshipped. With enough mojo from human faith, many of us can become like gods."

"He might be right," Ariel says. "There was a Phobetor in Greek mythology, and he had the same job. If more worlds have the same myth about a specific Cognizant, his powers would've grown beyond anything we can imagine."

I look around furtively. "How about we call him Collywobbles going forward? Especially when in the dream world?"

Valerian was insistent that we shouldn't say Phobetor's real name, and now that I've encountered him, I can no longer dismiss his concern as paranoia.

Kit nods. "No problem. Can you show him to us? Collywobbles?"

"I don't think I want to do that here either," I say. "I have this bad feeling. Like if I bring him about, he'll actually come to life."

"Hmm." Felix picks up a fallen leaf from one of the trees. Weirdly, it's shaped like a hexagon. "Could that be why he appeared to you in the first place?" he asks. "If your mom was taken over by him, as you theorized, that means she must've—"

"We agreed not to talk about that," Ariel snaps at him, casting a cautious look in my direction.

"I'm okay." I square my shoulders, ignoring the painful tension in my neck that somehow persists even in the dream. "If he's right, how about we don't talk about Collywobbles at all? At least not here."

Everyone falls silent.

"Maybe we should all sleep on this," I say. "If anyone has good ideas in the morning, get in touch."

They agree, so I let them go on sleeping and return to my cab.

When I get to my apartment a few minutes later, I collapse into my own bed. But I can't sleep, my mind replaying everything in a nauseating loop.

Finally, after what feels like hours, I drift off.

———

I'M WALKING through Times Square, doing my best not to touch the thousands of tourists and natives, which is harder than it should be. Above us loom skyscrapers adorned with screens playing flashy videos, most of them advertisements. All seems ordinary—until a vaguely familiar music begins playing.

It's "Dance of the Sugar Plum Fairy," the melody from a famous ballet here on Earth. In New York, they play it a lot around Christmas.

The screen nearest me stops showing the soda commercial, and a creepy-looking wooden soldier glares at me with a gaping mouth full of black teeth.

No, not a soldier. The Nutcracker—which is the name of the ballet where that music is from.

Unlike the usual depictions of this character, this one has real brown eyes inside a wooden head. Further adding to his creepiness is the way the face is painted, with a blood-colored grin framed by a tentacle-like mustache.

I stare at it, unable to look away.

The screen shimmers, and the Nutcracker is no longer inside it.

He's three-dimensional now.

Real.

My instinct for self-preservation kicks in, and I back away.

He leaps down, landing on a bent wooden knee, like some superhero.

I gape at the crater he's created in the spot where I stood a moment ago.

Suddenly, Pom shows up between me and the Nutcracker. His fur is black, his eyes wild. "Did you still want me to tell you when you're having a nightmare?"

A nightmare? As in, a dream?

I look at my empty wrist.

Of course. Pom is walking and talking—he can't be on my wrist.

"Thanks," I say to Pom, and will the music and the Nutcracker to disappear.

The music stops, but the Nutcracker stays where he is, the evil grin spreading wider. "It would've been easier to kill you if you didn't know you were dreaming," he says in a creepily melodic voice that reminds me of the music I just stopped. "Still, one has to make do."

What the hell? How is my own nightmare creature refusing to go away? Unless—

Extending his wooden, fingerless hand, the Nutcracker charges at me.

CHAPTER FOUR

INSTINCTIVELY, I duck.

The wooden ball of his hand smashes into a tourist, ripping through him and punching out his heart from his back.

"I'm sorry. This is too scary," Pom says and disappears.

Hey, that's a good idea.

I try to jolt myself awake—but feel a tug of power in the opposite direction. It's a bit like when I tried to wake up Mom, only I'm the one I can't rouse.

This supports a theory I've already started forming. "You're a dreamwalker."

The Nutcracker aims another punch at me.

I dodge it and two following swings, then smash a fist into his right eye.

He cries out but heals the damage I made instantly. With renewed fury, he lashes out, and his fist smashes into my shoulder, dislocating it.

Hot nausea sears through me, but before it can disable me, I leap out of my body and heal myself. I also consider doubling myself but decide against it for now —it's good to have an ace in my back pocket.

Returning to my body, I punch the Nutcracker's midsection. It hurts me more than him—his body doesn't just look like wood, it feels like it too. Note to self: Figure out how to make myself a dream body from something sturdier than flesh. It would be a lot like the fiery hair project, only bigger. For now, I make a blowtorch appear in my hands and aim it at my opponent's wooden chest.

A ten-foot cockroach materializes in the path of the flame, giving up its dream life to save my foe.

A yellow cab careens toward me.

I take flight—which is when the nearest skyscrapers grow taller, then fold sideways, creating a square box in the sky.

He thinks that will stop me?

I crash through the glass, steel, and concrete, and look down.

The Nutcracker is flying after me.

Stealing his own strategy, I make the One Times Square building lengthen and spear him with the spire from which the iconic New Year's Eve ball drops.

An elephant takes the strike.

Not wanting to be outdone, I make a great white shark appear, its jaws closing on the Nutcracker's head.

It doesn't get a chance to bite. In a blink, it explodes into a cloud of butterflies that flutter away.

I change our surroundings to that of another NYC tourist spot—the South Street Seaport.

Great. He hasn't stopped me yet—though I still don't know if he's fine with the change of scenery, or if he can't stop me.

Regardless, he takes advantage of it swiftly. A ship rises from the waters and nosedives at my head.

I try to make the ship disappear. His power annuls my attempt. I will the ship to morph into a ball of cotton candy. Nope.

Fine. I teleport behind the Nutcracker and make a baseball bat appear in my hands. As the ship crashes into the pavement where I stood, my bat breaks over the Nutcracker's head.

"You bitch!" he cries out.

I make the cobblestones levitate out of the walkway and fly at his head, one after another. As he dodges, I try jolting myself awake once more.

This time, it works.

———

SITTING UP IN MY BED, I order the lights on and frantically scan the room.

Nobody is here.

Leaping to my feet, I examine the whole apartment, just in case.

Empty.

I can't believe I now have yet another thing to worry about. I pace the living room for a few minutes before I decide that I must talk to someone about this. Maybe one of my friends is still dreaming? If they're on Gomorrah, it's still nighttime here and will be for a while.

The question is, do I dare go back into the dream world? What if the Nutcracker is waiting for me there?

It feels unlikely. It seems that part of his strategy was to catch me while I was still unaware of my dreaming, and for that to happen, I'd need to be dreaming naturally. Besides, if I give up dreamwalking completely, I'll be powerless.

And there's an extra precaution I can take—if Pom is willing.

Touching my looft's fur, I dive back into the dream world.

———

BEET-COLORED Pom appears at my feet as soon as I pop into my dream palace.

"I'm sorry for being such a coward," he says, his ears droopy.

"Don't say that." I muss the fur on top of his head. "That thing could've killed you. Then where would I be?"

Pom's fur darkens. "Killed?"

"Well, yeah. And I have no clue what that means for you. If he'd killed *me*, I'd have gone homicidally insane." I frown at him. "Can *you* go insane?"

He turns full black. "No idea."

"Then let's not find out. If the attack happens again, run away, exactly like you did."

"Okay." His fur lightens a bit. "But I will keep warning you about nightmares—else that thing could get a jump on you."

"Perfect. And there's something else I need you to do. If the Nutcracker shows up while I'm dreamwalking inside *your* dreams, you have the power to wake me up, so I'll need you to do that after you disappear."

"You got it." Pom turns teal and gives me a crisp army salute.

"Let's test it now."

With a nod, he disappears, and I find myself back in my apartment.

I touch Pom again, and once I greet him in the palace, I teleport us to the tower of sleepers and check the surrounding rooms.

Out of everyone, only Felix is here, so I connect with him.

He's dreaming of working with Itzel on a new robot suit. It's a memory, actually.

Banishing Dream Itzel, I explain to Felix that he's asleep and take him to my cloud office, where he paces the cloud as I tell him about the fight, finishing with, "When I woke up, there was no one there, which means this dreamwalker—if that's what that was—didn't touch me to get in. He or she either had a connection with me already, or set up one remotely, from outside my apartment."

Pom, perched on my shoulder, turns pitch black.

Felix stops pacing the cloud. He might already know what I'll ask, but I say it anyway. "If it's the latter, there's bound to be security footage of him—or her—creeping by my door."

His unibrow does a little dance. "I'll check on this as soon as I wake up. But are you sure this was a dreamwalker and not Pho—I mean, Collywobbles?"

"Well, the latter is extremely powerful and would've ended me quickly... Unless the idea was to just toy with me."

"And you don't know any other dreamwalkers, right?" Felix asks.

"If I did, I'd ask them to teach me how to wage a battle in the dream world. I got lucky this time."

Felix looks around, eyes bulging. "Can he show up here?"

"Should that happen, I have a plan." I pat Pom's furry feet, and he proudly puffs up. "Besides, I think the Nutcracker needs me dreaming naturally, to catch me unaware."

"How about doing something proactive in case he does show up again?" Felix asks. "I can help."

Good idea. I could, for starters, make my body more solid.

Gathering my power, I attempt to turn my flesh into metal.

Only my pinky solidifies—and I can't feel it at all.

With another effort, I force the metal pinky to bend. It does, and some feelings go back into it. It's a start. I bend the pinky some more, until it eventually feels like a regular one, only slathered in Novocain.

My index finger is next, then the whole arm, then finally my torso.

"What do you think?" I try to ask. The question doesn't come out. I guess the metal exterior is messing with the function of my throat.

It takes me a few minutes to fix that problem. When I finally master my newly metallic body, I ask, "Can you attack me?"

Felix walks over and gingerly pokes my midsection.

"You've got to do better than that." I create boxing gloves around his hands. "Punch me."

He does.

I feel the punch, but the impact is definitely dampened.

"The problem is that this takes up a lot of concentration." I create a baseball bat to replace Felix's gloves. "Hit me with that."

He smashes the bat into my midsection.

I barely feel it.

Felix smacks me again. "This is cool," he says when I don't flinch. "What's next?"

"Your call. What do you need?"

He grins. "Guns. Lots of guns."

I take us to a blank room with rows upon rows of weapons inspired by his movie reference.

Grin widening, he picks up a Beretta, loads it, and points it at my chest. "Are you sure?"

I inhale a big breath. "Shoot."

Bang.

My chest hurts as if I were punched, but the bullet just falls at my feet.

This is a workable strategy.

Arming Felix with other weapons, I experiment with different ways of fighting a dreamwalker—melting a katana instead of letting it slice me, increasing gravity to prevent a cannonball from smashing into my metal chest, messing with the chemistry of gunpowder to prevent an Uzi from firing, and so on.

"Those video game design courses have clearly given you an advantage," Felix says after we both tire of the exercise. "Practice like this some more, and I'm sure you'll defeat that Nutcracker—assuming he or she dares attack you again."

If only I were that optimistic.

"Thanks for the help. I'll let you sleep normally now," I say and leave Felix's dream.

Too wired to go back to sleep, I brew myself a soothing herbal tea and sip it leisurely for a while.

When I catch myself yawning, I get back into bed. It takes a while, but eventually, I go under, and this time, my slumber is dreamless.

———

IN THE MORNING, a message from Felix is waiting for me in VR:

Nothing in the security footage. The Nutcracker must've made a connection with you before.

Hmm. That does limit the pool of suspects somewhat, and is worrying. Some creepozoid touched me while I slept. Just thinking about it makes me want to hygieia myself.

With a slight pang of disappointment, I don't find a gushing apology from Valerian in my inbox—nor a message of any kind. Not even a "you suck." Oh, well. Sounds like that's it between us. I just hope he doesn't stop the development of the *Lucid Dreamer* game because of this—I need the power boost from that to rouse Mom.

At least I think I do. With Phobetor as a variable, having more power might not be the only thing I need. Still, it should help with the Nutcracker situation.

Unsure of what to do next, I check in on my rehab job and find a big backlog of clients waiting for my unique form of therapy, so that's what I do for the rest of the day.

———

OVER THE NEXT THREE WEEKS, I continue catching up on my workload at the rehab clinic. The Nutcracker doesn't show in my dreams, and Valerian is incommunicado.

Things get so routine with my clients that I wonder, not for the first time, if I should start a VR company to carefully craft VR experiences for common phobias that would mirror my dream therapy. It's actually one of the reasons why I took the game design classes in the past.

Maybe this is a project to look into after I save Mom. Especially if I patch things up with Valerian, a VR guru.

No, scrap that last bit. Valerian is not going to be in my life anymore, either as a love interest or a business partner—and I don't care how much I dream about his stupid, pretty face.

By the fourth week, I start to worry about the *Lucid Dreamer* project. If Valerian could throw me under the bus as he did with the Council, why would he continue all that expensive video game development for me?

To that end, I stalk the tower of sleepers until I catch Bernard there. Swiftly, I jump into his dream.

———

BERNARD IS DREAMING of a trip to the zoo with his daughter.

It's a memory, which means they've reconciled to the point of daytrips. Good for him.

I let him enjoy the dream, and when the next one starts, I direct it to a memory related to my query.

———

BERNARD—OR Bernie in this context—is sitting at the table with Ratridevi Bhairava, a.k.a. Rattie.

Today, Bernie looks more like Wario than his nemesis Mario, while Rattie is as attractive as he was when I saw him last, his symmetrical masculine features and strong dark eyebrows not at all rat-like despite the nickname.

"Let's talk replayability for *Lucid Dreamer*." Rattie activates the screens around them, and his Bangalore team joins the conference. "We want our user base to play the game over and over."

Bernie frowns. "Our plot is too linear, and that's hard to change. Nor do we have that many alternating paths or endings."

"Right. That's why I think the easiest way we can add some replay value is with multiple characters," Rattie says, and everyone on the screens nods.

Bernie twirls his mustache, villain style. "Maybe we use a character that's already in the game?"

"We could," Rattie says. "Our big bad would be a cheap option. He's got the same powers as—"

I tune the rest of it out. The villain in the game is the Rat King. I even tried fighting him in VR, though in that case he took on the guise of a spider with the head of a clown wearing a surgeon's mask. The playable version would probably look more like Rattie himself—as that's what his mischievous Bangalore team often makes their monsters' faces look like.

"And we don't need to involve another model,"

Bernie says, echoing my thought process. "If needed, you can just pop into the motion capture lab and—"

At the mention of the motion capture lab, I vividly recall being there with Valerian and the way he attached those dots to my face. Also, the way he—

Wait, why am I fantasizing about that traitor?

"—and the best part is that the release date won't change," Bernie says.

Everyone nods approvingly.

That is indeed the best part. Depending on how far back in the past this meeting was, the game might come out very soon.

"Now, if that's settled, we should talk about the feedback from the testers." Bernie opens a folder. "The most recurrent note is: Too many clowns and spiders."

The Bangalore team start laughing, and when Bernie gives them a questioning look, one of them explains that the clowns and spiders are Rattie's fault. Apparently, he has them overuse those elements in all the projects they've created.

Not interested in hearing more, I exit the dream and find myself back in my office at the rehab facility.

Doesn't seem like Valerian has halted the game design. Maybe he's not as much of a jerk as I thought.

As if waiting for that moment, a message shows up in my VR inbox.

It's from Valerian.

If you recall, I offered to take you out of the castle when we met.

What? He disappears for weeks, and his idea of

groveling is that? Pom turning red on my wrist, I compose my reply:

You offered to rescue me out of self-interest. If you recall, the vampires kidnapped me before I finished that job with Bernard. I guess your seer miscalculated—or it was all part of the big plan. Your offer to rescue me was as hollow as your current apology, and you know it. The vampires had my DNA, so taking me out of the castle would've only delayed the inevitable.

I wait for him to prevaricate his way out of that, but he doesn't reply.

Nor is there a reply on the next day, and the one after that.

Just as I figure he's done talking to me forever, I find a bouquet of flowers in my office with a small note:

I'm sorry.

The gall of the guy. He thinks he can kill some plants and make everything okay?

Still, I put the flowers into a vase and catch myself smelling them for the rest of the day with a dumb grin on my face.

The next day, I get a box of candy with the same note.

Unlike its Earth cousins, Gomorran candy is actually good for one's teeth, and is many times more delicious, which goes doubly so for the extremely expensive brand Valerian got for me.

Still. Just because I'm gobbling down the candy doesn't mean I'm ready to forgive and forget.

The next day, a box is waiting on my desk. There's a bracelet inside.

I put it on. It's pretty, even if it looks nothing like Pom's furry body on my other wrist. And no, just because I'm wearing the bracelet doesn't mean we're okay now.

By gift number seven, my resolve wavers a bit. That is, until I get a new message from Valerian the next day:

Felix told me everything. Can you put aside your silly misconceptions long enough to talk to me?

Silly misconceptions?

I remove his bracelet and toss it into the garbage disposal.

The nerve of that man.

And what was Felix thinking, talking to the enemy? He's lucky I'm not evil enough to sneak into his dreams and have him take a swim in a lake filled with blood. Or make him and Valerian screw themselves—and each other.

That last bit heavily inspires my reply, which, not surprisingly, is:

You and Felix can go puck yourselves.

Valerian doesn't write back, and there's no gift on my desk the next day.

Okay, so maybe I could've replied with something a bit more ladylike.

The rest of the morning passes in a blur of therapy appointments. Finally, feeling like I should treat myself, I go for lunch at White Fang, a restaurant run by a werewolf that serves various meat tartar and has a nice ambiance. Today, it's pretty much empty, which suits my mood just fine.

I'm halfway through my ri sashimi when someone sits down at my table.

It's Valerian, looking as unrepentant as can be.

CHAPTER FIVE

TALL AND BROAD-SHOULDERED, he's wearing a gnome-designed tunic that looks to have been tattooed on his muscled body. His expression is unreadable, the ocean-blue eyes serene, with not a twitch of emotion visible on those carved features.

Pom's fur turns coral pink.

Damn hormones. I forgot just how attractive Valerian is. He looks yummy enough to end up on the menu, and it's distracting me from my anger.

A server robot rolls over to the table, a plate of sashimi on his head. Valerian must've ordered it while I was staring.

I glare at him. "You're kidding, right? One of us is not staying."

He picks up a piece of sashimi with his bare fingers —proper werewolf table manners. Putting it in his mouth, he chews exaggeratedly slow.

I get up. "Fine. *I'll* go."

Suddenly, the other tables around us disappear, along with the restaurant's windows and entrance.

Valerian leans back in his chair and swallows his morsel. "We need to talk. What can I do to lower your hostility so you'll listen?"

Pom's fur is now the angriest red. "You can build a time machine and not puck me over."

He heaves a sigh. "Anything else?"

"Tell me everything you know about Soma. Let me see the precious black windows in your dreams, and maybe I'll hear you out."

His hands curl for a moment, but there's no hint of emotion on his face—that or he's tricking me with his illusion powers to think so. Sitting up straighter, he says, "This is important. I'm working with the Gomorran Senate and the Councils on Earth."

I plop back into my chair. If I try to flee now, I'll knock over a table or walk into a wall. Besides, if he's telling the truth, I don't want to anger the Senate or any of the Earth's Councils. Instead, I give him my most seething stare. "How many times do I have to get nearly killed before you leave me alone?"

He narrows his eyes, his serene mask gone. "I'm here to save your stubborn hide. You know you're in terrible danger, as much as you pretend otherwise. And I have arranged for your protection." He makes the illusion go away, returning the tables, windows, and entrance to visibility.

"Danger?" I ask, the sashimi feeling like a stone in my stomach. "What danger?"

"Seriously?" He shakes his head. "The one you call Collywobbles. You got on his radar—and lo and behold, someone is hunting you in your dreams. How long do you think it'll take before trouble comes for you in the waking world?"

That's an interesting point. Even I wondered if those events were related. But—

A strange duo walks into the restaurant. One of them is a man with dark glasses and one of those special walking sticks the blind use to navigate the streets on Earth. Next to him is a giant canine wearing a guide-dog getup—a job a robot would do here on Gomorrah.

Only that's not a dog.

It's a werewolf, in his or her animal form.

The maybe-blind man beelines for our table without using his stick and doesn't touch a single obstacle in his path, his guide werewolf lagging behind.

Without much ado, he sinks into the chair to my left and takes out a pair of tighty-whities from his pocket.

In a flash, the werewolf turns, becoming a naked man with sad eyes and unkempt facial hair that makes it difficult to determine his age. He snatches the underwear, robotically puts it on, then sits on the remaining chair and looks blankly into the distance.

The maybe-blind guy turns my way. "Hi, Bailey." His gaze cuts to my companion. "Hi, Valerian."

"Nostradamus," Valerian mutters, looking as discombobulated as I feel.

This is Nostradamus?

A legendary figure, he's said to be one of the most powerful seers in existence, and has been instrumental in saving all of the Cognizant kind at least once.

"At your service," Nostradamus replies. "And my companion is Marius. Nice to finally meet you both— outside of visions, that is."

Valerian glances at Marius. "Pleasure." Then his attention homes in on Nostradamus. "Everyone thought you disappeared with the rest of the seers."

The rest of the seers disappeared?

What's going on?

"I'll be gone too, after we talk," the seer says sagely. "But first, I'm here to tell you how to save Bailey's life."

CHAPTER SIX

SAVE *ME*?

No. Not again.

Valerian looks at the werewolf as if for an explanation, and when none comes, he says, "I'm here to protect her."

"Sadly, the protection you plan will doom her, and everyone else." Nostradamus grabs a piece of sashimi off my plate and tosses it into his werewolf friend's mouth.

The werewolf catches it and swallows without chewing, his sad eyes staring into the distance.

On autopilot, I move my plate toward Nostradamus and open VR to order the same thing again.

Valerian rubs the bridge of his nose. "The safe house the Senate prepared—"

"Will get broken into, the Enforcers overwhelmed," Nostradamus says. "And though my powers aren't as good when it comes to events that happen in dreams, I can tell you that most versions of the future you planned for her end with Bailey going homicidally insane."

I blink. "As in, the Nutcracker kills me in a future fight?"

"Not if you avoid sleep," Valerian says. "There's—"

"She'll refuse to live on vampire blood," Nostradamus says, and I nod emphatically. "But even in the rare futures where the choice is not hers, things end just as tragically."

Wait a second. He saw futures where someone force-fed me vampire blood? Who'd be—

"I hate seers," Valerian growls. "I assume you're going to tell us what to do?"

"I can show you a path." Nostradamus snatches another sashimi piece and eats it with an impressed look. "Take her and her friends with you to Necronia."

"And?" Valerian prompts.

"What's Necronia?" I ask.

Nostradamus rises to his feet. "Valerian will explain shortly."

Valerian jumps up too, his muscles bunching tight. "Wait, that's it?"

Shreds of tighty-whities fly everywhere as the werewolf morphs back into a shaggy beast and places himself between Valerian and Nostradamus.

Nostradamus lays a hand on the snarling wolf's head, scratching him behind the ear. "He's upset. It's understandable."

Valerian sits back down, all but vibrating with

tension. "Why won't you tell us what we need to do in exact detail? Why this charade?"

"Well, for one thing, if you know the future, you can change it," Nostradamus says.

I blink. "We can?"

"Sure. For example, what if I told you 'don't get dessert after I leave?'"

"If you said not to, we wouldn't," Valerian says.

"It's not that simple, though," Nostradamus says. "You'll see." He turns to leave.

"Wait!" I call. "Can you at least give us a few tips?"

"Sure," the seer says over his shoulder. "Take Chester with you—or another powerful probability manipulator. If the other side recruits one of his or my kind, he'd be a good counterbalance."

The other side? Does he mean the Nutcracker?

"Wouldn't Chester make it impossible for you to know our future?" Valerian asks.

"I don't know your future exactly anyway," Nostradamus says. "I'm here to offer you a path that doesn't lead to certain doom for you and everyone— but that doesn't mean I can guarantee a positive outcome."

Ugh. No wonder everyone dislikes seers.

A robot rolls over to the table with my new serving of sashimi. I take it on autopilot and put it on the table.

"Farewell," Nostradamus says. "Oh, last but not least, if you hear the Fate Motif, play the detective." With that, he strolls out of the restaurant, his werewolf on his tail.

I face Valerian. "What just happened?"

He scrubs a hand over his face. "I think we've officially gotten in over our heads. The Earth Councils have been trying to locate Nostradamus without any success—and he just waltzes in here, spouting prophecies like it's nothing."

"Uh-huh. Why are the Councils looking for him? Why did he keep hinting at some kind of apocalypse? What the puck is a Fate Motif? And what's Necronia?"

"First things first," Valerian says. "What do we do about the pucking dessert?"

I frown at him. "Didn't Nostradamus say not to get it?"

My appetite is history, and I bet the same is true for Valerian. Still, I summon VR and scan the menu. Today's only options for dessert are chef's choice of kibble with freeze-dried innards or a glazed *cheburashka* ear. No, thanks. The first option will no doubt taste like gourmet dog food, and the second sounds as appetizing as a baby koala ear would on Earth.

Valerian gestures in his own VR and wrinkles his nose. "Nostradamus's exact words were 'don't get dessert after I leave.'"

I dismiss the VR interface. "But he prefaced that with 'what if I told you.'"

"Right. That implies that merely saying the phrase 'don't get dessert after I leave' could, by itself, alter our future somehow. But that makes no sense. The only way it could be true is if we ordered the dessert out of spite."

"Which you won't do, right?"

He narrows his eyes. "I'm not the spiteful one."

"What's that supposed to mean?"

"Where do I start? You threw away the bracelet I gave you. Ignored—"

"You spied on me?"

Valerian doesn't reply. He's staring at the restaurant entrance.

Following his gaze, I gape at the dozen new arrivals —Cognizant of various types. Some are naked, some are only wearing underwear, and the rest have on a mix of nightgowns and pajamas.

All of them are armed with objects found in a typical kitchen: a few people with knives, a large female elf with a colander, a male dwarf gripping a spatula, a gargoyle with skewers, a dryad with scissors, and so on.

But it's not their clothing or weapons that make my insides freeze-dry like the dessert we'll probably never get the chance to order. Nor is it the lack of emotion on their faces.

It's their eyes.

There's a magma-like fire in all of them—the same exact peculiarity that Mom displayed when she killed my twin.

"Cast an illusion!" I whisper harshly as all fiery eyes lock in on us.

Valerian shakes his head. "Their condition makes it

hard to fool more than one, and to stop them, I'd need to fool all of them—or more precisely, the one controlling them. The one who sees through their eyes. If I had a team of illusionists to help me, that would be a different story."

His explanation raises many questions, but I don't get to ask them because at that moment, acting as one, the motley crew pounces.

CHAPTER SEVEN

A KNIFE whooshes by my ear, causing me to duck. A colander flies at my midsection, so I sidestep. A meat tenderizer smashes into Valerian's shoulder. He grunts, then leaps between me and a rolling pin, taking the blow on his chest.

"Stop getting hit!" I shout.

"Thanks," he pants. "I'll get right on that."

I pick up the tenderizer and launch it at the head of the dwarf with a spatula. It smacks him in the face, hard, but he keeps on coming. Not good.

Valerian catches a knife in mid-air and sends it flying into the eye of the elf woman. She drops her colander and collapses on the floor, presumably dead.

That's something. Seems like they can be defeated.

If we had a squadron of fighters with us, we'd stand a chance. As is, not so much. Not with their seeming imperviousness to pain, sheer numbers, and our lack of any weapons or useful powers.

A pair of skewers zoom by Valerian's head, then scissors. I curse myself for not carrying a sleep grenade to work as I dodge a dirty frying pan. Of all the unsanitary ways to go. Could this get any more nightmarish?

Valerian flips over our table and uses it as a shield. Good idea. That should buy us a minute, maybe two. Kitchen tools pound at the table like hail.

I cautiously peek out.

A new group of people zooms into the restaurant. Given their all-black outfits, super-fast movement and fangs, I have to assume they're Enforcers, or at least vampires impersonating them.

If this lot is with the weird-eyes group, we're going to be even deader.

But they don't seem to be. At least not the one I recognize. His name is Virgil, and he was Valerian's ally before.

Yep. Virgil disembowels a dryad while another vamp rips out an elf's heart.

A massacre follows. Soon, Valerian and I are the only people in the restaurant left alive, not counting the vampires. Their aliveness is a matter of debate.

"Why did it take you so long?" Valerian barks at Virgil.

Virgil licks a rivulet of blood from his hand. "You said you wanted privacy. Asked us to stay outside of the hearing range. That's a mile for me."

He can hear us from a mile away? Surely that's with a sound amplifier?

Then something clicks.

I round on Valerian. "You had them spy on me. Is that how you knew about the bracelet I tossed away?"

"They merely protected you," he says. "I knew about the bracelet because the rehab facility gave us access to the security camera in your office."

This is some Big Brother mooft dung. The folks at the rehab facility and I will have words.

Virgil hides his fangs. "You'd better take her to the safe house."

"There's been a change of plans on that front," Valerian says. "Instead of staying under your watch, she's going to come with me."

Virgil lifts an eyebrow.

Since it sounds like I might finally get some answers, I replace my initial angry retort with, "Where are we headed?"

Valerian looks at the bodies of our attackers. "Not here."

"Take that van." Virgil gestures at a vehicle nearby. "It's been vetted."

Nodding, Valerian strides to the car, and I follow.

This is one of those luxury limo-type rides that take people to weddings and the like. There's a bar and fridge here, a couch, and space enough to stand and move around.

As we get rolling, Valerian pours two drinks at the bar and hands me one of the glasses.

I take a small sip. Delicious. "Did that make any sense to you?"

He sits opposite me. "I'm sure you see what Nostradamus meant about the dessert. He mentioned it, and we started to argue about it when he left. If he hadn't said anything, we probably would've been out of the restaurant before the Overtaken arrived." At my blank stare, he explains, "The Overtaken is what I call the people with the strange eyes."

"The dessert is not what I was asking about. It's everything else. Who are the Overtaken?"

"It's only a theory." He puts his drink down on a small table nearby. "I believe they're possessed and controlled by Collywobbles." He makes air quotes around Phobetor's nickname. "As I was saying before, you're on his radar now."

Uh-oh. "So those eyes—"

"Are what reveal the control," he confirms.

"Which means my mom—"

"I'm sorry." He gently squeezes my knee.

I let out a shaky breath. Though I'd suspected something like this myself, I find it difficult, if not impossible, to accept that Mom was controlled by a god of nightmares. And killed my twin—let's not forget that impossible-to-process factoid.

"—Overtaken have started to appear in bigger numbers recently," Valerian is saying when I pay attention to him again. "That's what helped me convince the Senate and the Earth Councils to act."

Shoving aside all thoughts of my mom and my dead sister, I leap to my feet and begin pacing in the small confines of the car. "Start at the very beginning. Why did the Councils look for Nostradamus? When he hinted at doom and gloom, did it have something to do with the Overtaken? And what's Necronia?"

Valerian picks up his drink and takes a large sip. "Right. From the beginning. You remember Wrakar?"

I stop. "The necromancer who nearly killed us?"

I wish I could forget him. The last time I saw the guy, Kit had him cocooned in a spiderweb.

"The Senate had him questioned," Valerian says. "We learned a lot."

Ouch. *Questioned* is a polite way of saying *tortured*.

"According to Wrakar, Icelus is a multi-world organization," he continues, "all united in one goal: to make *you know who* stronger. Though we stopped the attack here on Gomorrah, the Cognizant in countless Otherlands weren't so lucky."

I sit back down, my knees suddenly feeling weak. "They blew up people?"

"On some worlds. On others, they instigated a war. And on some, they worked in a subtler manner. Remember Koshmar, the drug that gives nightmares?"

I nod.

"On one world that's a lot like Earth, they managed to start a pharmaceutical company and distributed a more lethal version of that drug as a sleeping aid. This has led to millions of deaths and billions of horrific nightmares."

I pinch the bridge of my nose. "I didn't realize Icelus is so widespread. How many members are there? How do they coordinate these atrocities across the Otherlands?"

"Many of the cataclysms were caused by the same cell. As for world-to-world communication, Wrakar claimed they have a dreamwalker among them for that. At first, it seemed farfetched, but after that attack inside your dream, I believe him on this, too."

Another dreamwalker.

An Icelus dreamwalker.

That must be who the Nutcracker is.

"How do you know it's a person?" I ask. "Couldn't a nightmare deity personally help them coordinate?"

He shrugs. "Seems like overkill. Besides, I think the Overtaken is what happens to people who get too chummy with the one you mention. Most Icelus are independent agents, not puppets with fiery eyes."

"Right. So you questioned the necro and told the Councils on Earth about your findings?"

"And the Councils on other easy-to-reach Otherlands," he says. "The idea is to coordinate a defense. This is why we looked for seers. Besides the obvious usefulness of their visions, they can communicate inter-world, albeit only with each other."

I recall Nostradamus saying how Valerian will never meet him again. "Let me guess. The seers foresaw your interest in them and ran away before they could get pulled into this mess?"

Valerian rakes his fingers through his hair. "Exactly. Which is when everyone started to *really* worry."

"What about that cryptic Fate Motif thing he said last? And, relatedly, how do I play detective?"

His upper lip curls. "Seers. I've heard of the *Fate Motif* in the context of music. Specifically, Beethoven's *Symphony No. 5*, also sometimes called the *Fate Symphony*."

I know the music piece he's talking about. It's one of the best-known compositions of classical music on Earth. One where the opening bars—and the motif— are Da-Da-Da-DUM.

"But what does it have to do with anything?" I ask. "And how do I play the detective?"

Valerian shrugs. "Let's hope you figure that out when the time comes. Playing the detective might mean using your reasoning skills or something like that."

"And Necronia?"

"That's Wrakar's home world—or more precisely, the world he was exiled from. He and the dreamwalker —whose identity he doesn't know—discussed that world at length, and Wrakar is convinced that it'll be attacked by a particularly nasty Icelus cell called the Pales. I decided to head up a team to go there to prevent the attack and capture the Pales."

I rub my temples. "And I wasn't going to be a part of this team, was I?"

He shakes his head. "I wanted to keep you safe on Gomorrah, but that's out the window now. Nostradamus is not a seer you can ignore."

Great, just great. If that dessert thing's taught me

anything—besides a fear of seers—it's that I'd better go on this stupid mission. "Did the necromancer say what kind of attack to expect?"

Valerian grimaces. "You won't like it. He thinks it'll be via a vicious virus, one that affects humans and Cognizant alike. The Pales apparently specialize in bioweapons and have used viruses on other worlds already."

A virus.

I can feel all the blood draining from my face.

Why couldn't it be anything else?

"You don't have to go," he says gently.

"He said I'd die if I don't."

"Actually, he said my current plans would lead to your death, but what about new plans? What if you stay on Earth?"

I stand up and pour myself a stiffer drink.

I have no idea what to do. Do I trust a seer? And if so, can I physically make myself go to a world where a scary virus is running amok?

What's really odd is that the idea of traveling with Valerian terrifies me almost as much as catching this virus. I don't know if I'll be able to stay mad at him while spending so much time together.

A part of me is already weakening. He did, after all, want to keep me safe before the seer messed it up.

Well, if I do go, I'll stay extra vigilant when it comes to Valerian. Surely, I can stop myself from lusting—or worse—with sheer iron will.

Yeah. Right. And maybe I can fight the virus with

my willpower while I'm at it. Even now—though it could be the alcohol talking—I want him to hug me and kiss me and tell me everything will be okay.

As if sensing that, he comes to stand next to me by the bar. "You barely survived the last encounter with Icelus," he says softly. "Think hard before you make your choice."

I down my drink. "There's not really a choice, is there? Nostradamus has spoken. Besides, if Collywobbles was behind my sister's death, I want to thwart him and his minions."

Valerian nods solemnly. "This will be a long journey. How about we start over?"

And so it begins. "Nice try. You know my price to let bygones be bygones." I face him squarely. "Tell me everything about Soma and let me into the black windows in your dreams. I want no more secrets."

He turns away. "That's too much."

A hysterical chuckle escapes my lips. "You served me on a platter to the New York Council. Now you want me to go to a virus-infested world, and you have the nerve to say *I* ask too much?"

"It's not me who says you should go. In fact, I'm still wondering if there's a way you *don't* have to go."

"There isn't." Not according to a legendary seer, untrustworthy though he might be.

Valerian exhales audibly. "Fine. You win. After we're done with this mission, you'll get what you want."

The car stops.

I look up at the hub building. "We're going to Necronia already?"

"Earth first." He exits and holds the door for me. "You'll be safer there."

As we cross through the lobby of the building, I spot Enforcers—no doubt our bodyguards in case the Overtaken strike again.

"How does Collywobbles Overtake people, exactly?" I ask.

Valerian gestures for me step into the elevator and presses the button for the top floor. "No one knows for sure. So far, the one thing all victims had in common is recurrent nightmares and other sleep problems."

"Do they retain their powers?" I ask when we come out of the elevator and head for the blue shimmering plasma gate that leads to Earth.

"Seems like it," he says. "And, as I mentioned, I can only fool a single one with illusions, which makes my power useless when dealing with a team of them."

We step through the gate and come out on the Earth side. The JFK hub is underground, so my voice echoes as I say, "I wonder if my powers would work on them."

"I wouldn't go into the dreams of the Overtaken," Valerian says. "*You know who* might be waiting for you there."

Right. I wonder if Mom counts as one of the Overtaken. She clearly did at one point. And I did face Collywobbles in her dreams.

We enter the corridors, but instead of leading me to

the secret door that opens into the JFK airport, Valerian takes a different turn.

"What's there?" I ask.

"A lab." He goes into a room at the end of the corridor.

I follow him.

A lab? More like a mad scientist's lair.

If a medical supply company were to battle a hardware store inside a space station, this might be the aftermath. A mix of Gomorran and Earth tech is everywhere, but particularly on a table where Itzel is building something, her attention fixed on her task.

Ariel and Felix are here too, engaged in an animated discussion.

"—no way Batman would beat Iron Man in a fight," Felix is saying. "Not unless they didn't have any gear on."

Ariel frowns, managing to still look uber-attractive while doing it. "If Batman had enough time to prep—"

"Hi, guys," I call. "What's going on?"

All three look at me as though I've appeared out of thin air.

Valerian smirks. He must've hidden us with his powers until now.

"I was working on something important," Itzel says, raising her head to pin me with a grumpy stare. "These two were supposed to test my work, but are really just interrupting."

I walk over to examine Itzel's "work." She's made a number of masks that are reminiscent of the one she always wears, being a gnome with breathing problems and all.

"I commissioned Itzel to make equipment for our Necronia trip." Valerian takes out a phone and types as he talks. "The Enforcers will take the prototypes to human labs and test them out."

I look around in confusion. "And she's working on a backwater world like Earth because…?"

"There's never been a major pandemic on Gomorrah. When it comes to virus protection and the like, this place is actually ahead." Itzel gestures at a nearby hazmat suit.

"Oh, please," I say. "We don't get pandemics thanks to the likes of hygieia and better sanitation. Earth is *not* ahead."

"We'll take hygieia devices with us," Valerian says. "But since the virus in question will most likely be airborne, we need masks too." He turns to Itzel. "Bailey needs a mask now as well. So do the rest of you."

"What?" Felix asks just as Ariel bursts out, "Why? Who?"

Valerian and I fill them in on our encounter with the seer.

"I can't believe things are so bad that Nostradamus got involved," Felix says. "The proverbial shit is about to really hit the proverbial fan. On an epic scale."

Ariel nods grimly. "Some kind of apocalypse is coming."

Itzel looks like someone crashed her favorite

spaceship. "I should've known that being your friend would one day bite me in the ass," she says glumly.

Of course. Nostradamus said my friends need to come with us on this mission. I've been too self-absorbed to realize what that means for the people in this room.

"I doubt he meant you," Felix tells Itzel. "Seers can't predict a gnome's future."

"Not directly," Ariel says. "But should we risk everything by *not* having her come?"

Wow. They're taking Nostradamus's words even more seriously than I did.

"I'm sorry about that," I say. "He didn't elaborate much, so if you guys don't want to—"

"I'm going," Ariel says firmly.

"It's a chance for me to test out my new suit," Felix says, a lot less firmly.

"If you *do* go, you'll be handsomely rewarded," Valerian says to Itzel before turning toward Ariel and Felix. "That goes for the two of you as well."

Itzel perks up. "Rewarded by you or the Senate?"

"Both," Valerian says. "And the Earth Councils too."

Felix and Ariel exchange impressed glances.

"I have a feeling we'll be able to work something out." Itzel bends over the mask in front of her with renewed enthusiasm.

Valerian checks his phone. "I have to go make some arrangements. The Councils have assigned you protection. They're waiting in a limo outside." Turning, he heads toward the exit.

"When do we start the trip to Necronia?" I call after him.

"In a few days," he replies over his shoulder.

"What?" I look at Ariel and Felix. They both shrug. "Where do I stay in the meantime?"

Valerian stops and gives me an exasperated look. "Your bodyguards should keep you safe anywhere."

"How about you crash with us?" Ariel suggests excitedly. "We have an unused room at the moment."

"And there's a domovoi at our place who can kill anything that might get inside," Felix adds. "Also, our doors and windows are bulletproof."

Huh. I wonder if the latter is something Bowser set up for Princess Peach, the original occupant of the room in question.

"Perfect," Valerian says. "We'll meet back here. I'll text you the details."

With that, he strides out.

"Text who?" I ask the remaining crew.

"Me," Felix admits. "We've been working together the last few weeks."

I level a look at him filled with pretend annoyance. "So that's how you had the time to spill all my secrets to him."

Ariel grins. "You've known Felix long enough to realize how big of a gossip he is. If there's something you don't want the world to know, don't tell him."

"I can *totally* keep a secret." Felix's unibrow seesaws on his forehead. "I never told anyone about—"

Noticing Ariel's death stare, he swallows audibly and mumbles, "Never mind."

"Can you shut your pieholes?" Itzel growls. "I'm working."

Ariel rolls her eyes. "Let's go see who the Councils assigned as protection."

She leads us out of the room and through the labyrinthine corridors into JFK, where an anorexic-thin woman is waiting for us.

"Thalia!" Ariel exclaims. "Great to see you again."

"Thalia is a nun from the Jinto mountains on Voikomlya," Felix whispers into my ear. "They're amazing fighters."

"Nice to meet you, Thalia," I say reverently. "I've been to your world and met some of your sisters." More specifically, I made dream connections to a couple of the warrior nuns so I could learn a bit of their fighting style, but since I never asked permission, I don't mention that part.

At the mention of her order, Thalia's thin face saddens.

"She's exiled and lives here on Earth." Felix further lowers his voice. "The reason she doesn't say anything is that she's under a vow of silence."

"See? Gossip," Ariel says.

Thalia takes out a phone and frantically types something out.

Ariel's phone beeps. Looking at it, she smiles and says, "Thalia said something not-so-flattering about Felix, then suggested we follow her to the limo."

The trip through the airport is uneventful, and when we exit, the palest woman I've ever seen is waiting for us outside. If she were human, she'd look to be in her late sixties, but I doubt human is what she is, as they rarely have such an unfathomable look in their eyes.

Nodding at the woman, Thalia takes out her phone and types up a storm.

Ariel checks the text and shows me the screen.

This is Edith. She's the oldest vampire on Earth. She's your protection. I'm just the driver.

A vampire, and the oldest on Earth to boot? Impressive. Given the woman's wrinkles and frown lines, I never would've guessed her nature—though it does explain those eyes and the paleness.

Cognizant who can become vampires upon their death are called pre-vamps. Not all of them turn, though. I've heard that drinking blood from a more powerful vampire helps their odds—with the side-effect being that they become sire-bonded to the donor vampire and have to do their bidding for a while. Living on Gomorrah hurts those turning odds, so you never meet pre-vamps there, only full vampires. Before they turn, pre-vamps are extremely long-lived, so Edith must've been ancient before her "death."

"You must be Felix, Ariel, and Bailey," she says with a slight German accent.

Felix and I reply that it's very nice to meet her, and Ariel just mumbles something unintelligible. Though she's kicked her vampire blood addiction, she doesn't feel comfortable around walking, talking sources of her drug of choice.

Getting into the limo, we pull out of the airport and promptly get stuck in traffic—New York at its finest. After a few minutes of the car alternating between crawling along and standing still, Edith stiffens and sits up straighter.

What the puck?

A woman in a nightgown steps onto the road. Then a man in silk boxers. Then more and more people in sleepwear.

My heartbeat picks up speed.

Their eyes are fiery, just like the Overtaken on Gomorrah.

This group is better armed, though.

As one, they raise their guns and fire at us.

CHAPTER EIGHT

I CRINGE, my eyes squeezing shut as the bullets slam into the limo, the deafening noise of gunfire blending with Felix's shrill screams.

Silence falls, followed by another round of gunshots.

By all rights, I should be holey, but I feel okay.

I open my eyes.

There isn't even a crack in the windshield.

"Bulletproof," Felix explains hoarsely, wiping the sweat from his brow.

To the side of me, Ariel is holding a gun. I have no idea where she pulled it from.

Thalia sets the car in "park" and reaches for the door handle.

"No," Edith says, her fangs extending. With a lisp, she orders, "Stay!"

Before we can argue, the vampire whirls into too-fast-to-track motion. I assume she opens the limo door, exits, and closes the door behind herself, but it's done with such speed I barely catch it—and not a single bullet has the chance to fly in.

Oblivious to the spray of bullets, she lunges at the nearest attacker.

The Overtaken fire again.

Edith doesn't seem to care.

An eyeblink later, the first Overtaken is a pile of gore.

A millisecond after that, another one is ripped apart. Then the next.

Two heartbeats later, all that's left are assorted body parts.

Edith turns away from her victims, her face taking on a strained, constipated look. Before I can wonder about vampire digestion, a bullet emerges from a bleeding hole in her neck and clanks onto the pavement.

Edith relaxes, and the hole heals right away.

"Wow," Felix mutters.

You can say that again. I knew that older vampires were powerful, but this is scary.

Edith's eyes take on the mirrored look of glamour, and she flashes to the nearest bystander car. She performs her vampire mind trick on everyone inside, then glamours all the rest of the bystanders as far as the nearest exit.

The glamoured drivers start their engines and head straight into the ditch by the side of the road, clearing it for us.

Edith whooshes back into the limo and orders Thalia to drive.

The nun floors the gas, and we leave the highway before anyone can say "dial 911." Edith takes out a phone and orders someone to "clean up" near the exit we've just left.

At triple the speed limit, we fly through the city streets until a police officer stops us—which is when Edith glamours him to be our escort. The cop gets back into his car, starts the siren, and clears the way for us until we turn onto the Brooklyn Bridge.

From there, the ride to Felix and Ariel's downtown building is uneventful. Leaving Thalia in the car, we step into the lobby. I half expect more Overtaken to attack again, but none do.

An elevator ride later, we reach the bulletproof front door of the apartment, and Edith says, "I'll wait outside."

Felix and I shrug while Ariel looks relieved.

As we step inside, two familiar furry creatures come to greet us: a chinchilla and a cat.

Hi, the chinchilla—Fluffster, who's really a type of Cognizant called domovoi—says in my head. *Good to see you again.*

The cat gives me and everyone else a once-over, then pretends she happened to check on the front door by accident. Her attitude seems to say, "A purebred Persian with a face as flat as mine doesn't *really* care if plebeians such as you exist."

Ariel scoops up Fluffster and hugs him to her chest.

"Bailey is going to stay with us for a bit. Isn't that awesome?"

The chinchilla looks at me unblinkingly, his eyes too intelligent for a rodent. *Are you going to be helping out with rent?* he asks mentally.

"Dude." Felix rolls his eyes. "If you must know, thanks to Bailey, Ariel and I are going to be 'handsomely rewarded' soon."

Fluffster demands to know why, so I bring him up to speed.

If I know Felix, he's not going to ask for money, Fluffster says mentally when the story is over. *This household could go completely bankrupt, and he wouldn't bat an eye.*

"I'll get money, don't worry." Ariel rubs the fluffy, frugal creature against her cheek.

"And I plan to ask for something that can totally be monetized," Felix says. "I want to start a VR game company on Gomorrah."

"Wait, don't tell us." Ariel lowers Fluffster to the floor. "You're going to build the Matrix."

"The Matrix was a prison," Felix says defensively. "I want to build a fully immersive VR game environment that people would want to visit voluntarily and stay in for months on end."

"Potato, potahto." Ariel saunters over to a linen closet and pulls out a set of sheets and towels. "Both are simulated worlds with lots of action and adventure." She glances at me. "Come, let's get you settled in."

She leads me into an empty room with a bed, table,

and bookshelves filled with paper books. Stripping the current sheets from the bed, she replaces them with the new ones and hangs the towels on the back of the chair.

I scan the books. They're all about magic—the performance art, that is, not powers. Makes sense. This is Princess Peach's room—or was—and she's really into this stuff.

"Is it okay that I'll be using her bed?" I ask Ariel, nodding at a nearby picture of Princess Peach herself.

"Oh, yeah," Ariel says. "She's on Atlantis, a world where time flows much faster than here. My math isn't so good, but I think in the time we've had this conversation, she's experienced a whole day of honeymoon bliss."

"So, if you know where she is, could we—"

"No. If Valerian were to go there with the intention of asking her for a favor, she'd see him coming and not be around when he arrives. And that's the best case. If he's not lucky, Valerian would catch her—which is when her hubby would kill him in the most spectacular manner. He really wants them to have this time to themselves and specifically warned against interruptions."

Right then. No help from Princess Peach or her "hubby." Not that either of them could help with the biggest problem of all— Collywobbles, who doesn't even exist in the waking world.

Unless he does. What does anyone really know about a god of nightmares?

"You hungry?" Ariel asks.

I reply in the affirmative, and she drags me to the kitchen before I can clarify my dietary hesitations.

I needn't have worried. Grinning like a maniac, Felix puts a large bunch of bananas into a salad bowl and places it ceremoniously in front of me.

He and Ariel get what he calls "his special," and the domovoi a bowl of oats with nuts. The cat receives a can of food that says "Fancy Feast" on it and has a picture of a feline very similar to her—but I think that's just weird marketing and not proof that cats are cannibalistic.

Is it true all you eat is bananas, like a monkey? Fluffster mentally asks me when I peel my first one.

"When on Earth, yes," I say with my mouth full. "It's the food I trust the most." And not very much at that, but I don't add that bit; Felix is already having too much fun at my expense.

I can live on oats and hay, Fluffster says. *Which, like bananas, is inexpensive.* He looks meaningfully at Felix, Ariel, and the cat.

Felix nearly chokes with mirth. "Don't worry," he says when he catches his breath. "If finances get tough, Ariel and I promise to live on bananas as well."

"And don't forget oats," Ariel says.

The cat gives everyone a look that seems to say, "If you don't get me my special food, I'll feast on your not-very-fancy eyeballs instead."

They tease me more with each banana I peel, and when I finish the whole bunch, Felix gets up, goes over to a cupboard, and takes out a couple of familiar packets.

I narrow my eyes at him. "You have manna?"

"Got a taste for it when we stayed on Gomorrah, so I smuggled in a bunch," Felix says. "It's all yours. I just wanted Ariel to see the banana eating at least once."

"Evil," I mutter, reaching for a packet.

"Genius," Ariel says, grinning.

Glaring at her, I dig into the heavenly food as they finish their boring, unsanitary Earth dishes.

For the rest of the day, I make myself comfortable in my new environment. We watch a movie and play violent video games, and I finally crash in the borrowed bed.

Nutcracker doesn't appear in my dreams, which is a relief.

The next couple of days pass by quickly; having roommates who aren't your mother can be pretty fun. On the third day, Felix gets a text from Valerian:

Be at the lab at 5.

When we notify Edith about this development, she's not surprised in the least.

Our limo ride to the JFK airport is blessedly uneventful. No Overtaken attack, and when we stop at the passenger drop-off point, Ariel asks Thalia, "You're not coming with us, right?"

The nun shakes her head.

"She's made a vow to stay on Earth or some such," Felix whispers.

Of course. I can see how staying on Earth is a form

of penitence, on par with a vow of silence or fasting. When I share this opinion with the others, Ariel starts violently defending her home world, and we argue about it all the way to the lab.

Valerian is already waiting for us when we walk inside, and he's not alone.

A number of unfamiliar people are here, along with some I've met before—besides Kit and Itzel, that is.

One such person is Chester, a probability manipulator who looks like a satyr. Another one is Nina, a woman with facial piercings and extremely powerful telekinesis abilities. Also here is Colton, a giant who is a small enough example of his kind to be able to live on Earth. All three of them are members of the New York Council.

"Welcome," Valerian says. "Let me make the introductions." He proceeds to name me and everyone I know, along with our powers. When he gets to the first stranger, I pay closer attention.

"This is Fabian," Valerian says, nodding at a man only slightly smaller than Colton. "He's the Alpha of the Berlin pack."

Impressive. A werewolf Alpha is as powerful as an ally can get.

"He's famous for his martial arts," Ariel whispers reverently.

"You're too kind," Fabian growls with a heavy German accent. "I invented wolfu, the first martial art performed in wolf form."

Nina tugs on her nose ring. "A wolf fighting? How would that even look?"

"Let's hope we don't get into enough danger to find out," Itzel grumbles.

"That's Stanislav," Valerian continues, nodding at a gray-haired man wearing all black. "Head Enforcer of the Saint Petersburg Council."

Felix eyes the man warily. "A chort?"

"*Da,*" Stanislav says with a frown. With a thick Russian accent, he asks, "You have a problem with that?"

"*Nyet, nyet,*" Felix says quickly. "It's nice to meet you."

It is indeed. Chorts can mess with their victim's organs and turn parts of their own anatomy insubstantial when attacked. Stanislav might be even more useful than an Alpha werewolf, and definitely scarier to touch.

Edith examines Stanislav very carefully, and he glares at her in return. I wonder what's up with that. I've heard something about vampires and chorts being at each other's throats but don't recall the details.

"Last but not least is Dylan." Valerian gestures at an attractive young woman in a leather jacket. "Though Cognizant, she doesn't have a power in a traditional sense. She'll be our science adviser."

Dylan lifts her chin. "If knowledge is power—and it is—I'm the most formidable Cognizant here."

"Don't forget the most modest," Itzel says with an eye roll.

Valerian gives Itzel a stern look. "Dylan has a genius-level IQ and doctorates in multiple disciplines—including virology."

"And don't forget my knack for languages," Dylan says. "I'm your translator as well."

"Gnomes are good with languages," Itzel objects. "I speak several."

"Yes, but unlike you," Valerian says, "Dylan was willing to spend the time to learn the language of Necronia from our necromancer prisoner."

Itzel stiffens. "I needed to design the masks."

"Which I helped with," Dylan says. "If you—"

"Speaking of masks," Valerian says. "Those of you who haven't, please try on yours."

All of us hustle over to the table where the masks await.

"I used hygieia on yours already," Valerian says, pointing at the middle one. "Go ahead and put it on."

I examine the mask. It looks overdesigned—like it might help out against a poison gas attack, not just a virus. A strap goes over the top of my head, and two others loop around my ears, creating a snug fit. When I put it on, I can smell something chemical and metallic, but my breathing doesn't slow down.

"This is an amazing design," I say, my voice muffled.

Ariel snatches her mask from the table. "It *is* really cool. Bailey looks and sounds like Bane."

"That's Batman's nemesis," Felix explains. "Leave it to Ariel to link anything and everything to her favorite caped crusader."

Ariel lightly punches his shoulder and puts on her mask. Immediately, she looks like a gnome. So does Felix when he tries on his.

Nina levitates her mask onto her face while everyone else puts on their masks more traditionally.

As if it's the most natural thing in the world, Fabian starts to strip, exposing rows upon rows of muscles that only the most potent of steroids can conjure up in non-werewolf folks. When he's down to his boxers, he turns his back to us and finishes stripping.

At the shameless display of his glutes of steel, Itzel looks away, Kit whistles like a cartoon wolf, Ariel waggles her eyebrows, and Dylan blushes like a medieval maiden. Conscious of Valerian's narrow-eyed stare on me, I pretend to be swooning as well.

"My mask is a special design," Fabian says without turning, his German accent even deeper. "Just wanted to test it one last time."

With a flash, he turns into his wolf form. The size of a bison and even more muscular than in humanoid form, it's a shaggy thing of terrifying beauty. And indeed, his mask has elongated to accommodate his canine face, making him look like a muzzled hellhound.

When he switches back to his man form, the mask contracts, but no one pays attention to that because this time, he's facing us, his family jewels and other bits out in full force.

Kit whistles again, Ariel fans herself, and Dylan looks on the verge of fainting.

"Great job, Itzel," the werewolf says, ignoring it all.

Itzel looks him over, swallows very loudly, and averts her eyes. I, on the other hand, gape for all I'm worth to annoy Valerian.

It must work, because his chiseled jaw tightens and he uses his powers to shield Fabian's bits with a fig leaf until the werewolf puts his boxers back on.

Acting disappointed, I turn to look at the leftover masks. There's at least a dozen of them.

"What about those?" I ask, nodding at the stash.

"They're for the second part of our team," Valerian says, still sounding irritated—much to my delight. "We're meeting them en route."

Puck. We've already got an ancient vampire, a giant, a telekinetic, an uber, a chort, a shapeshifter, an alpha werewolf, an illusionist, and a robot suit. Now it sounds like there are more reinforcements. By the time we get to our destination, we'll be a freaking army.

Grunting, Colton collects the remaining masks and stashes them in his ginormous backpack.

Itzel shows us some of the mask features—like being able to eat and drink without taking the mask off —and Dylan makes sure to point out which features were her contributions.

"You still have to make sure the food and drink aren't contaminated," Itzel says apologetically when she's done with the demo. "If I'd had to build a decontamination chamber, the project would—"

"No worries," Colton booms and turns to show us a

bag the size of an industrial refrigerator. "I'm carrying the supplies."

"Careful," Valerian says. "There are grenades in there."

Kit slides her mask up her forehead and transforms into a creepy plant-like creature without a mouth and nose, and with green cactus spines instead of hair. Returning back to her anime-character self, she says, "In a pinch, I won't need the supplies or the mask and could live off photosynthesis."

"*Nyechist*," Stanislav mumbles under his breath.

"That means something like *evil forces*," Felix whispers into my ear. "Usually said about chorts."

Stanislav's hearing must be good—he gives Felix a withering glare.

Chester also takes his mask off, revealing a devilish grin. "Shall we go?"

"Just one thing." Valerian unfurls a big hand-drawn map on the table. "Memorize the path to Necronia, in case we get separated."

"Done," Dylan says instantly. "I have a photographic memory."

"I hope you have the patience to wait for the more mentally challenged among us," Fabian growls through his mask, and Dylan takes a step back, proving she's got enough street smarts to be wary of an annoyed werewolf.

I memorize our path with ease; making sense of such maps is a course taught in middle school on Gomorrah. Felix and Ariel take the longest, and no wonder: Their teacher was Hekima, whose primary objective in his classes turned out to be causing nightmares.

"Now grab a weapon and let's go," Valerian says when everyone recites the map from memory to his satisfaction.

Ariel sprints over to the farthest corner of the room with all the excitement of a kid on Christmas morning. There are two piles there—one of blade weapons like knives, swords, and the like, and the other of guns.

"Remember, firearms don't work on every world," Dylan says as she watches Ariel cram pistols into every crevice of her outfit.

With a shrug, Ariel picks up a knife and a scabbard with a sword in it.

"I've got my own," Chester says and pulls out what looks like a sword handle from the back of his pants. He presses something, and the handle turns into a weapon I've never seen before—a sword made from a substance that looks just like the shimmering plasma of the gates.

"Wait," Felix says. "Isn't that—"

"A family heirloom." Chester winks and retracts the blade.

When it's Colton's turn, the giant picks up a claymore, which looks like a dagger in his massive hand.

Itzel forms a lightning ball on her palms. "I'm good."

Nina makes a scabbard and a scimitar fly into her

hands and attaches them to her waist. "I probably won't need these, but it doesn't hurt to have them."

Edith grabs an ax and straps it to her back, while Stanislav does the same with a saber.

Spotting a few Gomorran guns, I grab one, and Valerian and Dylan do the same.

"Should I distribute the grenades?" Colton booms.

"Not yet," Valerian says, picking up a pair of sai—pointy dagger-like weapons.

"What kind of grenades are we talking about?" I ask as I strap a dagger to my waist and a katana to my back. I'm no expert on the daggers, but I've studied how to wield the katana in the dreams of two Kendo masters who'd hired me to help them dream-spar 'to the death.'

"Sleep and poison grenades," Valerian replies. He seems to have finally gotten over his irritation with me. "The first in case we want you to dreamwalk in a group of enemies, the other in case we need a weapon of mass destruction."

"Wouldn't the poison kill us along with the bad guys?" Felix asks.

"Not if you keep the mask on," Itzel says.

"Got it." Felix walks over to a big contraption I hadn't noticed before. It must be a new version of his robot suit, and it boasts four arms, Hindu-goddess style.

"Keep the mask on," Itzel says when Felix starts to take his off.

"She's right." Dylan straps a rapier to her waist. "A

virus can penetrate the robot faceplate. If I had designed the suit for you, I would've—"

"We made the suit before we knew about this mission," Itzel says. "Besides, who cares? His head will fit, even with the mask on."

"Well, I care," Felix grumbles, climbing into the heap of metal. Through a speaker in his chest, he says, "I can barely breathe."

"You'll survive," Valerian says, then packs away the map and leads our ragtag procession to the hub room.

"How about I go first?" Chester says when we all approach the purple gate that is step one of our journey.

No one objects. His chances of getting randomly attacked are minuscule compared to those of us without his probability manipulation powers.

Once Chester steps through the shimmering plasma, the others follow. When it's my turn, I step in with some excitement. The one thing I've never really done much is Otherland spelunking, since that's more dangerous than visiting dream worlds, yet not that much more entertaining.

Or so I thought.

When I come out on the other side, I exhale in wonder.

CHAPTER NINE

THE SKY above us is a fluorescent purple, with pink cotton-candy clouds—a combination I've never used in my dream world creations because, ironically, I thought it was too unrealistic to exist in nature. There's also a Saturn-like ring around this planet, and two moons—one slightly smaller than Earth's and one twice that size.

As we hurry to the next gate, I notice that my steps are lighter, indicating a different gravity from that on Earth and Gomorrah.

The most worrying part is the air. Even through the mask, it feels unusually thick and sweet—but I figure if it were poisonous, Valerian would've planned for it.

"I've been on this Otherland before," Ariel whispers. "There's a gate to the Las Vegas airport nearby."

Felix glares at her. "You go into Otherlands to end up on the same world? The risk—"

"Beats an eight-hour plane flight," she mutters back.

Chester lets out a sigh. "Too bad Vegas isn't where we're headed. I love that place."

I'm sure he does. He can win at any game of chance, no matter how much the odds are stacked in favor of the house.

Felix is staring at the yellow shimmer that is our destination. "You know the gate we're about to take was on Hekima's list of 'dangerous ones to avoid,' right?"

"I'm sure that asshat was exaggerating," Valerian says coolly.

"Let's hope so," Itzel mumbles under her breath.

Oblivious to any possible danger, Chester steps into the new gate like I'd step into my favorite restaurant. The rest of us follow more cautiously. And it's a good thing we do.

When we emerge on the other side, Hekima's description doesn't seem all that exaggerated. For starters, the temperature and heat make the bathhouse from Valerian's dream seem chilly in comparison. Then there's the pterodactyl-like birds that circle in the sky like vultures above a desert.

Before I can ask Valerian to make us invisible to the fauna, a pterodactyl dives for us.

Almost casually, Nina extends her hand. With a pained shriek, the flying creature stops mid-flight and slams into a nearby cliff.

Stanislav mutters something in Russian in an impressed tone, and Felix replies, "*Da, da.*"

The rest of the flying creatures must not be choosy

eaters; they swarm around the body of their fallen comrade with loud shrieks of glee.

My enthusiasm for Otherland spelunking fades a bit as we continue. The next world is a never-ending desert with a strangely starless night sky. The one after that is a gray tundra.

"What are we expecting on Necronia?" I ask, the tension in my shoulders easing when nothing attacks us for another two worlds.

"It's run by necromancers," Dylan says, taking on a professorial tone. "They have a religion that revolves around souls, and they use reanimated corpses to run their economy. That keeps humans grateful by letting them live in luxury. According to—"

"That reminds me." Valerian looks at Kit. "They have some sexual taboos I wanted to warn everyone about."

Everyone who knows Kit well follows Valerian's gaze with curiosity, while the woman herself minces forward as if "everyone" didn't mean "her."

"They are deeply homophobic," Valerian says, and Kit slows her pace. "Also, there's a strict anti-adultery law."

"Which is why Wrakar was exiled," Dylan chimes in. "He had an extra-marital affair."

Kit stops and morphs into an androgynous person of unspeakable beauty. "What if they're single?" she asks in a voice that's as masculine as it is feminine.

The corners of Chester's eyes crinkle. "How about you just keep it in your pants?"

Pouting, Kit looks at Dylan. "Fine. But maybe someone can help me scratch the itch on the way?"

Dylan's ears turn a deep red, and she gracelessly sprints into a blue gate in front of us.

Fabian growls something in German, and Itzel replies in kind.

"Well, I just figured sex is something else she might have a doctorate in," Kit says defensively and steps into the gate after Dylan. The rest of us follow, and I can't help but notice how Ariel is doing her best never to be near Edith.

Speaking of Edith… Isn't she going to be a problem on a world of necromancers? In our morgue encounter with Wrakar, a group of Enforcers was a major hindrance.

I mull this over for a couple of worlds before sharing my concern with the team, Edith included.

She huffs. "I'm too powerful for any necromancer to control."

"I'm sure," I say. "But won't they know what you are and get upset? Didn't your kind drive them off most worlds?"

"They won't even sense that I'm a vampire," Edith says. "The plan is to say that I'm an uber. My lack of youthful looks should help with the deception."

Chester smirks. "True. Vamps aren't known for their need of Botox injections."

"Still," I say. "It's a little worrying."

Falling into step beside me, Valerian places a hand on my shoulder and squeezes lightly. My treacherous stomach feels wobbly all of a sudden. "Edith's ability to glamour necromancers overrides the risk of discovery," he murmurs in my ear. "You don't need to worry."

Ignoring the warmth spreading through me, I remove his hand from my shoulder and turn to Edith. "Is that true?"

"It's how we got so much information out of our necro captive," she says proudly.

Hearing this, Ariel backs away from the vampire and changes the topic by asking about the team that Valerian mentioned will be waiting for us.

Oh, yeah. I almost forgot about that.

"Since Icelus is operating on multiple worlds, we're trying to organize a cross-Otherland defense," Valerian replies. "The people you're asking about are from the worlds that have decided to participate thus far."

"Wow," Ariel says.

"That's cool," Felix says.

Itzel bobs her head. "A historical achievement, indeed."

If I weren't mad at Valerian, I'd join their praises. Cognizant worlds usually stay out of each other's business.

Falling into step beside me again, Valerian touches my arm. "There's actually someone waiting for us who you might be interested in."

I not-so-subtly step out of his reach and lift an eyebrow.

Annoyingly, Valerian doesn't look put off. "Since Icelus uses a dreamwalker to coordinate across worlds, we decided to do the same and located a willing one on a world called Raira."

My second eyebrow joins its twin, and they both shoot up my forehead. "You know another dreamwalker, and you're just telling me now?"

His lips press together. "We just recruited him a few days ago."

"You might want to give Valerian a break," Kit says just as I'm about to say something snide. "The Council of Councils wanted to use *you* to coordinate across worlds, but he said it was out of the question."

I blink up at Valerian's ocean-blue eyes. "You did?"

"I wasn't going to throw you under the bus for a second time," he says, his face unreadable.

"Hmm," is my genius reply. I look at my friends, but they all avoid my gaze.

Fine. I jump through the next gate and end up on an icy plain under a toxic-looking green sky.

No one bugs me for the next two gates. Felix and Stanislav speak Russian, Itzel, Edith, and Fabian banter in German, while Felix and Dylan discuss computer science in what might as well be a foreign tongue.

And surprise, surprise—Dylan has a doctorate in that too.

The next world is a green savannah with waist-high grass.

Ariel catches up with me. "Am I the only one who thinks Necronia sounds like Narnia's dead sister?"

"Hush," Edith hisses. "Something's coming."

Everyone stops talking.

Thunder—or something like it—rumbles in the distance. The grass vibrates as the ground shakes.

"An earthquake?" Felix whispers.

"Run!" Chester yells and hoofs it to the gate.

I finally see the danger—a herd of mammoth-like creatures, only bigger and fiercer-looking. If they reach us, we're all meat tortillas.

As one, we launch into a sprint. Edith, Ariel, and Fabian are soon in the lead. The herd is gaining on us. To my shock, Nina sits down on the ground in a lotus pose and closes her eyes, a serene expression appearing on her face.

What the—

Everyone, Nina included, floats up off the ground.

Ah. She's using her powers again.

Floating like this is an eerie feeling that I've experienced once before and hoped never to feel again, but it beats the alternative.

The creatures stampede under us.

When they're gone, Nina gently lowers us back down. "You guys might want to start pulling your own weight," she says, jumping to her feet.

Ariel follows her into the gate, and the rest of us walk in after them.

"Is this your home world?" Chester asks Colton after I exit on the other side.

It takes me a second to figure out why he singled out the giant.

The primitive huts in the distance are the size of four-story buildings on Earth. Oh, and there are a dozen giants behind Chester. They're coming toward us from the direction of the next gate we need to take.

All are big but one is especially so.

A giant giant.

Itzel gasps. "Look at their eyes!"

"Crap," Felix mutters.

You can say that again.

That fire in the giants' eyes means only one thing.

They're also Overtaken.

CHAPTER TEN

BEFORE ANYONE CAN BLINK, Ariel is already holding a gun in her hand. Aiming at the giant, she presses the trigger.

An empty click sounds.

Puck. A world where firearms don't work. Isn't Chester's luck supposed to rub off on us?

But hey, that's Earth technology. I yank out my Gomorran gun, set it to stun, and shoot the giant giant.

Nothing happens.

Heart racing, I switch the setting to lethal and shoot again.

Still nothing. I guess since giants aren't allowed on Gomorrah, no one bothered to calibrate these guns to impact one.

One of the giants stoops to pick up a stone.

Puck.

He hurls it at me. I duck. Colton catches the stone

and pelts it back at the bigger giant. The Overtaken giant stumbles but keeps on coming.

"Stay back!" Valerian jumps in front of me, as if he can somehow shield me from giants. Inspired by his example, Felix steps protectively in front of Dylan, who looks paler than Edith.

Edith herself, along with Chester, Stanislav, and Ariel, charges forward, and Colton follows, while Fabian strips off his clothes and morphs into his impressive wolf form before joining the fray as well. Kit, too, shifts into a copy of the giant giant and lumbers after everyone.

"Valerian, use your powers to hide us from them!" Dylan shouts.

He grimly shakes his head. "I can't. I'd need to trick them all, but I can only handle one. Best I can do for you is make you not see the violence."

"No, thanks," Dylan says, but I can tell she's tempted.

I'm tempted too, but I'd rather know what's going on, so I can help.

Itzel, who's stayed by my side, shoots the smallest of the Overtaken with a ball of her gnome lightning. It smashes into his forehead, and he drops to the ground.

Score.

Itzel tries doing it again, but her new target dodges the projectile.

To my right, Nina extends her hand and visibly concentrates.

The second-smallest giant lifts off the ground an

inch, then plops back down, which causes him to stumble. The ground shakes as he crashes down, nearly squashing Fabian—who jumps away on hind paws with a grace I wouldn't expect from an animal his size.

A rock smashes into Nina's head, and she drops to her knees, blood trickling down her temple. "Seriously, start pulling your own weight, people."

Ignoring her, Edith swings her ax at the giants, who try to grab her.

One loses an arm, another a finger. But her victory comes at a cost—the giant giant grabs Edith by her legs and yanks hard. Her ax drops to the ground as she curses and flails.

Ariel throws a dagger at the giant giant's head.

Bullseye. Or rather, giant's eye, as that's exactly what the dagger pierces.

The Overtaken giant doesn't react to the injury. He simply grabs Edith's head with his free hand and pulls with a twisting motion.

Fearing for her, I leap out from behind Valerian and throw my own dagger at the giant's other eye. Sadly, my aim isn't as good as Ariel's. I hit the wrong giant, and in his shoulder, not the eye.

Activating the gate sword, Chester slices at the giant giant's leg.

The leg is severed, but it's too late for Edith.

By the time the giant crashes to the ground, the vampire's head and body separate and fly in different directions, spraying blood and bits of flesh everywhere.

Valerian yanks me behind him with a curse as I

gape at Edith's remnants, my stomach churning with equal parts horror, pity, and disgust. No matter how ancient, a vampire can't survive a beheading.

Stanislav slashes at the next biggest giant with his saber, slicing off a chunk of his leg. Seemingly oblivious to the injury, the giant swings a massive arm at the chort, but his grasping hand goes through Stanislav's suddenly incorporeal torso—which is when Ariel chops it off at the wrist with her sword.

Oblivious to the fountain of blood gushing from his injured limb, the giant pivots to snatch up Ariel with his remaining hand, but Kit finally catches up with everyone and smashes a car-sized fist into the attacker's face.

The giant crashes to the floor.

With a roar, Colton beheads another one with his claymore. Fabian and Stanislav help Ariel down another, while Chester and Kit get yet one more.

At that point, the fight turns, and one by one, our allies kill or incapacitate the rest of the Overtaken giants.

When it's all over, Nina makes her way to Edith's remains, her expression somber. "To live so long just to perish here," she murmurs, shaking her head. "What a shame."

Equally grim, Colton scoops up nearby dirt, his enormous hand creating a hole worthy of a shovel. He keeps digging until the pit is six feet deep. At that point, Fabian picks up Edith's head and removes the mask, while Kit, still in her giant form, lifts the torso.

Gently, they lower the vampire's remains into the grave.

Kit and Colton cover Edith with dirt as Fabian puts on his clothing. Then Fabian hands Edith's mask to Colton, who wipes the blood and stashes the mask in his backpack.

"Anyone want to say anything?" Valerian asks, sweeping a grave gaze around our congregation.

"More giants might be on the way," Itzel says. "We should go."

I approach the grave on unsteady legs. I feel sick, both from the adrenaline overdose and the senseless slaughter I just witnessed. Bending down, I find a patch of ground that *isn't* soaked with blood and toss some dirt into the grave. "Phobetor has a lot to answer for."

Though my voice is barely above a whisper, Valerian's jaw tenses. "Don't say his name." He walks over and hygieias my hand before I can do so myself. In a softer tone, he adds, "But you're right. He does."

"We should listen to the wise gnome and go before more trouble catches up to us," Chester says.

Everyone mutters their agreement, and we plod to the gate, disinclined to talk for the next six worlds.

———

"I'M STARVING," Fabian says when we enter a hub located in a lush forest meadow. "As the German proverb says, 'Hunger leads the wolf to the village.'"

Kit morphs into an adorable girl wearing a red

riding hood. "I'm also hungry… like a wolf."

"Let's make camp," Valerian says. "I'll make us invisible to any predators that might lurk in the forest."

"I doubt they'd dare show up here." Removing his boxers again, Fabian takes on his wolf form and stalks into the bushes.

"I'm also going to get something to eat," Stanislav says, holding his saber. "Anyone care to join?"

Chester, Kit, and Nina tag along with the chort while the rest of us build a couple of fires.

Felix steps out of his robot suit and plops in front of the largest fire. "Am I the only one who finds the idea of a necromancer world creepy?"

I crouch to Felix's right. "I do too."

"It could be worse." Ariel folds her legs into a lotus pose across from me. "It could be a world full of vampires."

"That wouldn't be sustainable," Dylan says, joining us. "I've run the numbers. If a world has a greater than five percent vampire population—"

I don't hear the rest because Valerian strides over and takes a seat next to me.

I scooch away from him.

Shaking his head, he walks over to Colton's backpack, gets something out, and sits next to me again.

"Seriously?" I scoot away once more.

"Here." He slides next to me yet again and hands me a packet of manna, along with a water bottle from Gomorrah.

I snatch the food and drink without a thank-you, which is harder than it sounds. Mom raised me to be polite.

Valerian starts to say something, but Stanislav and his group of hunters show up, carrying a bleeding furry creature.

Gross. They're going to skin it and actually eat the meat. Did they forget all the gore we just saw on the giants' world? Leaning toward Valerian, I whisper, "Can you use your powers to prevent me from seeing their meal?"

Smirking, he does as I ask. After that, I can't bring myself to chase him off, so we sit side by side as I eat and drink through the special openings in the mask—a task that requires a surprising amount of concentration.

When I finish, I tell Valerian I don't need the illusion anymore, and he removes it. Through the mask, the smell of charred flesh isn't as bad as I feared, though watching everyone shove that unsanitary meat into their masks is nauseating.

"What do you think the Overtaken want?" I ask, mostly to distract myself.

Dylan lowers her meat skewer. "I guess they want whatever *you know who* wants."

"We call him Collywobbles." Felix wipes his greasy fingers on his shirt, and I almost ask Valerian to reapply the illusion. "But yeah, what does he want?"

Valerian tosses a log into the fire. "In the long run, more nightmares. Or more precisely, power."

I frown. "But how does killing my sister accomplish that? Or attacking us?"

"Not us." Valerian's forehead creases. "So far, I'm only aware of the Overtaken attacking you and Maxwell."

"Who's Maxwell?" Ariel asks at the same time as I exclaim, "Me?"

"Maxwell is the dreamwalker with the other team. We're going to meet him soon," Valerian says. "As to why—something about dreamwalkers must be a threat to Collywobbles, and he doesn't seem to trust Icelus to deal with it."

I turn to him—and can't help but notice that we're close enough to kiss, or would be if I were ever insane enough to let that happen. Well, and if there were no masks in the way. "How do you know it was me the Overtaken want?"

Valerian heaves a sigh. "The mess in the werewolf restaurant wasn't the first time they came after you. The Enforcers thwarted five attempts prior to that— two by your apartment and three near your work." Eyes gleaming, he places a hand on my knee. "That's why I wanted to put you in a safe house."

"Great." I not-so-gently remove his hand. "Now I'm on the priority kill list of a god."

No one replies. They just sit there, looking at me with pity.

I shiver, and not just because of the brisk evening breeze. As if to make things worse, I overhear Chester telling a scary story to his fellow New York Council members at the nearby fire. On the word "eviscerate," I tune the rest out.

"I wonder how many Overtaken there are?" Ariel asks after she finishes with her hunk of meat and tosses her skewer into the fire. "Also, do we know *how* Collywobbles turns people into them?"

"Maxwell might know the answer to the latter, but I can tell you about the former," Dylan says, again taking on that professional tone. "Thousands of people on Gomorrah have reported symptoms consistent with what we've dubbed the Overtaken. But the number of the affected is harder to puzzle out on Earth and other similar places since the condition has only affected the Cognizant thus far, and we can't report supernatural-sounding details like fire eyes to human doctors. So we still don't know if humans are immune, or if Collywobbles just hasn't bothered with them."

Ariel shakes her head, her expression subdued. "So many people turned into mindless puppets."

"That's not exactly what happens," Dylan says. "When awake, the Overtaken are actually normal. Even at night, they only get up and sleepwalk on rare occasions—when Collywobbles has something for them to do, we think."

Felix's eyes widen. "So if we'd woken up the giants and the other people who got killed, they—"

"Those deaths are on Collywobbles's conscience," Ariel says sharply. "When it comes to self-defense, don't second-guess yourself or you'll be the next corpse."

On that cheerful note, the conversation peters out until Dylan yawns loudly, creating a chain reaction with the rest of us.

"Someone should watch me at night," I say, not meeting anyone's gaze. "If the Nutcracker attacks and wins, I might be a danger to you all."

"I'll take the first shift," Ariel says. "Felix can go next, then—"

"No." Valerian crosses his arms over his chest. "I'll watch her."

I open my mouth, then close it. I'm not sure how I feel about Valerian watching me sleep. Definitely *not* aroused. Or intrigued. Also, why does he want to do this? Is it because he doesn't trust me to be asleep at the same time as him—worried I'd waltz into his dreams and steal his precious secrets?

When no one argues with him, he puts out the fire, fishes out a sleeping bag from Colton's backpack, hygieias it, and puts it a perfect distance from the coals.

I stomp over to the sleeping bag and climb in. Puck him and these little acts of kindness. If he keeps this up, I'll feel like a jerk holding on to my grudge, which I bet is his evil plan.

Before I can stop him, he zips up my makeshift bed. "Sweet dreams," he murmurs, gazing down at me. "I'll be here if you need me."

"Whatever," I say, glad he can't see Pom turning coral pink on my wrist.

Closing my eyes, I instantly drift off.

CHAPTER ELEVEN

I'M STANDING in front of my video game design class, naked as a mole rat.

Everyone stares at me, some giggling and some rolling their eyes. My left hand moves to cover my groin area, and as my right one goes to hide my breasts, I realize something is missing from my wrist.

The furry bracelet.

Pom.

In an eyeblink, I use my powers to clothe myself and make the audience disappear.

Ah, the good old 'naked in public' dream. If I had a gold coin for every time I've stumbled into one of these, I'd be richer than a dragon.

Speaking of dream invasion—no Nutcracker here. Does he need me unaware that I'm dreaming for his strike? Just in case, I turn myself metallic before teleporting to the tower of sleepers.

"Hi," Pom says, appearing next to me as I examine

the people whose dreams I could potentially sneak into.

"Hey, bud. Hope you weren't awake during that fight with the giants."

When he says he wasn't, I update him on what's happened so far.

"So what now?" he asks when I'm done.

"I want to check on Mom," I say, spotting the gargoyle nurse I've been using for this purpose. "Want to join?"

He turns gray. "I don't like seeing Lidia like that."

He doesn't like it? It's *my* mom we're talking about.

Biting back an unnecessarily sharp retort, I touch the nurse and nudge her into a dream memory about Mom.

In this one, she's making sure there's enough goop available for Mom's feeding tube. Mom herself is lying there ashen and unmoving, for all intents and purposes a living corpse.

A hollow ache takes residence in my chest, and I let the nurse slip into her next dream while I teleport to my memory gallery. I know replaying a memory where Mom is fine doesn't change the reality of her current situation, but it's comforting nonetheless.

Once I'm calmer, I walk around the paintings depicting events from my life to see if there was any hint that I'd had a sister. I locate only the one that I already knew about, where I break a vase on which my twin and I had left our handprints.

I replay the memory.

Mom was sad, but it's unclear if she knew *why* she was sad. Thanks to a black window in her mind, she doesn't consciously recall killing Asha—or that Asha existed at all.

I strain to recall something—anything—else, but there's nothing. My theory is that seeing Mom kill Asha in front of me was so traumatic that I blocked the whole thing out, along with the majority of my childhood. But shouldn't there be at least a few stray memories?

Feeling heavier than before, I leave the memory gallery and reunite with Pom in the tower of sleepers, where I locate a few of my patients and provide some therapy sessions.

Making others feel better is a mood booster for me.

"You might want to create some exposure therapy for yourself," Pom says as we fly into the lobby and hover below a mosaic depicting an archery-target-like mandala made out of multicolored glass. "Your adrenaline levels are through the roof."

I grimace. "That would be tricky. The main source of my fear is going to a world with a nasty virus."

Pom nods sagely. "Of all the ways to perish, that one would be the worst for you."

"You can say that again." I swoop down and land on my metallic feet with a thud.

"Won't you be safe with the mask Itzel made?" Pom asks, following me down.

"No mask is perfect."

He wiggles his ears. "So how about that therapy then? To calm you down?"

I roll my eyes. "What would that even entail?"

"You can have a dream where you lick doorknobs in a bathroom."

Ugh. I suppress a shudder at that mental image. "No, thank you. And in any case, this is a deadly plague. I'm justified in my paranoia. Any other bright ideas?"

"We can talk about you and Valerian," he says hopefully, his coat turning a light orange hue as his pupils transform into hearts.

"Nope," I say and jolt myself awake.

UNDER THE LIGHT of four moons, I see Valerian sitting there, vigilantly guarding my slumber.

For some reason, the sight makes me smile.

Closing my eyes, I drift into sleep again—this time without any dreams.

IN THE MORNING, we have a hearty breakfast— another Valerian-smuggled manna for me, leftovers from dinner for the rest of the crew—and continue on our journey.

"Maxwell and the others are just through there," Valerian says as we approach a pink gate that, according to the map we memorized, leads to the world just before Necronia.

When we step through, we end up in an underground hub that looks just like the JFK one we started from.

Instead of a team, one person is waiting here for us. He's wearing a surgical mask with a plastic face shield on top. He looks us over with sad eyes, his forehead creasing in worry.

"Maxwell?" Valerian asks.

Nodding, the man turns away. "Those masks look like good ones, but it'll still be safer if we talk outside."

He hurries out of the hub, and we follow him through a maze of corridors right into what looks like a train station on Earth.

Except there aren't usually any corpses on Earth train stations, and I spot a dozen here. The dead—at least I assume that's what they are—are all dressed in odd clothing, their skin a strange purplish hue.

I suppress a shudder.

"What happened here?" Dylan asks, looking at a nearby man, whose face looks to have been contorted by agony before he perished.

Maxwell doesn't stop to explain. He carefully circles around the corpses in his path and picks up the pace again as we near an exit.

We follow him out. The buildings and the storefronts outside remind me of Midtown in Manhattan—except there are no people here at all, just more corpses.

"Stay there." Maxwell walks about fifteen feet away from us, looks back, and backs up one more step. "This should do it."

"Do what?" I shout. "Where's your team?"

He takes out a handkerchief and wipes at his eyes.

Puck. Is that blood on the handkerchief?

Before I can ask, he pockets the hanky with a somber expression. "They're dead."

On some level, I expected him to say something like that, yet it's still a shock. They must've been as formidable as our team, so for all but one to be dead—

"Dead?" Fabian steps toward Maxwell, but Dylan grabs his shoulder.

"Keep the distance," she says tensely. "If this is what I think—"

"They're not the only ones dead." Maxwell gestures at the nearest corpse. "The majority of this world's population are doomed too. Just as I am." He wipes his eyes with his bare hand and displays his fingers.

Yep. It was blood I saw.

Blood from the eyes.

If I were Maxwell, I'd be hysterical now.

"Haemolacria," Dylan mutters. "It's usually benign."

"It's the first symptom." Maxwell wipes the blood on his shirt. "Soon I'll have heart palpitations, then upset stomach, then just around the time my skin turns purplish red, I'll perish."

Pucking puck. Itzel's masks have a huge design flaw. There's no way to puke without taking them off—

which is why I just swallow the bile down and do my best to even out my breathing.

"When?" Valerian asks, his brow furrowed.

"Depends on one's immune system," Maxwell says. "The orc from my party lasted four days while the elf was dead the day after."

Slow breathing is out the window. I begin to hyperventilate.

"Does anyone else find it suspicious that he's the last person alive?" Chester asks conversationally. "Or that he has whatever the plague is, yet has a mask on? Or is it not airborne?"

"No, the virus transmits through air droplets," Maxwell says. "My team and I wore protective gear as we waited for you, but then the Overtaken attacked." He takes out the handkerchief again and dabs some of the new blood away. "It's my fault. It's me the Overtaken wanted, and everyone protected me as well as they could. The Overtaken killed some of them outright, and ripped off masks from the faces of the others. I was the only one who managed to keep my mask on. And one of the Overtaken must've been sick because the team displayed symptoms soon after."

"Then how did you catch the virus?" Dylan asks.

He shrugs. "Perhaps the virus can penetrate a mask like this, or maybe I caught it when I ate or drank. I was staying at the hospital with my team"—he gestures at a building across the street—"and in hindsight, that might've been a bad idea."

I'm only partially listening as the word *virus* repeats

on a loop in my mind. I want to run until my legs cramp up, then take a hygieia device and use it from head to toe, over and over and over again.

"So that's why you wanted to keep the distance?" Itzel asks.

Maxwell nods.

"This has to be the same virus we came to prevent on Necronia," Dylan says. "Icelus must've already let it loose on this world."

"That's what we assumed." Maxwell rummages through his pocket and takes out a couple of beakers. "These are blood samples from my team. Do you think you can figure out a cure using them? There's a lab at that hospital and—"

"Where?" Dylan's eyes gleam with excitement.

Maxwell tells her how to locate the lab in question, and Dylan sprints across the street.

"I'll make sure nothing attacks her," Fabian says and rushes after her.

I try to rein in my panic. "We should give Maxwell one of the better masks. This way, when he goes to the lab with Dylan, she's less likely to get infected."

Everyone likes the idea, so Valerian takes out a mask from Colton's bag and places it on the pavement.

We all step away as Maxwell approaches. Keeping his back to us as a precaution, he swaps his old mask for Itzel's design. When he's done, we return to our previous positions and wait for Dylan.

"We have a question for you," Valerian says after a

period of uncomfortable silence. "How do the Overtaken come to be the way they are?"

"It's also a virus, of sorts." Maxwell's voice sounds muffled by the new mask. "A person somewhere—let's call him Dreamer Zero—had a very special nightmare, one that allowed *you know who* in. Thus, Dreamer Zero was the first Overtaken, most likely without knowing it. Then, because the special nightmare was so memorably nasty, Zero felt obliged to tell a friend, or a relative, or a therapist about it. What he probably didn't know was that this particular nightmare is unique—hearing its details plants something like a virus in the subconscious in such a way that when the person who hears it goes to sleep, they *also* dream the exact same nightmare, thus giving access to *you know who*. From there, the nightmare spreads exponentially, far and wide."

Chester casts a nervous glance at Kit, Colton, and Nina, who look shell-shocked.

"How long between the nightmare and the sleep walking?" Nina asks in a strangely unsteady voice.

"A couple of nights," Maxwell says. "Why?"

"What was the nightmare about?" Chester asks, sounding equally strange.

"I'm not one of the Overtaken, so I haven't seen this particular nightmare," Maxwell says. "But even if I had, telling you about it would mean I'd turn you into an Overtaken, so I'd have to keep quiet."

Valerian examines the New York Council members with a frown. "Why are you asking all this?"

Colton shifts from foot to massive foot. "Chester told us about a nightmare he had last night. Then, when I went to sleep, I had the dream myself."

"So did I," Nina says grimly.

"Same," Kit says, glaring at Chester with narrowed eyes. "I can't believe you infected me—and not with something sexually transmitted at that."

Chester shakes his head. "My daughter couldn't sleep because of a nightmare." His voice is hollow. "She told me what it was, and I thought it curious when I dreamed the same thing."

"How long ago?" Maxwell asks sharply.

Chester scratches behind the back straps of his mask. "Two days. I've had the nightmare twice so far—which made it more notable and is the reason I told others about it."

Maxwell shakes his head. "You have two more days before you need to take precautions. I suggest having someone lock your room for the night." He looks at the other Overtaken-to-be. "You have three more days—unless you start messing with your sleep cycles to stall it."

"We have experience with people who are dangerous when they sleep," Nina says. "Gertrude, our fellow Council member, is a gangrene-giver who sleepwalks."

At the prospect of being treated like Gertrude, Colton, Kit, and Chester look glum.

"How much of the nightmare story do you need to hear to get into trouble?" I ask, recalling my eavesdropping from the other day. "I think I overheard Chester talk about his nightmare, but only caught a few words."

"If you didn't have the nightmare, you're fine." Maxwell gets his hanky out and dabs at his eyes again. "Make sure not to hear any more, though."

Puck, yeah. The idea of getting a mind virus, or whatever the term, has never even occurred to me, but now that it has, it goes to the top of my things to avoid, up there with crunching on kitty litter.

Kit morphs into Chester but with fiery eyes. "How could this even happen? Isn't your luck power supposed to protect you?"

Chester shrugs. "Bad things still happen to me. The universe is too chaotic to avoid that."

"Guys. Isn't that a person?" Ariel points into the distance.

Everyone looks.

A woman in a surgical mask is creeping around a block away from us. When she sees us looking, she bolts as if worried we'd catch her and turn her into soup.

Maxwell follows the woman's retreat with his sad eyes. "Not everyone here is dead. There are whole continents on this world where the governments shut down all incoming travel. The virus hasn't spread there as much."

Valerian's eyebrows meet in the middle of his forehead. "More like Icelus hasn't yet spread it everywhere."

Felix's robotic neck turns with a screech. "If Icelus are still here on this world, it gives us a chance to help the people on Necronia save themselves."

"Ever the optimist," Itzel says. "Icelus might've infected this world by accident—and could already be done with Necronia by now."

"Nostradamus didn't think so," Felix says defensively.

"He also wanted us to take Chester, yet look what happened," I say.

"Whatever Nostradamus said will no doubt benefit *him* most of all," Chester says. "Seers can't be trusted. I bet he never said the people of Necronia will be saved."

That's true. He didn't. The only clear-cut thing the seer said was that I will perish if I don't go to Necronia. Given the virus situation, I'm tempted to take my chances with not going and let the chips fall where they may.

"We're not just trying to save Necronian lives." Valerian's eyes gleam with menace. "We have to catch Icelus agents so they can be questioned."

Kit morphs into a giant spider I've seen once before. "Questioned, tortured… who wants to split hairs?" she growls through a set of mandibles.

Seeing Maxwell's terrified reaction, Kit becomes herself again and winks at the poor guy.

"Our walking-talking encyclopedia is done," Stanislav says, looking across the street.

Sure enough, Dylan is sprinting toward us, Fabian on her tail.

"So," Maxwell says when she reaches us. "Can you cure me?"

Panting, she shakes her head. "That lab isn't equipped for research. If I already knew the chemical formula for the cure, maybe I could make it there. As is, it would take longer than the time you have left. I think we'd better follow the protocol we established in the case of contamination."

Ariel lifts her eyebrows. "We planned to get sick?"

"A medical team of vampires and quarantine rooms are waiting for us at the hub on Gomorrah," Dylan says. "If Maxwell rushes back, he can be there in a day."

"Unless the Overtaken kill him," Itzel says. "Or the virus makes him too weak."

"He'll need an escort," I say. "Which could actually solve our other problem." I wave at Chester, Kit, Nina, and Colton.

"I agree," Valerian says. "Chester has a day before he turns, the others even longer. That gives them time to escort Maxwell to Gomorrah."

"Good plan." Kit transforms into that creepy plant-like creature without a mouth and nose.

"It's an outstanding plan," Nina says. "Except for the part where we walk with the sick guy."

"Kit and I can stay close to him while you and Colton keep your distance," Chester says. "With two masks and my luck, I shouldn't catch the virus."

No one has the heart to tell him that if his luck had worked, it would've protected him from becoming an Overtaken.

"Here." Chester hands Ariel the handle of his gate sword. "Your group will need this more than ours."

Ariel takes the artifact reverently and gives Chester her own sword in return.

"This actually works out," Felix says.

Everyone looks at him like he's lost some mission-critical marbles.

"Maxwell will take himself and samples of infected blood to Gomorrah." Felix folds his pinky. "They develop a cure." He folds his ring finger. "We tell Necronians how to make it." He folds his middle finger. "Then all we have to do is catch Icelus and go back." He triumphantly folds his index finger.

"How simple," Itzel says with an eye roll. "Maybe it should've always been the plan to kill half our party?"

"We'll need a way to stay in contact," Maxwell says. "To that end, can you please lie on the ground?"

Everyone looks at everyone else. No one wants to say what we're all thinking—the virus has clearly gotten into his brain.

"I meant Dylan," Maxwell says. "Please, I don't have much time."

Gingerly, Dylan lies on the ground.

Maxwell extends his hand and closes his eyes.

Instantly, Dylan's eyes also close, and her body relaxes.

Wait. She can't be—

But she is. My new senses confirm it. Maxwell has not only made Dylan fall asleep; he's put her right into REM cycle.

"How did you do that?" I exclaim excitedly.

Maxwell doesn't reply. He's clearly setting up a dreamwalk session with Dylan.

Would I meet him if I set up a link myself? I've never dreamwalked in someone who already had another dreamwalker in their mind, and the idea sounds interesting.

If it weren't for the virus, I'd try it. As is, though, I feel irrational repugnance at the idea of ending up face to face with Maxwell, even in the dream world. It's probably my fear of germs, but I can't help feeling that there's more to Maxwell than it seems, that he's hiding some secret.

Hold up. He's a dreamwalker. Could *he* be the Nutcracker? His job is to coordinate communication between Otherlands the way the Icelus dreamwalker does, so how ironic would it be if they were the same person? He could then anticipate every move against Icelus—the perfect spy.

I need to talk to Valerian about this. Soon.

"Done," Maxwell says, bringing me out of my suspicion-filled fugue.

Looking disoriented, Dylan gets up from the ground.

"Let's go," Maxwell says.

"How did you put her into REM sleep like that?" I ask.

Maxwell looks at me as though for the first time. "That's something we dreamwalkers can just do."

"Not me, and I'm a dreamwalker."

"No one taught it to you on… your home world?" he asks haltingly.

"You mean on Soma?" I ask on a hunch.

Maxwell's eyes nearly bulge out of their sockets. "We really have to make haste," he says hurriedly. "It's literally a life-and-death situation."

With that, he rushes into the station.

"Good luck," Chester says to us and follows the dreamwalker.

Colton takes off his backpack and hands it to Fabian, the only member of the party big enough to carry it. With a farewell, the giant lumbers after Chester. Lacking a mouth in her plant form, Kit blows us an air kiss before she goes, while Nina just waves and follows the others.

As soon as they disappear into the station, I notice Valerian glaring at me.

Of course. I said the forbidden word. *Soma.*

Was that why Maxwell bolted so fast too? Is Soma something you never talk about—like Fight Club from that Earth movie? Or is it because Maxwell is the Nutcracker and didn't want to teach an enemy dreamwalker any new skills?

Puck. If he *is* the Nutcracker, what if his whole team hadn't died of the virus?

What if he'd killed them?

I rattle out my concerns out loud, ending with, "Should we run after them?"

Fabian shakes his head. "They have Chester's probability manipulation to keep them safe."

"But he couldn't keep *himself* safe," Itzel says.

"Maxwell was vetted," Valerian says with finality. "I say we've wasted enough time on this world. Let's head to Necronia."

"What?" Itzel exclaims. "We're still doing that? Our group is half the size we were supposed to be, and we just lost our most powerful allies."

"Bullshit," Stanislav says, his accent thicker than usual. "Your most powerful ally is still here."

"The chort is right," Fabian says. "Assuming he means me, of course."

"We can't not go," Felix says, almost regretfully. "Nostradamus's prophecies are not something you want to mess around with."

"Fine." Itzel readjusts her mask. "I just want to go on record saying this is a bad idea."

Felix mimes writing something in an imaginary notebook. Pretending to close it, he says, "Noted."

Valerian turns on his heel and strides into the train station. The rest of us follow, vaulting over corpses when necessary. I do my best not to think about dead bodies decomposing and whether the virus is still live in the air around them. Because terrifying. And super gross. A sprint down the corridors later, we find ourselves in the hub and in front of the purple gate that is our destination.

"Ready?" Stanislav asks.

Everyone nods, though some, like Itzel, less enthusiastically than others.

"Let's go then," the chort says and enters the gate.

Fabian and the others follow, and I go last.

Stepping out on the other side, I realize Chester's probability manipulation powers hadn't failed him. Far from it.

If this is Necronia, he's lucky to have missed it.

CHAPTER TWELVE

WE'RE INSIDE A SMALL CANYON, surrounded by gray mountains, with a sky blocked by gloomy clouds up above. My eyes have to adjust to the lack of light, and when they do, I realize a legion of people are crammed into the hub like rotten sardines.

They're wearing masks with nightmarish designs and loin cloths, along with itchy-looking bras on what might be the females. Their skin is ashen, and they have tattoo-like carvings all over their bodies that glow from the inside.

The only place free of these people is a two-foot-wide tunnel that leads from the hub canyon into a crack in a mountain ridge—a crack that looks like a gap in the teeth of a dead titan.

My teammates gingerly advance into the people-tunnel. Behind us, the tunnel fills with silently moving bodies, cutting off the way back—which doesn't fill me with warm fuzzies, not even a little bit.

"These must be corpses," Ariel whispers. "I can't believe this is happening again."

She's probably right. Now that she's said it, I could swear there's a stench of death seeping through my mask's powerful filters.

"For their sake, I hope they're dead." Felix points at one of the carvings. "Doing that on a live person would be against the Geneva Convention."

"We're far from Geneva," Ariel mutters.

"Well, yeah," Felix says. "Nor are we in Kansas anymore."

Nobody replies to him, and we continue through the tunnel in silence until Felix speaks again in a loud whisper. "Those masks look like they were designed by H.R. Giger." Without waiting for a follow-up question, he explains, "He did design work on *Alien*."

I know the artist he's talking about and have to agree. The masks depict people and steam-powered machines interlinked in an eerie, almost sexual symbiosis.

Dylan says something in an unfamiliar language, seemingly addressing the corpses.

"What did you say?" Felix asks her. "That sounded like a mix of German and Vietnamese, with some Klingon thrown in."

"It sounded nothing like German," Fabian says, giving Felix a cold look. "If anything, it reminded me of Russian."

Stanislav glares at the werewolf. "*Sobaka*. That's nothing like Russian."

Stern-looking LEGO letters appear in front of my eyes, and I assume in front of everyone else's also:

Let's stay quiet and figure out what they want.

We follow Valerian's suggestion, and it soon becomes clear that what the corpses want is to herd us through the crack in the rock.

When we step out of the crack, we find ourselves in a bigger canyon, which is filled to the brim with more animated corpses, thousands upon thousands of them.

Valerian's LEGO letters appear again:

Dylan, try speaking with them.

She begins yelling in the same language, facing this way and that.

At first, there's no response. Then every single one of the thousands of corpses replies in unison. Their speech—a strange dry rustle, like dead branches rubbing against each other—creeps into my bones, chilling them below zero kelvin. This is what hell would sound like, I imagine, and though the corpses seem to be using the same language as Dylan, through their withered vocal cords, it sounds exponentially uglier and more terrifying.

"They asked why we're here," Dylan announces.

Tell them, Valerian commands via LEGO letters.

Dylan shouts in Necronian for a few seconds.

Almost anticlimactically, the corpses respond with just two words.

"You lie," Dylan translates.

"Ungrateful bastards," Fabian growls.

Persuade, Valerian orders. *Tell them about Icelus and the virus. Tell them what the symptoms are.*

Dylan tries—or at least, she speaks in Necronian for a while.

The reply from the corpses is a little longer this time, but given how Dylan whitens, I doubt we'll like the translation.

The corpses step aside, creating a tunnel, this time leading back the way we came.

"They said this is our last chance to go back and never return," Dylan says, her voice shaking. "If not, and I quote, 'I'll turn you into helpers.'"

"Helpers?" Felix asks.

Ariel examines the masked corpses with a shudder. "I bet it's a euphemism for *zombies*."

"I say we do leave." Itzel glances the way we came. "We told the necros about the threat, so our consciences are clear."

Valerian glares at Dylan. "Tell them we'd like to talk to someone in charge."

Felix chuckles humorlessly. "Good old 'may I speak to the manager?'"

"More like 'take me to your leader,'" Ariel says.

"Shut up," Stanislav says. "They might speak English."

Ignoring everyone's back-and-forth, Dylan yells out a short phrase.

The response through the zombie mouths is curt.

"Time's up," Dylan says with a stutter.

Her translation wasn't necessary. With a shuffling of naked feet, the tunnel leading back to the hub closes, and the so-called helpers assume aggressive postures—ready to leap and claw at our faces.

In a coordinated move, the zombies attack.

CHAPTER THIRTEEN

"WEAPONS OUT!" Ariel shouts, pulling out a big gun with one hand and her plasma sword hilt with the other. Without a second of hesitation, she shoots the zombie closest to her in the middle of his mask.

Boom.

Mask in tatters and face a mangled mess, the zombie stumbles back before recovering and lunging at her.

Ariel activates her sword and slashes at her attacker. The gate-like substance of the blade effortlessly cleaves the zombie from head to groin. Not surprisingly, the already-dead creature doesn't die, but since each half can't balance on one leg, they fall and get trampled by the next set of zombies who attack Ariel.

She shoots one and slices another in half with all the speed and grace of an uber while I unsheathe my katana. My heart drums furiously in my chest as I swivel my head from side to side, taking in the battlefield.

To my left, Dylan fires her Gomorran gun. The zombies are unaffected, as I knew they would be, having once tried this move on their kind myself.

"Valerian, do your illusion thing!" Dylan shouts.

He's already got his sai out and is stabbing both of them into the throat of the zombie nearest to him. "Necros can see through the eyes of all the zombies," he yells back as he yanks the weapons out before plunging them back into zombie flesh. "My powers won't work here!"

Back to back with Valerian is Felix. With his upper right robotic arm, he catches a zombie by the throat and keeps her there. His upper left hand grabs the zombie's head, while the lower arms hug the zombie's torso.

Metal creaks, and the zombie's head separates from her body.

Another zombie lunges at my throat, but a ball of lightning hits him in the chest, sending him flying.

"Thanks!" I shout to Itzel, who blasts another zombie with a second lightning ball.

One more zombie leaps at me—a female one, if the bra is anything to go by. I swing my katana and slice her hand off before it reaches me, then behead her with a strike I've practiced in my dream.

To my surprise, it works from the first try. Whatever this katana is made of is amazing. It goes through flesh and bone as if through sponge cake.

Whoever provided these weapons knew what they were doing.

To my right, a male zombie with talon-like nails takes a swipe at Stanislav's arm. All the nails get is empty air—the chort uses his power to make his flesh insubstantial just in time.

The zombie swipes again, aiming at Stanislav's head. His nails scrape the mask as the chort makes his head insubstantial and sidesteps the next strike.

The zombie is left holding Stanislav's mask. With a twist of his wrist, he tosses it like a frisbee back at the chort's head. Stanislav's face phases in and out of substantiality, and the mask whooshes through him to the other side of the canyon. A moment later, Stanislav retaliates, beheading his opponent with his saber.

Two more zombies attack Stanislav.

He phases over and over, slicing with his saber all the while.

In the meantime, Fabian is already naked, the backpack at his feet. With a flash, he morphs into his wolf form and starts hopping from paw to paw as though dancing, while at the same time swinging his limbs around. Each time one of his massive paws connects with a zombie, the zombie loses an important part of his or her anatomy. It must be the wolfu martial art he mentioned. It's deadly, and probably would be more so if it weren't for his muzzle-like mask.

A large male zombie jumps at me. I slice at his Adam's apple with the katana. The head rolls at my feet, and I do my best to catch my breath. This beheading felt harder. My arms are growing tired.

A few more zombies later, my arms feel like lead, my muscles screaming in exhaustion. The most discouraging part is that no matter how many reanimated corpses I or my teammates dispatch, there are thousands more to take their place.

Puck this. I'm not giving up. Panting, I swing harder, beheading another zombie just as a squadron of shadows appears in the sky.

What the puck?

They're flying creatures, each the size of a roc bird, but they look like a hybrid between a pterodactyl and a bat. In the claws of each flying creature is a masked person.

In a blink, the squadron swoops down, delivering more zombies into the already-impossible battle.

We are beyond pucked.

CHAPTER FOURTEEN

GRITTING MY TEETH, I will my leaden arms to move. *Swing, swoosh, don't think about gore and germs.* I'm a zombie-beheading machine, taking out one after another, not thinking about how sweaty and numb my palms are getting or how my lungs are struggling to drag in enough air through the mask.

Still, no matter how determined I am, my body is beginning to give out. I stumble, nearly dropping my katana as a zombie lunges at me, teeth snapping like a rabid dog. Gasping, I lop off its head, and as I pivot to face a fresh onslaught of attackers, I realize none are coming.

The attack has suddenly stopped.

The zombies open their mouths and begin to speak.

All eyes swing toward Dylan, staring at her with hope.

"That's odd," she pants, wiping the sweat from her

forehead. "They're asking what the first symptom of the virus is."

"Tell them." Stanislav's Russian accent is thicker than ever.

Dylan shouts a reply in Necronian.

The zombies speak once more.

"They said his name is Nulen. He swears that if we put our weapons down, he'll talk to us face to face."

Everyone exchanges worried glances.

"I don't see harm in it," Valerian says, tossing his sai on the ground. "It's only a matter of time before we lose."

Everyone solemnly nods. I guess I wasn't the only pessimistic one.

The zombies back away, creating a wider circle around us.

I toss down my katana, then the gun.

Ariel drops empty gun after empty gun on the ground. Then she disables her gate sword and gently places it on the rest of the weapons.

When everyone's disarmed, the zombies speak again.

"He's asking Fabian to turn back into man form and for Felix to be turned off," Dylan says.

In a flash, naked Fabian stands before us. He picks up his clothes and starts to dress.

The robot suit opens up, and Felix reluctantly steps out of it.

Stepping aside to create a tunnel, the horde speaks again.

"Step away from the weapons," Dylan translates.

"I have a better idea." Felix shoots the robot with a ray of magenta energy. The robot starts to move of its own accord. It picks up the backpack and stashes it inside itself, where Felix's body would usually be.

Catching on, we help the robot stash the other weapons inside it. When our armory is hidden, the robot closes shut, and Felix makes it walk through the tunnel the zombies created. It reaches all the way to the edge of the nearby mountain, and when the robot gets there, it sits on the ground and grabs its legs with all four arms, slumping forward.

We wait in tense silence. And wait. And wait. After what feels like an hour, a new zombie tunnel opens up, and a man steps out of it—presumably Nulen. As pale as a pre-vamp, he's dressed in strange leather clothing and has lines of black paint on his face.

He walks over to us, and when he's within touching distance of me, he stares me in the eyes so intently, it's as if he's trying to see who blinks first. But no. He just steps over to Itzel and does the same thing, then repeats the process with everyone else.

A weird greeting ritual perhaps?

Finally, he opens his mouth and speaks.

"He's asking what kind of Cognizant we are," Dylan translates. "Should I tell him?"

Valerian nods, and Dylan speaks for a few seconds.

Nulen frowns and replies in rapid-fire Necronian.

Dylan pales. "He's asking which of us can make someone cry blood."

"Tell him the truth," Valerian says. "Such power doesn't exist, and he probably knows this."

As Dylan speaks in Necronian again, Nulen's frown deepens.

This is when I notice it—and realize the reason we're still alive.

In the corner of Nulen's right eye, a red droplet is gathering. A bloody tear that can only mean one thing.

The virus we came to stop is already here.

CHAPTER FIFTEEN

"STANISLAV NEEDS TO put his mask back on," Dylan blurts, her gaze following mine.

The chort touches his face as if realizing its nakedness for the first time. "It flew there." He points at the other side of the canyon.

"Do we have another mask in Stanislav's size inside the backpack?" I ask urgently.

Eyes wide with horror, Dylan shakes her head.

"What about one for him?" I gesture at the necromancer.

"Maybe," she says, helplessly glancing toward the robot.

I take a breath, trying not to panic. "Tell him to get his 'helpers' to bring Stanislav his mask and to let Felix go get one for him."

Dylan and Nulen go back and forth, looking increasingly agitated. Finally, the necromancer nods, and the zombies reopen the tunnel that leads to the robot.

As Felix sprints for the backpack, the zombies pass a mask over their heads is if it were a stage diver at a rock concert.

Stanislav's mask arrives first, luckily intact. He carefully puts it on, letting the necromancer see how he works the back straps.

Felix comes back and throws Nulen his mask.

The necromancer puts it on and speaks in a muffled voice.

"He asked about a cure," Dylan says. "I told him we don't have it yet but are working on it. He then stated that we're lucky. He indeed has never heard of a Cognizant power that would cause blood tears, particularly at a distance, so he has to give us the benefit of the doubt. Ultimately, it's up to the Parliament to decide if we're telling the truth. He'll take us to them."

"Good," Valerian says. "Let's hope Maxwell survives his trip back, and that the scientists on Gomorrah work out how to make the cure posthaste."

If we're throwing around hope, mine would be *please let us not get sick*. No, make that *pretty please, with a cherry on top*. Valerian still has a good point, of course. Without a cure or some other counterbalance to bad news, the Parliament might well treat us as the proverbial messengers to shoot.

Nulen strides toward a big opening in the canyon,

and the zombies part for him in the widest tunnel we've seen yet. He waves for us to follow.

"What are the chances Stanislav caught the virus?" I ask in a low voice as we walk after him.

"Depends on a lot of factors." Dylan's professorial tone is back. "We're outside, and Stanislav and Nulen didn't stay close together for long. Also, chorts have excellent immune systems—though not pre-vamp levels, of course. If I had to guess, I'd say infection is unlikely."

"I'll keep my distance from everyone, just in case," Stanislav says and falls back.

Valerian looks at Dylan. "Did you ask Nulen how *he* might've gotten sick?"

Dylan smacks her forehead, then talks to Nulen for a few seconds.

"He doesn't know," she says when they finish. "He'd never heard of a virus like 'ours' before today."

"Did he talk to anyone else who came through the gates?" Valerian asks.

Dylan checks.

"No," she translates a moment later. "The reason he was there by the hub was to enforce the policy their Parliament put in place many years ago. No one from the Otherlands is allowed on Necronia."

Not friendly, but understandable in light of how necromancers are treated on vampire-biased worlds like Earth and Gomorrah.

We don't talk the rest of the way, and when we exit from the canyon, it's into yet another canyon that's big enough to fit a small city. Once we're out of that canyon, a big herd of zombies spills out of there, following us.

Glancing to make sure Nulen isn't looking, Felix turns back and sends a blast of magenta energy behind us.

A few seconds later, his robot suit crawls out of the canyon on six limbs.

Without turning, Nulen shouts something.

"Leave that there," Dylan translates.

"Dude." Ariel waves at the hundreds of corpses all around. "He can see through the eyes of his dead minions."

With a sigh, Felix makes the robot sit on the ground by the smaller canyon's entrance.

"You think it'll be safe?" Ariel looks wistfully at the robot. "I want the gate sword back."

Felix gives Nulen a suspicious once-over. "Depends on whether they have any high-end blowtorches on this world."

Fabian places a hand on the small of Dylan's back and loudly whispers, "Tell our necromancer friend to be careful of the self-destruct mechanism inside that machine. That should keep our stuff safe."

"You want me to lie?" Dylan asks, her face flushed.

The werewolf pulls his hand away and tilts his head like a curious puppy. "You can't lie?"

"Of course I can," Dylan mumbles. "Just prefer not to."

"Well, it's not really a lie," Itzel says. "If they were to

apply a blowtorch in the wrong place, the suit *could* explode."

Placated, Dylan delivers the message to Nulen, and he doesn't respond with so much as a grunt, just keeps on heading toward a large contraption that resembles a wooden raft, only large enough to carry an army.

Odd. Is there a river I'm not seeing?

Reaching the "raft," Nulen and two dozen of his helpers step onto it. Looking at us, he shouts a command that Dylan translates as "get on."

After everyone cautiously steps onto the wooden platform, its purpose becomes clearer. Zombies walk over and grab what turn out to be wooden handles, lifting us and the "raft" off the ground.

"A zombie-powered carriage," Felix mutters as we begin to move.

"A litter," Dylan says. "I'd get used to zombie-powered things if I were you. We'll see a lot of it soon."

At first the ride is rocky, but then we reach a relatively even terrain and it feels like we're floating. When we exit the big canyon, we gape at the gray mountains around us like a bunch of tourists.

"What the hell?" Ariel exclaims, looking at Nulen.

I follow her gaze, trying to make sense of what I'm seeing.

If you unfocus your eyes, Nulen is just on a chair. But if you look closely, it's clear that his chair is made entirely of people. Dead people. Each zombie must've twisted like a contortionist to make the structure.

Noticing our attention, Nulen speaks in Dylan's direction.

Before she can translate, the zombies that aren't part of his chair begin to move. Some kneel, some twist around, and soon, eight more macabre chairs join Nulen's human throne.

"He said 'take a seat,'" Dylan says. "In case that wasn't obvious."

We all stare at our "chairs." I don't know about the others, but if it were a choice between a gun to the head and this furniture, I might just opt for the gun.

Like it's the most natural thing in the world, Stanislav plops onto one. "Clever," he says. "The soft belly of that woman makes a cushion."

Right. I'd *gladly* choose the gun.

Stepping as far away from the "furniture" as I can, I pointedly stand and watch the mountains to keep my mind off my battle-fatigued muscles.

"I have a surprise," Valerian says, approaching me.

Startled, I turn and see him holding a hygieia device.

Wow. I can't believe he's managed to keep it through the whole ordeal. I've got to say, he's good at the suck-up game. If it weren't for the masks, I think I wouldn't kick him in the balls if he tried to kiss me right now.

Eyes crinkling above his mask, Valerian sterilizes a large circle of the platform beneath us.

"Thanks." I sit cross-legged in the middle of the circle. "If you want, you can join me here."

Is he looking smug? It's hard to tell with the cursed masks.

He sinks to the floor a perfect distance from me, and just like that, the landscape around us seems more romantic than gloomy. That is, until we leave the mountains and see a field of some kinds of native vegetables.

A field that's crawling with the masked dead.

I guess if you don't care about the eek factor—and that's a big if—it makes sense to use this free workforce on difficult agricultural tasks.

As we keep riding, we spot a herd of goat-like animals that graze inside a pasture that's walled off by zombies. Later, we see zombies performing even more functions: fixing roofs, chopping down trees, and even building a pyramid the size of the ones in Giza, but with creepy designs carved into the sides that remind me of the masks that the zombies wear.

An hour after the dirt road underneath us becomes paved, we enter a village.

A big village.

"Are all those pale people alive?" Ariel asks, studying the crowds that stare at us with unabashed wonder.

Dylan exchanges some quick words with Nulen. "He says they're predominantly human, with just enough necromancers to keep things running. You can recognize his kind by the leather clothing they wear. The humans revere them—hence all the waving."

Indeed, the majority of the people are wearing

clothing made of cotton-like material, with only an occasional leather-clad figure here and there.

Nulen says something else.

"We're stopping for a meal and a sleepover," Dylan explains. "He'll stay in special necromancer quarters, while we'll rest in an inn designed for humans."

No one objects, and when we reach the town square, our zombies lower the litter to the ground, allowing us to step off.

Dylan has another quick exchange with Nulen. "We go there." She points at a large structure to the side of the square.

Felix looks around dubiously. "Don't we need money or something like that?"

When Dylan translates this question to Nulen, he looks at Felix disdainfully and delivers what sounds like a tirade.

"We won't need money to stay at the inn," Dylan says. "The owner is a necromancer, and the staff are helpers. That means that food and drinks are free, as are the lodgings. In general, all basic human needs are provided for on Necronia, free of charge."

Around us, I spot people reverently nodding when they see Nulen's outfit. Not surprising, given what we've just learned.

"They really love their necros here," Fabian says, echoing my thoughts.

Stanislav nods. "There's a good word for that: necrophilia."

We chuckle as we head for the inn, but then we spot a herd of zombies on our tail.

"Seems like Nulen wants to make sure we stay at the inn and nowhere else," Felix says.

Valerian lifts his broad shoulders in a shrug. "Since we weren't going anywhere else anyway, let him."

When we step into the establishment, a leather-clad woman looks warily at our masks, but is overall cheerful. However, when Dylan speaks up, the cheerfulness disappears. I guess she's detected an accent and doesn't like strangers.

Still, she has a zombie seat us in the restaurant area, and I thank the stars for the wooden table and chairs.

Valerian uses hygieia on my chair and part of the table, and I reward him by not telling him off when he sits by my side.

The other patrons sit far enough away that I can't tell what they're eating or hear their speech. Like most humans I've seen here, they're pale, wear cotton clothing, and seem to be really happy considering they live on such a dreary world.

Masked "helpers" bring out appetizers in the form of a big bowl of fruit.

Valerian examines the fruit, then samples one, peeling and stuffing pieces into the proper section of his mask. He repeats this a few times, and when he comes across one that reminds me of a yellow orange, he catches Dylan's gaze. "Can you ask the innkeeper for a whole bowl of these for Bailey?"

When the bowl arrives, Valerian hygieias one fruit and hands it to me.

I gingerly peel the thing and stick a piece through the mask's opening.

It reminds me of a slightly tart banana, only fruitier.

"Thanks," I say and pick up another.

After about seven more of the round banana approximations, I feel full. These must be more nutritionally dense than my favored Earth fruit.

My teammates, in the meantime, are much more adventurous/suicidal with their food choices. They gobble down bowls of pink soup made from who knows what, skewers of an unknown meat that smells like feet, and bread from a mystery purple grain. Oh, and they chase all that down with fermented drinks that make the meat smell like flowers in comparison.

For everyone's sake, I hope Dylan can make antibiotics in a pinch.

Bellies full, everyone yawns.

Dylan compliments the innkeeper, and the woman smiles and replies in rapid-fire Necronian.

Stammering something back, Dylan reddens and looks at us with a horrified expression.

Before she can translate whatever was said, a group of strange zombies steps into the room. Their masks don't have the scary imagery. Instead, they depict very generic, good-looking human faces. Their bodies are atypical too: The men are muscular and cut, and the females have curves in all the right places—and no bras.

"She's offering them to us as, um… bedroom companions," Dylan says, reddening further.

Okay. I'm starting to really want that gun to the head.

"You were wrong before," Ariel whispers to Stanislav. "*That's* necrophilia."

Felix eyes one of the bustier zombies. "In a way, they're like sexbots, so…"

Ariel rounds on him. "Seriously? Did you forget about Maya? Plus the whole necrophilia thing?"

Felix draws back, offended. "I wasn't going to say yes. I was just comparing—"

"Please thank our host and tell her we're all too tired for companions today," Valerian says with a straight face.

When Dylan conveys this, the woman shrugs, and her bizarrely sexualized zombies scram.

She then has a regular male zombie show us the bathroom facilities, which are primitively water-based, like those on Earth. After that, the zombie leads us to a cluster of rooms. To my huge relief, the open doors reveal beds made from wood instead of dead people.

The zombie leaves us in the hallway, and Valerian points to a room with a chair. "This will be Bailey's. I'll be standing watch."

Oh, right. I completely forgot. I could get killed by the Nutcracker in my dreams and go homicidal on everybody's ass. A gift that keeps on giving.

"I'll take that one." Stanislav points at the room farthest from us. "And I'll keep the mask on as I sleep."

"Everyone should keep their masks on," Dylan says. "I get that it's uncomfortable, but we know the virus is already out on this world, so why take any chances?"

I don't know about anyone else, but taking my mask off was never on the agenda.

As the other rooms are chosen, I clear my throat. "I need a volunteer."

Fourteen eyebrows and a half of a unibrow lift in unison.

"Remember how Maxwell was able to make Dylan fall asleep?" I ask.

Reluctant nods.

"I want to do that too… to one of you."

Silence.

I put my hands on my hips. "You're going to sleep anyway."

Ariel steps forward. "Fine. I'll be your guinea pig."

Grinning maniacally under my mask, I follow Ariel into her room.

"Do you mind waiting outside?" she says to Valerian.

If he minds, he doesn't voice it.

As soon as she shuts the door in Valerian's face, Ariel strips, revealing a body that's impressive even for an uber. Talk about an unattainable standard of beauty. I don't exactly have poor self-esteem, but if I stare at her enough, I'm certain to develop it.

With a yawn, she gets under the covers. "This might actually work out. Sometimes I have trouble falling asleep."

"Okay," I say. "Close your eyes."

She does.

Now what? I had no idea dreamwalkers could do what I'm about to attempt. Now that I know it's possible, I still have no clue as to how.

I start by looking intently at Ariel and wishing her to sleep with all I've got.

"Is this going to take long?" she says, yawning again.

"No clue."

Extending my hand, I picture Ariel sleeping in as much detail as I can, a bit how I initiate dreamwalking from a distance.

Nothing.

Then it hits me. Before I could make dream connections from afar, I needed skin-to-skin contact. Maybe this power works the same?

I carefully approach the bed. "Do you mind if I touch you?"

Ariel opens her eyes. "You're lucky I'm not Kit. Or Felix, for that matter."

Chuckling, I gently put my hand on her wrist and wish her asleep.

Nothing happens. I try an imagination exercise. I picture Ariel sleeping so vividly I could create a painting of it in my memory gallery. Still nothing. I'm about to pull away in frustration when I do something purely on instinct, calling on a strange hint of a feeling, one that reminds me of having a word on the very tip of my tongue.

It works.

Ariel is asleep. No, not just asleep. I can feel that she's in the REM stage of sleep, which she wouldn't be in if she just fell asleep out of boredom.

With a fist pump, I tiptoe out of the room.

Now if I only knew what I did so I could repeat it. It would mean the end of subdreams, just to name one huge benefit off the top of my head. And if I do this quickly enough, I would be like a sleep grenade myself.

Walking into my room, I catch Valerian waving his hygieia device over my bed.

Wow. And he didn't even know I'd see him being super nice like this.

Walking over, I place the hand that touched Ariel under the sterilizing rays.

The problem is I get too close to Valerian and my treacherous heartbeat speeds up. "Thanks," I say breathlessly, nodding at the bed.

"I'll do the same to your clothes after you take them off," Valerian says, his voice husky.

I step back, ignoring the flush spreading over my skin. "Nice try. Turn around."

With a sigh, he obliges.

"Actually, leave the room."

He walks out the door.

"How do I know this isn't just an illusion?" I ask the empty space around me. "For all I know, you're standing there staring at me."

The empty air doesn't respond, so I undress, put my clothes on Valerian's chair, and hide under the blissfully sterilized blanket. "You can come back in."

Valerian returns and cleans my clothes as promised, ending with my underwear.

"Perv," I mutter when he hangs the last article—my bra—at the head of my bed. "You liked touching my undies. Admit it."

His eyes crinkle above the mask. "I admit that and more. For instance, I'd like for my hands to do the job your bra usually does. Panties too."

I'm speechless—and so hot I may combust on the spot.

"What would you say if I took off my clothes?" he asks softly.

The heat inside me intensifies.

"I can hygieia every single part of my body and get in there with you," he says temptingly.

"Um, no…" I clear the hoarseness from my throat. "I don't do that with people I barely know."

He strides over to the chair and sits. "You know me."

"No," I say pointedly. "I don't know where you grew up, or if you have siblings, for that matter. I don't know if—"

"Nice try," he says in a perfect imitation of my tone. "I'm not ready to speak about Soma. If that's all you want, you should just go to sleep."

"Fine." I close my eyes and turn over, giving him my back.

Then something dawns on me. Did he just admit that Soma *is* where he was born?

I lie there, unable to sleep, my mind churning.

Eventually, I feel someone in the distance go into REM sleep. Lucky for them. I want to be dreaming right now.

Since I can, I make a connection to whoever it is. Then I use Pom to visit my sleep palace and find that it's Stanislav I've just connected with.

Awesome. My remote connect range is farther than I thought.

Since I'm here, might as well sneak a peek at the chort's dream. I've never dreamwalked in his kind before.

Making myself invisible, I dive in.

____

CHAPTER SIXTEEN

STANISLAV'S current dream is a memory. He's standing in front of a round-faced woman who must be the descendant of whoever was the original model for the matryoshka dolls. In Stanislav's hands is a tiny kitten of the Siberian variety. It's not as cute as Pom, but extremely close.

It's clear the chort is loath to let the little creature go, so the woman eventually snatches it away with a wide grin.

He marches over to the fridge, opens it, points at the milk, and says something in Russian. Grinning even wider, she nods and replies placatingly in the same language. Stanislav grabs her hand and leads her to an adjacent room, where he points at an enormous box of kitty litter.

She nods solemnly, then pantomimes putting the kitten into the box.

"*Molodetz*," Stanislav says. He then pecks the woman

on the cheek and the kitten on the top of its head and walks out of the apartment.

I decide this is as good a moment as any to tell him he's dreaming, so I make myself visible and do just that.

"What are you doing here?" he asks once he adjusts to the idea of talking to me in a dream.

"Wanted to ask you how you're feeling." I take us to a white-sand beach. "Didn't want to put you on the spot in front of everyone."

"I'm healthy as a bull." He takes off his shoes and buries his feet into the sand.

"Okay then. I'll leave you be."

"Wait. You saw my earlier dream, right?"

I smile sheepishly. "Yep. Sorry about that."

"Can you walk into my girlfriend's dream? That's who the woman was. I want to know how Murzik is doing."

"Is Murzik the kitten?" I ask.

He nods, a tender expression stealing over his face.

"Sadly, I can't just dreamwalk in a random person," I say. "I have to make a connection with them first, and that requires proximity."

"Ah," he says, looking extremely disappointed. "Then go."

I wave and leave his dream.

———

I LIE in bed for a while longer, making connections with the rest of our party, just in case. I don't invade their dreams, though. Stanislav took it well, but I'm not sure if some of the others would. Plus, Fabian, being a werewolf, would be way too difficult.

Finally, I fall asleep.

———

I SIT on a throne made of bones. There's an army of vampires kneeling at my feet.

"Next," I say imperiously.

A vampire crawls over to the throne, slashes his wrists with a ceremonial dagger, and squirts blood into a glass chalice.

A servant picks up the chalice and hands it to me.

I gulp down the liquid like a Slurpee. A wave of pleasure smashes into my every nerve cell with the force of an opiate concentrate.

"Next," I say again, my voice somehow steady despite the bliss.

Another vampire worshipper makes a donation.

I drink this too. The pleasure grows stronger. I say "next" again and again. When the pleasure blurs into pain, I notice something odd as I raise the chalice to my lips.

No furry bracelet.

No Pom.

This is a dream.

Obviously a dream, now that I think about it.

I will the pleasure away.

The pleasure doesn't leave. If anything, it gets *more*

intense. Less like the vampire blood effect and more like an orgasm, but not quite. It feels as though my whole body has turned into an erogenous zone, and someone is stroking me all over.

What the puck?

I exit my body the way I do when I want to heal it.

The pleasure doesn't stop.

I duplicate myself and put my consciousness into the two bodies. Both of me feel the pleasure now, but it doesn't stop.

Going back to a single body, I try counterbalancing the pleasure with some pain. I make a thick needle appear in my hand and stab my palm with it.

I might as well try to stop a hurricane with an umbrella.

Puck. What a weird predicament.

Can intense enough pleasure kill? And if so, could this be a very unusual form of attack from the Nutcracker?

Pom appears in front of me, his fur black and his face worried. "What's happening?"

"I have no idea," I try to say, but it comes out as a moan.

"Ah, you want privacy," he mumbles and disappears.

I want to call him back, but I just moan again.

Fine. It's not like he could've helped with something like this.

Impossibly, the pleasure intensifies again.

That does it. If this is a dream attack, waking up should snap me out of it.

Gritting my dream teeth, I jolt myself awake.

———

I'M BACK at the inn, but the pleasure is with me, stronger than ever. It now feels like some energy is pouring into me—an energy that brings pleasure as a side effect.

I soon discover that here in the real world, it's harder to keep my responses under control. Case in point: A moan escapes my lips without my consent. Then another one. Then a scream.

I'm vaguely aware of Valerian rushing to my side.

Writhing, I groan louder.

Strong arms wrap around me and soothing words are whispered into my ears, but the pleasure assault continues.

"You're going to be okay," I hear Valerian whisper before something finally short-circuits in my brain and my consciousness winks out.

CHAPTER SEVENTEEN

I COME to my senses on the bed, where I'm held in a spooning position. Valerian's arms are wrapped around me, his hands on my belly.

Whew.

I feel better.

I never thought I'd find a *lack* of pleasurable sensation a relief, but here we are.

A part of me knows I should wriggle out of Valerian's hold, but a much bigger part of me needs the comfort and thus tells that first part to shut up and enjoy this.

"What just happened?" I whisper—and realize my throat is hoarse, presumably from all the moaning and screaming.

"Did you feel really good for no apparent reason?" Valerian asks, his breath tickling the back of my neck.

I exhale, trying not to react to *that* pleasurable sensation. "Understatement of the year."

"I think I know what happened," he murmurs into my ear. "The game must be in the hands of the players."

The game. Of course. How could I forget?

Last I checked, Bernie and Rattie had kept working on the *Lucid Dreamer* project. The game features me as the heroine who openly uses her powers, and the hope was that it would leverage human belief mojo to make me a stronger dreamwalker.

Seems like the game has been released, and our idea has worked. When beta testers had first used the game, I'd also felt pleasure, just less of it. If the intensity of what I experienced tonight is anything to go by, this was a more significant boost.

"What now?" I ask hoarsely. "What can I do that I couldn't do before?"

"No idea." Valerian's breath tickles my ear again. "But hopefully you can jolt your mom awake the next time you try."

Right. With my pleasure-addled brain, I hadn't thought of that yet, even though that was the whole point of the project.

I cover his hands with mine. "I want to hurry back to Gomorrah."

Valerian stills, then exhales slowly. "I'm sorry. Even if we didn't care about this world dying from the virus, Nulen would fight us again—and we'd lose."

I do my best to conceal my disappointment. "Of course. Need to finish saving Necronia first."

"That's right. Besides, it will probably take you a

few days to internalize your new power. Also, as more users get the game, you'll grow stronger yet."

I stiffen. Experiencing the boost isn't something I want to relive.

"Don't worry," Valerian says softly. "My guess is, now that you've achieved a certain threshold, adding more will feel like a good mood, or even nothing at all."

Huh. Is that why I'm in such a good mood right now? Or is it because of the spooning?

An unexpected yawn tugs at me, and I hear a soft chuckle against my hair.

"Go back to sleep. You need it."

I close my eyes, though I'm doubtful I'll be able to fall asleep after all that's happened—not to mention, with his arms around me.

Wrong.

The sleep is instant, dreamless, and extremely deep.

———

WHEN I WAKE in the morning, to my huge disappointment, Valerian isn't spooning me anymore. Instead, he's back in his chair, watching me with an unreadable expression.

Did I dream the whole power boost and his comforting me?

He moves to the edge of his seat, his gaze warming slightly. "How are you feeling?"

I sit up, holding the blanket against my chest. "Was it all a dream?"

A faint smile touches his eyes. "No. It happened."

I check to make sure Pom is on my wrist.

He is. Not dreaming *now*.

"Look away," I say and realize my throat feels better.

He complies, and I quickly put my clothes on, then head for the door.

"Breakfast is already downstairs," he says. "You're the last to wake up."

I guiltily examine the dark circles under his eyes. "Did you get any sleep?"

He shakes his head. "I stood watch, as promised."

"Then you'd better get some sleep soon. I can tell you from experience, sleep deprivation blows."

He cocks his head. "I *could* sleep on the litter. But you'd have to promise not to sneak into my dreams without my permission."

I place a hand over my heart. "I swear not to go into your dreams without your permission when you sleep on the *litter*. But if you don't let me in soon, eventually I'll catch you sleeping elsewhere and not be able to help myself."

He nods, eyes gleaming. "I'll take that under advisement."

———

THE BREAKFAST IS identical to dinner, with banana-like fruit for me and questionable items for the crew. As we eat, Dylan tells us she was visited by Maxwell in her dream. He and the others have reached Gomorrah safely, and the scientists there have started working on a cure.

"In the meanwhile, a healer is keeping him alive," Dylan says as we get up from the table. "In hindsight, maybe we should've brought one with us as well."

"Isis refused to go," Valerian says. "Same with the others we asked."

"What about Kit and the rest?" Ariel asks. "Did they become Overtaken?"

"They did," Dylan says somberly. "But with proper care, they can continue to lead normal lives."

Valerian holds the door for me. "So long as they sleep under lock and key, and stay far away from Bailey."

"Well, yeah," Dylan says. "That's what I meant."

When we get outside, Nulen's zombies are still there. They escort us to our strange transport, where the necromancer himself is already lounging in his zombie chair.

Upon Dylan's request, Nulen makes a bed of zombies for Valerian. Valerian sterilizes a spot for me on the wooden floor, then stretches out on the bed and closes his eyes.

Ariel comes up to me and nods at Valerian conspiratorially. "Someone had serious fun last night," she whispers.

I give her a blank stare. "I don't know what you're talking about."

She rolls her eyes. "Your moaning and screaming was loud enough to wake me up."

I fight a flush. "It's not what you think." I tell her what really happened, and she seems to believe me. *Barely.*

When she leaves, I examine myself to see if I feel any different now that my power is boosted.

I don't, at least not much.

Touching Pom, I go into the dream world and experiment with my powers there.

Still no difference. Maybe I can make more sleeper connections per day now, but that's not something I need at the moment.

Back in the waking world, I sense it when Valerian enters REM sleep. The feeling that informs me of this is stronger now, but not qualitatively different.

It takes all my willpower to resist the temptation to dreamwalk in him. Stupid conscience. If I were a sociopath, I'd break that promise in a heartbeat.

To distract myself, I observe our surroundings. We pass by a coal mine where a zombie strapped with dynamite is blown to bits—presumably not for fun but in order to break solid rocks into pieces. Later, we pass another large pyramid construction site, and after that, more farms. At some point, I spot a steam locomotive in the far distance. No doubt zombies are the ones tossing coal into the furnace there, too.

I'm diverted from sightseeing when Dylan asks Nulen something. The necromancer replies in a sharp tone that wakes Valerian and makes Dylan pale to pre-vamp levels.

Looking at her, Fabian frowns. "What was that?"

Dylan darts a furtive glance at Nulen. "I was wondering how his virus is progressing, so I asked if he felt any heart palpitations or had an upset stomach."

"And?" Fabian asks, his frown deepening.

"And he said never to ask again. Also threatened me."

Fabian looks on the verge of turning into his wolf form when Valerian puts a hand on his shoulder and whispers something into his ear.

"Fine," Fabian growls. "Don't ask the asshole again. It's *his* health, after all."

Dylan nods.

We ride in dour silence for a while after that. Eventually, we reach a town that's at least twice the size of the village we visited. We have lunch at another inn and resume our journey.

In the evening, we reach an actual city and eat dinner at the nicest inn thus far.

"Thank you," I tell Valerian after he sterilizes my bed yet again.

His eyes gleam above the mask. "Don't make me turn around or leave the room, and we'll call it even."

Heat floods my cheeks, making me grateful for my mask. Worse yet, I suddenly don't know what to do with my hands—they're itching to take off my top.

"Hey, I'm kidding." He turns around, giving me his back. "We'll pick this up when you're ready."

Whew. I can't believe I was actually considering getting naked for his viewing pleasure.

What is wrong with me? Why do I keep forgetting what he did?

Stripping as quickly as I can, I dive under the covers before he gets any ideas, such as turning around.

"You can look now," I mutter.

He goes to sit in the chair, where he winks at me.

Huffing, I close my eyes.

As is usual in Valerian's presence, sleep eludes me for a while, but eventually, I drift off.

————

I'M in the Intro to Programming class, and the professor slaps a final on my desk.

Puck. I thought I dropped this course, but I was mistaken. A couple of minutes ago, I realized I forgot to actually drop it. Now I have to somehow pass this exam even though I didn't attend a single lecture or read a page of course material.

Dread spreading through my very being, I open the paper and Pom pops out.

"You're dreaming this again?" His fur turns light orange. "Why?"

Oh. He's not on my wrist, so this is a dream—one I've had countless times for some reason.

Out of the corner of my eye, I see the professor throw an eraser at me.

Odd.

Instinctively, I dive under the desk—and it's a good

thing I do. On the way to my head, the eraser becomes a foaming-at-the-mouth pit bull.

What the puck?

Leaping from under the desk, I glare at the professor—who morphs into the dreaded shape of the Nutcracker.

"You're hard to ambush," the creepy creature says in his melodic voice. "It won't save you, though."

A gun appears in his hand.

Leveraging my earlier practice, my body becomes metal.

Bang.

My shoulder screams in agony, but the bullet falls at my feet.

"Oh, that won't work," he says. "I know what you actually look like."

He does something, and my metallic body turns back into flesh.

Oh, puck.

He aims his gun again.

CHAPTER EIGHTEEN

AS FAST AS I CAN, I mess with the chemistry of the gunpowder in the Nutcracker's weapon.

He squeezes the trigger.

The gun clicks, but no bullet comes out.

He hurls the gun at my chest.

I sidestep and make his feet heavy while weakening the structure of the floor underneath him.

The Nutcracker crashes through the floor.

"This is too scary," Pom says and disappears.

I change my surroundings to those of the lobby in the gorgeous Harpa Reykjavik concert hall located in Iceland. If the Nutcracker isn't from Earth—or is but has never visited this place—I might have an advantage.

He doesn't appear.

Score.

I try to jolt myself awake.

It doesn't work, and I soon hear why. It's that

cursed music—*Dance of the Sugar Plum Fairy*—blasting from all around.

He must be here and is somehow preventing me from waking up.

But how? I'm supposed to be more powerful now. Has the Nutcracker also gotten more power since our last encounter? That doesn't seem likely. Valerian was probably right when he said I need to internalize what I've gained.

Assuming I survive this encounter, that is.

In an eyeblink, the Nutcracker appears ten feet away from me and launches an angry tarantula at my face.

I leap to the side, then run up the wall, changing gravity and the traction of my feet as needed.

The Nutcracker chases after me with the clickety-clack of wood hitting metal and glass.

When I reach the windows facing the harbor, I make the glass melt under my feet. Swiftly, I fly out, landing on the cold waters of the Atlantic Ocean.

The Nutcracker lands on the water nearby with ease. I guess he's practiced walking on water as much as I have, or is a natural at it.

Without much ado, he throws a scorpion at my head.

I make a katana appear in my hand, a replica of the one I fought zombies with the other day. With a *whoosh*, I slice the scorpion in half, then lunge at my opponent.

My hope is that by walking on water and having to

defend a close-up attack, he won't have the bandwidth to mess with our environment.

My plan almost works. The katana strike lands, but the metal only cuts a shallow gash in the wood that is his chest.

Right. Wood is harder to penetrate than flesh.

A saber appears in the Nutcracker's wooden hand just in time to parry my next strike. Puck. My own strategy is working against me now. When I try to melt his weapon, it doesn't work.

A close-up fight was a mistake; unlike him, I'm made of flesh.

Maybe I can turn him corporeal to even the score? He gave me a clue as to how when he said he knows what I look like.

I swing the katana. He sidesteps and unleashes a barrage of his own attacks.

As I parry the onslaught, I realize I have a slight problem when it comes to making him corporeal.

I have no clue what he looks like.

Or do I?

The last dreamwalker I met was Maxwell, and he seemed suspicious to me.

Could this be Maxwell?

Parrying the next attack, I will him to take Maxwell's shape—sad eyes, the mask, and all.

Nope. He's still in the Nutcracker guise and must know what I failed to do because his already-evil grin looks infinitely more wicked.

Okay. Either this isn't Maxwell, or I misunderstood

how this works. Or he's just more powerful. Or I need to know what Maxwell's face looks like to get this right.

Ow!

All my ruminations have made me lose my battle concentration, giving the Nutcracker a chance to slice open my right forearm.

Ignoring the bleeding, I parry another dozen strikes as I attempt to control the environment again. Except a whale I try to conjure up doesn't swim from under the water, nor does the water itself want to turn into magma under the Nutcracker's feet.

Pucking puck.

My muscles are tiring from all the frantic Kendo moves I'm using. If I don't do something soon, I'll make a fatal mistake and that'll be that.

No. Not when Valerian is guarding me in the outside world.

Not when I have a real chance to wake Mom.

Exiting my body, I play an ace I've been saving for the right moment. Instead of wasting time on healing my wound, I duplicate myself and jump into both bodies.

The me that is behind the Nutcracker slashes at his saber-holding wrist, effortlessly cutting through the wood. The Nutcracker's human eyes widen—which is when both of me try the wake-up jolt.

It works this time.

A single me opens my eyes on the bed inside the inn.

Panting, I sit up.

Valerian leaps to his feet. "What's wrong?"

Wiping the cold sweat off my brow, I tell him.

"That bastard," he says through gritted teeth when I'm done. "This is why we need to catch a leader of one of the Icelus cells. They meet via this dreamwalker, so they should know his identity."

"Unless he disguises himself even with them," I say, still shaken.

He waves dismissively. "One leader would lead us to another, until eventually we'd find him."

"The Nutcracker said he knew what I look like. That narrows our list of suspects drastically."

"Right." His dark eyebrows furrowed, Valerian adjusts his mask. "Either Icelus have a dossier on you, or someone you know is a dreamwalker who's hiding that fact."

"Or it's Maxwell," I say.

"He didn't see your face, so he doesn't *really* know what you look like."

Oh, yeah. I had the mask on when I met him. But wait— "He could've seen me in Dylan's dreams. Or yours if you connected with him."

"Highly unlikely. Maxwell hates Icelus even more than I do."

"How do you know?"

"The vetting," Valerian says. "During it, Maxwell allowed himself to get glamoured by an ancient vampire and was thoroughly questioned. I don't know of any way to fool that."

The adrenaline is leaving my body, and the tiredness is kicking in. "Fine," I say with a half-yawn. "But I can't help the feeling that there's more to Maxwell than meets the eye."

Valerian peers at me intently. "You think you'll be able to fall sleep again?"

"I can try." I close my eyes.

Minutes later, I'm out.

———

AT BREAKFAST, Dylan tells us she saw Maxwell in her dreams again, and he informed her that the work on the cure continues. He also said he dreamwalked in his contacts on all the collaborating Otherlands, and the news he got there is mixed. The deadly Icelus virus hasn't shown up anywhere, which is good, but the Overtaken threat is spreading exponentially everywhere, which is not so good.

"That tells me the Icelus cell we're after is the driving force behind the spread of the plague." Valerian gesticulates with a breakfast sausage made out of a local creature. "We stop them, we stop it."

"And then we'll 'only' have to deal with legions of the Overtaken," Itzel says.

We all ponder Itzel's point for the rest of breakfast, but no one comes up with anything good enough to share with the group.

The rest of the day is identical to the one prior; we ride through the countryside and witness ever more ingenious uses for a zombie labor force. By the next day, the roads become better, and in the afternoon, we see a city that sprawls from horizon to horizon in the distance.

Nulen says something.

"That's Necropolis," Dylan translates. "Our destination."

The city looks more curious the closer we get. There are flying creatures crisscrossing the skies, tall trees that have somehow been made part of the skyline, and skyscraper-high gothic-looking buildings.

Soon, though, the city isn't what draws everyone's attention. What we're gaping at is the truly mind-boggling number of zombies in our way.

Not thousands but millions, they surround Necropolis like an impenetrable wall. Their faces are covered by the same masks as Nulen's zombies, but these specimens were clearly taller and beefier people when they were alive.

"Cream of the undead crop," Ariel says, awestruck.

"The best of the zombie best." Felix's tone echoes hers.

Everyone else stays mute.

When we approach the zombie wall, the dead clear a path for us and close ranks behind us once we get through.

"Even less chance of going back now," Fabian mutters.

"Great," Itzel says in that grumbly manner she's

adopted for most situations on Necronia. "We're even more screwed than before."

Further debate is drowned out by a horrible screeching sound as the gates of Necropolis are drawn apart by thousands of zombie arms.

Inside the city, we see that we're not the only ones using zombies for transport; a lot of Necropolis residents seem to be doing the same. Some ride piggy-back on zombies, like overgrown children, while others sit inside a single-person palanquin or hammock.

What's different in this city is that there don't seem to be any humans in sight—only leather-clad necros.

When I ask Dylan, she confers with Nulen and confirms my supposition.

Necropolis is a necromancer-only city.

We ride through the streets until we reach a gloomy-looking building. A zombie opens a door for us as Nulen says something to Dylan.

"He's asking us to wait here," Dylan translates. "He'll go to explain the situation to the Parliament."

Felix clears his throat. "Does he look purplish red to anyone else?"

We all stare at the necromancer with varying degrees of concern.

Puck. He does indeed look purplish red—like Pom would if he were equal parts happy and mad.

"There's not much we can do for him," Valerian reminds us, stepping into the house.

We follow his example, and as soon as we're all in,

the door to the house closes and locks from the outside.

"Are we under house arrest?" Ariel asks.

"More like jail," Felix says, looking around.

He's right. Our surroundings are more reminiscent of a dank dungeon than a house.

As he usually does, Stanislav walks as far away from everyone as he can—since we still don't know if he's infected and all. "At least we get a reprieve from the constant presence of zombies," he says, perching on a chair in the corner.

"And there's normal furniture," Itzel says, plopping on an ancient-looking chair.

Valerian sweeps away cobwebs and dust from another chair, hygieias it, then gestures for me to sit.

Gratefully nodding, I do so.

"I guess we wait," Ariel says to no one in particular.

So we wait again in a tense silence.

And wait.

And wait some more.

At some point, I have to use what passes for the bathroom in this house—and experience another bout of gratitude for Valerian's hygieia device.

After about four hours, I'm both thirsty and hungry. An hour after that, I start complaining, and soon after, I have to explain to Felix that I'd rather die of thirst than drink the water of questionable potability that comes out of the faucet in the grimy bathroom.

Two hours after that, Valerian captures some of said

water, waves the hygieia device over it, and convinces me to drink.

Four hours later, I haven't developed dysentery, but I'm hungry enough to gnaw on my own arm.

"Should I break a door or a window?" Fabian asks, yawning.

"Let's play nice for a while longer," Valerian says. "There are millions of zombies outside. We don't really stand a chance."

And the interminable waiting continues, with more yawns coming in, followed by naps.

"You should also sleep if you can," Valerian says to me. "I'll make a clean surface for you."

He does, and I drift off—luckily without a visit from the Nutcracker.

———

WHEN I WAKE UP, our situation is unchanged, my hunger is stronger than ever, and the question of breaking out is at the top of everyone's agenda.

Just as Fabian walks over to test the strength of the door, the lock clicks.

We all leap to our feet, eyes glued to the door as it opens.

The person who walks in isn't Nulen. It's a good-looking young woman with heavy eyeshadow and a black line drawn horizontally across her face below the eyes. Her leather outfit has a worn look to it, as though she got it from a necromancer thrift store. Half of her hair is jet black, while the other half is bleached white, and it's all held back by a pair of goggles on her head— an accessory that wouldn't look out of place at a steampunk convention.

"You're not Nulen," Dylan says to her, forgetting to switch to Necronian.

"Amazing powers of observation," the woman says in unaccented American English. "Anyone want to say something even more obvious?"

"Who are you?" I blurt.

"Where's Nulen?" Valerian says at the same time.

"My name is Rowan," the newcomer says. "Nulen is dead."

"Dead?" we exclaim in unison.

"Well, yeah," she says. "I figured you'd know, seeing as how the Parliament are convinced it was your evil schemes that killed him."

CHAPTER NINETEEN

EVERYBODY STARTS SHOUTING AT ONCE, with Dylan babbling in Necronian.

Rowan frowns at her. "Did you not hear me speak your language a second ago?"

Dylan winces. "Sorry. All the stress is getting to me."

Stepping up to her, Fabian places a comforting hand on her shoulder.

Rowan scratches the bleached side of her head. "Stress sucks. I heard that when an octopus is overstressed, she'll eat herself, and sadly, not in a dirty way."

"That's not actually accurate," Dylan mutters under her breath while I grin internally. The necromancer seems to share my often-inappropriate sense of humor.

"I have a question of my own," Rowan says, ignoring Dylan. "What's with the masks? Are you all gnomes?"

"I'm the only gnome," Itzel says. "With the others,

it's a long story, which will have to wait until you've answered some of our questions."

"Right, about that." Rowan shifts from one booted foot to the other. "I don't have many answers for you. I'm only here because I speak your language—and because the Parliament wouldn't be too sad if you killed me." She looks us all over. "With that in mind, how about you don't kill me? Please?"

Everyone continues to shower her with questions, but they speak too fast for anyone to understand anything, plus Stanislav and Fabian might actually be speaking their native tongues.

Rowan loudly clears her throat, and silence finally falls. "I wouldn't recommend you make the Parliament wait."

"They want to speak with us?" Dylan asks.

"Right. I think I'll call you Ms. State-the-Obvious." Rowan glances at Fabian, then at Dylan. "Or is it Mrs. State-the-Obvious?"

"Why does the Parliament want to talk to us?" I ask. "Or is that also obvious?"

Rowan's expression turns more serious. "From what I've been told, Nulen died in the process of explaining your visit to them. They questioned his corpse afterward as well. I wasn't given any details; it's not as if I need to know who you are to bring you to them. Or how much danger I'm in. Or—"

"If Nulen told them everything, they should be glad we're here," Dylan says.

"Sounds like someone wants to be renamed to Ms. Naivete." Rowan looks at Fabian. "Or is it Mrs.?"

Ariel's pretty eyes turn flinty. "Her name is Dylan. And remember how you asked for us not to kill you just seconds ago?"

Looking more intrigued than intimidated, Rowan examines Ariel. "With that bravado, I take it your name isn't Ms. Hotness McSexyBod either? Because that's what I have in my head."

Ariel stands up from her chair and gives its seat what seems to be a light squeeze.

With a loud crack, the wood shatters into tiny splinters.

Rowan's eyes widen. "You're one of those Strongmen types, aren't you?"

"An uber," I say. "And I wouldn't piss her off. Or any of us for that matter."

As if to highlight my words, Fabian crushes his chair as well, while Stanislav passes his hand through his.

Valerian must also show her something really impressive because her eyes widen and she mutters, "Is it possible to learn this power?"

A smile touches Felix's eyes as he deadpans, "Not from a Jedi."

Rowan grins. "I like you. What are you called? All I got so far is Skinny McUnibrowPants the Second Jr."

He rolls his eyes. "I'm Felix." He points at his roommate. "That's Ariel. And that's Valerian, Bailey,

Itzel, Stanislav, and Fabian." He points at each of us in turn.

"Well," Rowan says, "now that I know your names, I feel more invested in your fate—which is getting more dire with every wasted second."

"Right," I say. "How about we go?"

"Hakuna Matata," Rowan says and exits through the door.

"Do we trust her?" Dylan asks.

Everyone shakes their heads.

"Do we trust this Parliament?"

The shakes are even more vigorous this time.

"Great," Dylan says. "But I guess we have to go anyway."

We head out of the prison-house one by one. Once outside, I spot Rowan standing next to a group of drab-looking zombies, plus a creature that reminds me of an Earth's opossum, only creepier and cuter at the same time.

"Say hello to my little friend," Rowan says, following my gaze.

The creature scurries over and grins toothily at me.

I step back.

"Oh, don't worry. Frank won't hurt you," Rowan says. "He's under my control, like the rest of the helpers. Aren't you, Frank?"

Frank scurries back to Rowan's side and looks exaggeratingly zombie-like.

"You have a dead pet?" Dylan asks.

"Are you sure you'd mind if I called you Ms. State-the-Obvious after all?" Catching Fabian's narrow-eyed stare, she quickly adds, "Or it could be Mrs. State-the-Obvious, of course."

Our translator visibly bristles. "I insist you call me Dylan. But allow me to state more obviousness. You lived on Earth?"

Rowan brushes imaginary dust from her leather jacket. "What gave it away: my skills with the tongue or my amazing mastery of American pop culture?"

"But isn't your kind banned?" Dylan asks.

"I was incognito," Rowan says. "Kept my head down. Pretended to be human. Didn't raise corpses and have them stroll down 42nd Street willy-nilly. That sort of thing."

"Aren't we in a rush?" Valerian asks, looking impatient.

"Right." Rowan's face grows serious, an expression that I suspect doesn't show there much. "Follow me."

Briskly, she strides northward, and we follow.

Over her shoulder, Rowan asks, "Do you want me to play the tour guide?"

No one replies.

"That"—she points at a magnificent castle-like structure to our left—"is the church of Mor. He's the god everyone here believes in. Oh, and they worship him hard, so don't say things like *Mor be damned,* or *by Mor,* or *Mor take me,* and so on. Especially not in front of anyone in the Parliament. They don't like it. I speak from experience."

Stanislav groans. "Do you ever shut up?"

Rowan turns and peers at him intently. "Something's off about your eyes. I can't quite put my finger on it."

The chort snorts, and Rowan proceeds to explain the local religion, which, among other things, preaches that when a soul leaves the body, the proper way to revere the leftover shell is to turn it into a helper.

"How convenient," Felix says. "I bet humans willingly bring you corpses to turn into zombies."

"Don't use the z-word in front of the Parliament," Rowan says. "They don't like that either."

Two good-looking women in nice leather clothing cross the road and give Rowan the evil eye. When she ignores them, they say something in Necronian—and though I'm no linguist, I catch a distinct nasty undertone.

Rowan smirks and responds with something equally snide.

The two women upgrade their evil eyes to death glares. One even goes as far as to spit in Rowan's direction—a gesture that should be outlawed throughout the Cogniverse, as far as I'm concerned.

Frank, the weird opossum, rushes at the spitter and promptly bites her toe.

The woman shouts something, grabs her friend, and rushes away.

"What was that about?" Felix asks Dylan.

"Something about some person named Keyser making a huge mistake. What she"—Dylan nods at

Rowan—"replied with must've been some slang I didn't recognize."

Rowan wrinkles her nose. "They were talking about their husband and my betrothed."

Felix stares at the escaping women openmouthed. "You guys have polygamy on this world?"

"Polygyny, to be exact," Dylan says.

Rowan's upper lip curls as she looks at Dylan. "You're so useful. Mor forbid we use the wrong term."

"But is it true?" Felix demands, and I recall that Uzbekistan, the country on Earth that his family's from, is supposed to have something along those lines. Or had—what little I know about this is from Ariel's teasing.

Rowan bares her white teeth. "To put it in terms you can understand, members of the Parliament and other powerful male necromancers take multiple wives under the pretext of a eugenics-like program to increase the number of powerful necromancers overall. For better or worse, my own necromantic potential is high—which is allegedly more important than, say, intellect or looks. So yeah, I drew the short straw. And no, I can't have multiple husbands; that would make some minds implode."

Ariel stares at her in fascination. "And your hubby-to-be is named Keyser?"

"Yeah. I know. Like from *The Usual Suspects*," Rowan says. "You're about to meet him. He isn't as cool as his name would imply. Kind of the opposite."

No one speaks as we walk a few more blocks—that

is, until Valerian's LEGO letters appear, presumably for everyone except Rowan:

If things go south, we take one or more members of this Parliament hostage and get the puck off this world.

Fabian flexes his fists. I guess he realizes that with our current lack of weapons, he's the most dangerous in the group.

We step onto a large circular plaza where a large building stands in the middle, and ten mansions are located along the plaza's circumference.

"This is Decagon Square. The Parliament meeting room is in there." Rowan points at the middle building. "And each member of the Parliament resides in one of those." She gestures at the surrounding mansions.

As we head to the center building, I overhear Dylan talking to Fabian about the word *decagon*. She mentions such practical pearls of wisdom as "a decagon is a figure with ten straight sides and angles," and "the name 'decagon square' is a contradiction of terms," and last but not least, "each mansion is inside an angle that is exactly 144 degrees."

The biggest zombies I've seen yet open the doors of the center building for us, and Rowan leads us down a posh corridor with walls decorated by creepy art à la the zombies' masks.

"Through here is the Parliament meeting room," Rowan says, nodding at a set of ornate doors. She peers at Stanislav again. "Seriously, what's going on with your eyes?"

I follow her gaze and see what she's talking about.

My heartbeat skyrockets.

There's a tiny gathering of red moisture in the chort's tear ducts.

Stanislav must see me whiten because he wipes at his eyes and stares at his fingers in horror.

It's blood.

CHAPTER TWENTY

I BEGIN HYPERVENTILATING as a million thoughts rush through my mind.

I want to run. Barring that, I want to grab Valerian's hygieia device and use it until its batteries run out—even though the rational part of me understands that we have our masks for exactly this reason. Both my mask and Stanislav's should prevent any viruses from going in or out, so there's double protection.

In fact, everyone—besides Stanislav—should be fine, even the maskless Rowan.

Still, it's hard not to spiral. Stanislav was only briefly without the mask, yet he's already having his first symptom.

The virus is extremely contagious.

I'm not the only one freaking out either. Everyone on the team is a little wild-eyed, their foreheads clammy. The only person looking more confused than scared is Rowan. Staring at the blood on Stanislav's fingers, she asks, "Is that normal for your kind?"

Stanislav ignores her. I imagine he must be in shock.

"What do we do?" Dylan's voice is barely above a whisper.

LEGO letters instantly appear in the air:

There isn't much we can do. Let's talk to this Parliament.

"Seriously, what's going on?" Rowan demands.

"Long story," Valerian says. "Just stay as far away from Stanislav as you can."

"Uh-huh, sure." She stares at us, and when no explanations are forthcoming, she heaves a sigh. "Fine. Ready to go?"

At our nods, Rowan has her zombies open the doors for us.

Stanislav trudges into the room. Rowan waits a few seconds to let him get far enough away, then follows—with the rest of us on her tail.

We end up in a room large enough to play football in, with a neck-straining, sixty-foot-tall ceiling.

Rowan's zombies close the doors behind us.

Like the surrounding square, this room is decagon shaped, and in each of the ten angles stands a massive throne with a masked figure.

"These helpers were giants in life," Rowan whispers, in case we couldn't guess by the zombies' size. "The masks are designed to look like each member of the Parliament."

Sure enough, the masks have people's features

depicted on them, a bit like the sex-worker zombies' masks did.

"So the members of the Parliament aren't here in person?" I ask, my eyes darting from giant to giant.

"Nope," Rowan says. "Each Parliament member sees through the eyes of the helper dedicated for his use and hears through his ears. Think of it as a videoconference, only designed to make you feel small and insignificant."

Felix whistles. "Zoom has nothing on this."

Puck. There goes Valerian's plan to kidnap one of these people in case things go south. Despite Rowan saying she's engaged to one of them, it's clear that kidnapping her wouldn't do much good; as she said, they don't seem to care about what happens to her. If they did, they would've asked her to use a zombie proxy instead of dealing with us face to face.

The best we can hope for now is that things don't go any more south than they already have.

One of the giant zombies stands up and says something in a booming voice.

"Should I translate?" Rowan asks Dylan.

Dylan shrugs.

Taking it as agreement, Rowan points at the zombie with a mask that has a hawkish nose. "That's Keyser, and he insists I use the word 'demand' when I ask you why you came to this 'magnificent' world."

We all look at Dylan.

"That's pretty much what I heard," Dylan says.

"Except the original had more aggrandizements and flowery language."

Valerian steps forward. "We came to help. An organization called Icelus is trying to rouse fear throughout the Cogniverse. Their agents are on this world, trying to infect your citizens with a deadly disease."

Rowan's shoulders tighten. "Is that what the masks are for?"

"Exactly," Dylan says.

Rowan rounds on her. "And *that's* the long story? I could've made time for that—especially since it took you all of two seconds to explain." She pivots to stare at Stanislav with widening eyes. "Is he—"

"We learned that at the same time as you," Dylan says. "He caught it from Nulen. You should be safe because he has a mask on."

Keyser's booming voice drowns any further discussion.

"He demands to know what we're talking about," Rowan says.

Valerian plants his feet wide. "Translate what I said, but not a word about Stanislav."

"Disobey him, and I'll rip you to shreds," Fabian adds, his German accent stronger than ever.

"Since you ask so nicely, how can I refuse?" Rowan says and starts to translate, with Dylan hanging on to her every word.

I feel a little guilty about the threat on Rowan's life, but desperate times and all that.

Keyser's reply is curt and loud.

"You lie," Rowan translates. "I assume you want me to skip the accompanying insults."

Valerian's hands flex as he looks up at the giant. "You saw Nulen die of the virus with your own eyes."

"They saw him through their helpers' eyes, but I'll translate," Rowan says and speaks Necronian for a few seconds.

Keyser's reply is a bit longer but no less angry.

"He insists you killed Nulen with your vile otherworldly powers," Rowan translates.

"Why would we come here, putting ourselves at your mercy, and do that?" Valerian shouts.

A giant with a small goatee replies this time.

"Even if there is a virus, how do we know the organization you're talking about exists? How do we know you didn't bring the disease with you?" Rowan darts a furtive glance at Stanislav as she says this last bit. "Most importantly, what do you want?"

Valerian looks at Stanislav, then at the currently standing giant. "I want you to capture the Icelus agents and give them to us. In exchange, we'll provide the cure for the virus."

"Wait, what?" Felix says. "Didn't we want to catch Icelus ourselves?"

"These necros seem to hate outsiders too much to let us do that," Valerian says, and Rowan nods in confirmation. "More importantly, we need to take Stanislav back to Gomorrah as soon as possible. As much as I hate Icelus, they're not worth his life."

"Must be nice to have friends," Rowan mutters. Louder, she asks, "Can I translate now?"

"Please," Valerian says.

Rowan speaks Necronian.

The giants begin a discussion among themselves.

As they go on, Dylan whitens. I'm guessing we won't like the translation when it comes.

Indeed, Rowan gives us an uncomfortable look when the giants stop speaking. "Some of them say your deal is so outrageous, they don't see why you'd come here to make it," she says. "Keyser, on the other hand, says you're either crazy or very clever—and has called for a vote to decide your fate."

"A vote?" Ariel adjusts her mask.

"If the majority of them stand up, you're going to be killed," Rowan says, not meeting our eyes. "Otherwise, they'll hear more about your deal."

How fun. My fate is again tied to a ruling body's vote. I'm definitely getting the next one for free.

Keyser's giant stands up.

The one with a small goatee follows.

Then another. And one more.

When the fifth one stands up, everyone tenses.

If one more joins them, that will be a majority against us.

The sixth giant stands.

Puck.

We're officially screwed.

CHAPTER TWENTY-ONE

SOMEBODY LOUDLY KNOCKS on the doors that lead into the meeting chamber. The pattern of the knocks is strange, something like *Da-Da-Da-DUM*.

The giant zombies and the rest of us look at the door.

The banging repeats, again going *Da-Da-Da-DUM*.

Wait a second. Isn't that how the *Fate Motif* from Beethoven's *Symphony* goes? My arms prickle with goosebumps. This must be Nostradamus's cryptic prediction finally coming into play. Which means I'm supposed to play the detective—whatever that means.

Keyser barks an order at Rowan, and a moment later, she has her zombies open the doors.

A man rushes into the room. He looks haggard, with black bags under his eyes. More notably, his skin is purplish red, and there are steaks of blood on his face.

Rowan wisely backs away from the guy. Without her mask, she's in mortal danger from him.

Ignoring us, the newcomer haltingly monologues in Necronian.

LEGO letters appear in the air in front of me:

Are you playing the detective?

So Valerian has also noticed the connection to Nostradamus's words. Good. For a second, I was worried the adrenaline spike was making me hear things that weren't there.

I nod at him, then close my eyes and do my best to "play the detective."

Except I don't know where to start, and the presence of yet another victim of the virus is making me want to run away screaming.

Hold on.

The virus.

I bet playing the detective implies I should figure out who or where the Icelus are.

Assuming they're on this world in the first place.

No. They have to be. Nulen was sick when we met him, so he must've gotten infected by someone before we arrived, thus proving Icelus presence on this world. Not much detective skill required to figure *that* out.

Although… when we met him, he had only the very first symptom. That means he'd gotten infected recently. Also, the Parliament doesn't believe us about the virus, so they couldn't have heard reports of it, which also points to it being a recent arrival on this world.

So what does Nulen being one of the first cases tell me? Not much yet—but hold on. Going back to Icelus being on this world... Wasn't Nulen guarding the hub with a force of zombies to prevent any arrivals?

Another round of goosebumps ripples down my spine. That's exactly what he was doing. Which means one of two things: Either Nulen let Icelus agents in and was infected by them in the process, or someone else let them in and that someone else got Nulen sick too. Given that Nulen is dead, the only useful option is the second one. Which means—

The newcomer collapses, seemingly mid-sentence.

"Dead," Rowan says somberly. "I can feel it."

The six standing Parliament members sit back down.

One of the ones who didn't vote to kill us—a giant with a mask that features a cartoonishly strong chin—begins to speak.

"He wants me to bring the messenger back," Rowan says. "If that sort of thing is going to make you puke, I suggest you look away." And as I look on, Rowan shoots the dead guy with a stream of multicolored energy.

A moment later, the messenger is back on his feet.

Members of Parliament attack him with questions, and the messenger answers in a robotic monotone.

"What did he say?" I hiss at Dylan.

Dylan looks to be in shock, so Rowan answers in her stead. "There was an outbreak of the virus in the province he's from. Humans and necromancers are dying in droves."

"And what's the Parliament talking about now?" Valerian asks.

"Shegan is asking the messenger if the eight of you have been seen in the province," Rowan translates. After the messenger zombie replies something, she adds, "Apparently not."

"Of course not," I say. "Nulen brought us here straight from the hub."

Rowan chuckles humorlessly. "Silly rabbit—you expected the Parliament to use logic?"

"Kind of," I say. "Can you translate something for me?"

Rowan nods.

"Was Nulen the only person guarding the hub against newcomers?"

"I can answer that myself," Rowan says. "There's a whole team of us who share that particular chore. Right now would be my turn, but I'm not at my post thanks to all this brouhaha you've created. Thanks for that—and I mean it."

My pulse speeds up in excitement. "How long do each of you spend on your post?"

"A few days," she says. "Depends on weather and things like that."

"And whose turn was it right before Nulen?"

"Exozar's," Rowan says.

"Then logic says this Exozar is working with Icelus,"

I announce triumphantly before explaining my deductions.

Just as I finish, the Parliament demands to know what we're talking about, and Rowan loops them in.

As she speaks, Dylan looks at her admiringly, but it's unclear why.

After Rowan is done explaining, Shegan speaks up.

"If you can get proof of what you say, they'll take your deal," Dylan translates.

Keyser speaks up next—and talks for a while.

Rowan rolls her eyes when he's done. "The great humanitarian that is my husband-to-be says you can't be trusted, and that the proof wouldn't prove anything as far as he's concerned. He also says the virus isn't such a big deal; it will just grow the number of available helpers, thus improving the quality of everyone's life. He also says we can use helpers to quarantine impacted areas— which is no doubt a euphemism for 'burn everything to the ground' and contradicts his 'more helpers' point."

Shegan speaks again.

Rowan nods approvingly. "This more reasonable dude says their job as the rulers is to do everything they can to get people the cure. He also worries the virus might be spreading through Necropolis now, thanks to this messenger. Finally, he says they should vote on this."

Yay. Another pucking vote.

The Parliament confers, and Rowan explains that if the majority of the giants remain seated, we'll be allowed to get the proof we need. Otherwise, the default ruling stands—as in, we get killed.

We all watch with baited breaths.

Keyser stands up.

A colleague of his does the same.

This is it.

History is about to repeat itself.

CHAPTER TWENTY-TWO

NO MORE GIANTS STAND UP.

The vote has just gone in our favor.

A relieved exhale escapes my lips as Shegan speaks rapid-fire Necronian at Rowan, who nods and replies in a respectful tone.

"I'm to head the investigation," she translates. "Let's go before they change their minds."

We hurry out of the room and head down the corridor in silence.

When we enter the lobby, Dylan looks at Rowan. "You didn't have to put your neck on the line for us in there."

"What are you talking about?" Felix asks.

"When she told them Exozar was guilty, she said she was suspicious of him too—that he's been acting strange lately," Dylan explains.

"As in, I lied," Rowan says. "Exozar and I haven't spoken in months."

Dylan nods. "And after she said that, Keyser told her to be sure she means what she says and made it clear that by doing this, she's aligning her fate with ours."

"I'm beginning to have a feeling that he doesn't want me even as a seventh wife," Rowan says ruefully. "I don't know if I should cheer or be insulted."

Ariel stares at the necromancer as if seeing her for the first time. "You shouldn't have done that. Our chances aren't good."

"But thank you," I say hurriedly. "I bet you helped the vote."

"Yeah, well, I wasn't as self-sacrificing as you might think. I can use logic just as well as anyone—and it says my fate is already tied to yours." She nods at Stanislav. "More precisely, his."

"You think the messenger has gotten you sick, so you want the cure," Stanislav says, wiping at his slightly bleeding eyes.

Rowan nods. "Bingo."

"That room was spacious and you stood far away from the messenger," Dylan says reassuringly. "Your viral load would've been small and chances of infection insignificant."

Stanislav holds out his bloody fingers. "Isn't that what you told me at the hub?"

"And I wasn't wrong," Dylan says. "Given how long it took you to develop your first symptom, the viral load you must've inhaled *was* small."

He glares at her. "Yet I'm still sick."

Rowan bends down and scratches her dead pet

under his whiskery chin. For a zombie, Frank looks too much like he's enjoying the grooming—but what do I know of such things?

"There's something more important we should discuss," Rowan says after she's done with her pet therapy. "How are we supposed to figure out if Exozar is guilty or not?"

Everyone exchanges startled glances. Everyone except Valerian, that is, who pointedly looks at me.

"If you could get me access to him, I could determine his guilt," I say, doing my best to sound more confident than I feel.

Felix and Ariel still look confused, so I say, "I'm supposed to be playing the detective right now, and in the past, that's always involved my powers."

Rowan has her zombies hold the doors as we exit. When we're outside, she says, "What's your power?"

I explain about dreamwalking as we make our way south, with Rowan's helpers lumbering after us like extras in a horror movie.

"New question," Rowan says when we stop next to a drab building that looks eerily like the one we were imprisoned in. "How will you understand his dreams if you don't speak Necronian?"

I grin under my mask. "Good point. You or Dylan have to volunteer to go in with me."

"Rowan volunteers," Valerian says firmly. "She's more familiar with local customs and such, so she'll make a better translator."

LEGO letters show up in the air as he speaks, and they say:

Also, this way we can check two necromancers for the price of one.

I nod. "Rowan it is."

"And I guess Rowan agrees," she says dryly. "Though the word 'volunteer' clearly means something different in English than it does in Necronian."

"Is this our target's home?" I ask, looking at the drab structure in front of us.

"Yep, that's Exozar's quarters," Rowan says. "Now what?"

Valerian looks at the door. "Can you get him to open up for you?" he asks Rowan.

"Sure," she says.

Valerian turns to me. "And could you do that sleep-at-a-distance trick Maxwell performed on Dylan the other day?"

I bite my lip. "Maybe. When I pushed Ariel into REM sleep that time, I was touching her skin. But that was before the power boost…"

"I don't understand," Rowan says.

"Sounds like we need a plan B," Dylan says, ignoring her.

"Plan B will be for me to knock the guy out," Stanislav says. "Then tie him up so Bailey can touch him as much as she needs."

"Touch him where?" Rowan asks with a smirk but is ignored again.

"I really hope we don't have to resort to plan B," I mutter under my breath. "I'm not eager to touch a stranger who might be spreading the virus." Or any stranger for that matter. Or even people I know.

"I'll hygieia his skin if we end up going that route," Valerian says. "That will kill anything." He looks at Dylan, who vigorously nods.

I still don't want to touch anyone, so I'm going to do my best to get plan A to work.

"Don't we need a way to make sure he doesn't see our team as a threat?" Felix asks.

"We can disguise you all as helpers." Rowan gestures at her zombies.

"I'm not putting on a mask that's been on a corpse," I say with a shudder. "There's a limit."

"You don't have to do that," Rowan says. "Follow me."

She leads us a couple of blocks over, where we enter an empty store filled to the brim with brand-new masks and different clothes, all designed for zombie wear. We pick masks big enough to fit over our current ones and robe-like garments to hide our non-Necronian attire.

After Valerian sterilizes my choices, I put them on.

The rest of the team does the same, and we totally end up looking like a bunch of zombies—a pretty eerie development.

"The helpers wear these masks to spare the family of the deceased the pain of seeing their loved ones walking around," Rowan explains as we walk back. "Not sure who decided the design should be this disturbing, though—or why."

When we get back to our original destination, Rowan gives us a thorough once-over. "Don't draw attention to yourselves," she says. "If Exozar puts his mind to it, he could figure out that you're not helpers."

I guess I'll have to do my part quickly.

"Ready?" Rowan asks.

I nod, and she knocks on the door.

A minute passes.

The door opens. A pale, disheveled head peeks out and says something in Necronian. Rowan replies in kind. The guy steps out, and they begin talking.

I close my eyes and concentrate. I don't bother wishing my target asleep or doing any imagination exercises. Instead, I try to replicate what I did to Ariel on instinct.

Nothing happens.

Maybe the wishing and imagining helps?

I do both while seeking the tip-of-the-tongue sensation. Still no results. Meanwhile, I can hear the necromancer conversation petering out.

I open my eyes and see Rowan darting glances at Stanislav, who's standing near Exozar.

Catching her drift, Stanislav sends his fist at Exozar's chin.

Bam.

Stanislav's strong arms catch Exozar before he falls.

"Finally," Rowan says. "I was seriously running out of things to say to the guy."

Grunting, the chort drags the necromancer inside, and the rest of us follow.

"Let my helpers do the rest," Rowan says. She has her zombies put Exozar on his bed, locate a rope, and tie up his arms and legs. "Your turn," she says to me when the bondage is complete.

True to his earlier promise, Valerian sterilizes a patch of skin on Exozar's wrist.

I touch the area gingerly, doing my best to suppress a strong desire to gag as I seek the prerequisite feeling.

It takes me a couple of minutes, but eventually, I get that sensation.

I metaphysically push.

Finally. Exozar is in REM sleep.

I switch gears and drop into his dream. As soon as I appear in my palace, I exit my trance.

There's one more step before I can properly dive in.

"Your turn," I tell Rowan in a low voice. "Oh, and you might not want to be standing next to sharp objects for this."

Rowan stretches out on the floor at the foot of the bed. She gives Valerian a caustic look when he cleans her wrist with the hygieia device.

I approach and make skin contact again. Rowan makes a goofy face and closes her eyes. I also close mine and search inside myself. The feeling is a little easier to locate this time; practice makes perfect and all that. When I catch it, I push, and Rowan is in REM sleep immediately.

I grin. I've officially mastered a new dreamwalker power. At least the touch version of it.

Without removing my hand, I enter Rowan's dream. Time to see if our alleged ally can be trusted.

CHAPTER TWENTY-THREE

FINDING myself in my dream palace lobby, I gape at the scene in front of me with a mixture of fear and confusion.

Two feet from me stands a frozen-in-place Nutcracker, with pitch-black Pom glaring up at him.

What the puck?

"Pom!" I shout. "Get away from him."

The Nutcracker disappears and Pom turns toward me, the fur on the tips of his ears going from black to beet. "You weren't supposed to see that."

"See what?" I ask, though a part of me already knows.

"That wasn't the real Nutcracker," Pom says, confirming my suspicion. "He just scares me so much, I figured I'd use exposure therapy to become braver." The beet color moves from his ears to the rest of his body.

I smile and fluff up his fur. "It's brave of you to even try. Especially on your own."

Pom's ears take on a brown tinge. "You mean it?"

"Sure. I usually have to badger my clients to try exposure therapy, and once they agree, I have to hold their hand every step of the way."

He hugs my leg and grins. "Thanks. Maybe I'll join you in whatever you came here to do—no matter how scary."

"Good idea."

I don't tell him that my investigation isn't likely to uncover frightening dreams. Let him believe he's being brave. Besides, one never knows what can come out of other people's subconscious.

Pom perches on my shoulder, and I make us invisible before teleporting to the tower of sleepers. Locating the nooks of both of my new necromancer connections, I enter Rowan's. "We'll start with her."

———

A MAN WEARING a Necronian zombie mask is chasing Rowan through the streets of Manhattan. Though this isn't a memory dream, it does prove she's been to New York City.

I make the pursuer evaporate, more for Pom's sake than Rowan's.

As Rowan stops running and looks around in confusion, I debate how to proceed. What I'm about to do works best if I have something like an alibi to check.

Answering a question such as "is this person part of Icelus?" is much harder and therefore time-consuming. Basically, I have to put Rowan—and later Exozar—in different dream scenarios, and as they fill in the details from their memories, I might spot something incriminating.

Or I might witness them knitting socks.

The worst part of this is that I can never prove anything with one-hundred-percent certainty. Even if I spend days without discovering an incriminating memory, it could just be due to bad luck.

Oh, well. All I can do is my best.

I start with the simplest trick I know. I make a random stranger on the street whisper the word "Icelus" and watch Rowan's expression.

She looks confused for a second. Then her mind takes over, and she strolls right into a nearby cinema to get a ticket for a movie in *The Fast and the Furious* franchise.

I switch to mental communication and tell Pom, *So far, this doesn't look suspicious.*

I don't think this woman is evil, Pom replies as a voice in my head. *And my intuition is never wrong.*

I'm not staking our safety in the real world on anyone's intuition, so I change the surroundings to a warehouse, a setting where I imagine shady conversations might occur.

Rowan's mind doesn't generate anything suspicious in response.

I put her in a few more shady places, with a similar lack of results.

After more futile digging, I recall an extra clue that I have in this case. The Nutcracker is someone who knows what I look like—and if he's the Icelus dreamwalker, Icelus members might know him in the real world.

Excited, I have Rowan meet dream versions of anyone I can possibly think of, from nurses at Mom's hospital to all of my rehab clients.

Nothing.

Then I get an idea. If Rowan is in Icelus with Exozar, putting them together in a dream might yield memories of them conspiring.

When Rowan is not paying attention, I change her current surroundings from a back alley to Exozar's house, then add Exozar himself.

Rowan's subconscious takes over, and suddenly, the room looks different, though clearly, we're still on Necronia.

My guess is this is Rowan's own living room. Her pet, Frank, is here as well, and Exozar is smiling and pointing at the creature.

They speak Necronian for a bit.

Puck. Valerian and I hadn't thought this through. In hindsight, I should've brought Dylan in too. Though it's pretty clear the conversation is about the pet; they're not looking anywhere else.

As I watch, Exozar crouches and feeds the creature

a couple of local nuts. He's rewarded with a lick from Frank and a grin from Rowan.

This must be from a time when Frank was alive— that or I've just learned something new about the zombie diet.

I think she's clean, Pom mentally informs me.

You're probably right, I reply.

Since we're still in a memory dream, I let it play out.

Exozar leaves, and Rowan plays with Frank for a while longer.

We should play more, Pom says in my head.

I pet his furry foot. *You're right. Once I'm out of deadly peril, we'll make playing a regular thing.*

The door Exozar left through opens again, and a new person steps in.

The hawkish nose and the other facial features match those on the mask that a giant zombie wore when we faced the Parliament.

Of course. This is Keyser, Rowan's betrothed.

And he doesn't look pleased. Quite the opposite.

Turning, Rowan asks him something, her tone playful.

He shouts at her.

Eyes narrowing, she shouts back.

His nostrils flare, and he grits something out— clearly an insult.

Rowan looks like she's been slapped.

Frank advances on Keyser, baring his very sharp teeth.

Keyser shouts again and kicks the poor creature like a football as Rowan lunges forward with a cry.

Frank smashes into the wall and slides down in a limp heap.

Pom's feet dig painfully into my shoulder.

Rowan rushes over to her furry friend, her face a mask of such grief that I almost make myself visible and give her a hug. I can't even imagine what she's feeling. If I ever lost Pom—

No, I can't even think about it.

Looking unrepentant, Keyser shouts one more time and slams the door on the way out.

Rowan kneels next to her pet, tears streaming down her face.

"Please, please, please," she whispers in English. "Don't be dead."

There's no response from the creature, and from the way Rowan's face crumples, it's obvious her plea wasn't answered. Bending over the pet, she sobs, rocking back and forth and muttering a mix of English curses and harsh-sounding Necronian words.

Then her sobs cease and her jaw sets in a stubborn line. "I'm going to bring you back," she whispers raggedly. "It'll be our little secret."

Standing up, she extends her hands, pointing at the little corpse. A blinding energy beam shoots out of her fingertips, one that looks very different from what she used when she resurrected the messenger earlier.

Frank stirs.

Kneeling over him again, she pets his fur, a watery smile appearing on her face.

Frank's gaze is unfocused, but he's clearly not dead anymore.

"Thank goodness," Pom exclaims. "I was worried she'd lost him for good."

Dude, you spoke out loud, I mentally answer.

Rowan looks up from Frank, wiping the wetness off her cheeks. "Is someone here?"

I debate if I should answer.

"Can the books be true?" she asks Frank. "Is Mor already punishing me for my sin?"

Frank doesn't reply, but I've made my decision now, so I make myself visible and clear my throat.

She looks at me, eyes wild. "By Mor, where did you come from?"

"You're dreaming," I say soothingly. "Remember how I was going to pull you into Exozar's dreams to help me translate? Well, I'm here, and I caught you reliving a painful memory, that's all."

She rubs her forehead. "You saw the whole thing?"

I nod somberly. "Sorry about Frank."

"Me too," Pom says.

Her gaze darts to my shoulder, and her eyes widen to comical levels.

I explain what Pom is in the simplest terms I can. When I finish, Rowan gives me an imploring look. "Please don't tell anyone what you saw."

"I'm not actually sure what I saw," I say. "Is Frank an unusual zombie or something?"

Rowan bends down and grabs the opossum-like creature off the floor. "He's not a zombie at all."

"I meant a helper," I say.

"He's not really a helper either." She strokes Frank's fur. "Only the most powerful necromancers can do what I did, and all of us are forbidden from doing it. Usually, when we raise a body, the soul—or consciousness—is gone from the resulting entity, letting the necromancer have control. But it *is* possible to do something different with a very fresh corpse. You just bring the life back without taking control. It's forbidden, but I'm a horrible excuse for a necromancer." She glances at the door, and I get the feeling that must be one of the things Keyser yelled at her.

"As far as I know," she continues, "Frank is the only being that has been brought back in this forbidden way. If the others found out about it, they'd kill me and destroy Frank."

Pom eyes Frank warily. "Is he the same as he was before he died?"

Averting her gaze, Rowan sets her pet down. "There *have* been changes. I'd rather not talk about it, though."

"It's fine," I say before Pom can insist. "We should jump into Exozar's dreams."

I teleport us to the tower of sleepers, leaving Frank behind.

"Wow." Rowan twirls in place, gaping at our surroundings. "Where is this?"

I explain it as well as I can and fill her in on how the investigation is going to proceed.

"Wait," she says. "You did that to me, didn't you?"

"We've just met," I say unapologetically.

"Fair enough. But won't Exozar see me? Or hear when I translate for you?"

I mentally say, *How about we talk like this?*

She doesn't look as shocked as I expected.

"That's cool," is all she says. "Are you hearing me do the same?"

Pom giggles. "You're still talking out loud."

"I was trying something," Rowan says defensively. "How about you tell me what to do?"

"Try to have a dream where you can talk to me telepathically," I say. "I'll help you."

She strains until her face turns red, and Pom helpfully informs her that she looks like someone dreaming about pooping rather than speaking mind-to-mind.

How about now? Rowan asks mentally.

There you go, I reply in kind. *In dreams, the impossible becomes possible.*

I was the first to get this to work, Pom chimes in.

You were. I tickle his paw. *But you're going to stay silent the whole time we're in Exozar's dreams, or you have to stay behind. Okay?*

Deal. Pom hops over onto my other shoulder.

I grab Rowan's hand, make all of us invisible, and touch Exozar's forehead.

A moment later, we're in the necromancer's dream.

CHAPTER TWENTY-FOUR

EEK. Exozar is having a wet dream.

This isn't scary, but I'm out, Pom informs me, and I can no longer feel his paws on my shoulder.

Well, this is awkward, Rowan announces.

No kidding. The woman bent over in front of Exozar is none other than Rowan herself.

She must notice that bit only now because she adds, *This never actually happened, but it does put a new spin on the phrase 'in your dreams.'*

Yep. I can confirm this isn't a memory.

Since Exozar's attention is on the naked Rowan, I change the environment from that of a bedroom to a shady warehouse.

Maybe he's dreaming this because you were the last person he saw before falling asleep? I ask.

I think he's fancied me for a while. That's why he opened the door so readily for us. And it's partly why Keyser was so jealous when he walked in on us on that fateful day. He must've passed Exozar on the street and guessed where he was coming from.

I ignore what she says next because Exozar grunts in pleasure, pulls away from his lover, and starts to dress.

When he's looking away from the naked and blissed-out dream Rowan, I swap her for a broken wooden mannequin.

I can't believe he hasn't noticed that switch, the real Rowan complains. *Maybe he doesn't like me as much as I thought.*

This is just the way dreams work, I reassure her.

I wait a few beats, but Exozar's subconscious doesn't fill in any details. If he had shady conversations with Icelus, it didn't happen in a place like this.

Then something occurs to me. Unlike with Rowan, I actually know one place where Exozar would've had to meet Icelus at least once. Smiling in anticipation, I change the surroundings to the Necronia hub—canyon, zombies, and all.

Now for the tricky part.

To really jar Exozar's subconscious, I make a figure step out of the gate we came from. I don't give this mystery person any distinct facial features or anything—the hope is that Exozar will.

Eureka. The newcomer suddenly develops a pale thin face, a pointy chin, and pitch-black eyes.

Another person follows him out of the gate, then a bunch more.

All are dressed in black leather outfits, and all look relieved when Exozar approaches them.

"Percival," Exozar says to the pointy-chinned one and follows it with a Necronian phrase.

Percival must be that guy's name, Rowan translates. *Exozar is happy to see him 'again.'*

Percival takes a backpack off his shoulders and rummages inside. Taking out a gallon-sized flask, he hands it to Exozar with a few words in Necronian.

Percival's accent is barely noticeable, Rowan comments. *He says the flask contains vampire blood, and that Percival has to drink a glass per day to keep the virus at bay.*

Huh. *Could this Icelus cell be vampires?* I ask, eyeing the flask warily.

I doubt a vampire would show up on this world, especially if they're trying to stay incognito, Rowan replies mentally. *Any necromancer worth the title would feel them from a mile away. Not to mention how much vampires fear our ability to take them over and make them do our bidding. There's a reason they made sure we're unwelcome on worlds like Earth.*

Exozar takes the flask and says something.

He's asking if vampire blood is how the rest of Percival's team will keep themselves alive while they infect people, Rowan translates.

Carrying on in Necronian, Percival continues to rummage in his backpack.

He says his team are all pre-vamps, Rowan says. *Their*

immune systems can keep this virus at bay indefinitely, which is why they've been chosen to spread it.

Pre-vamps. I wasn't that far off. I examine the pale faces of the arrivals. *I take it your kind can't detect or take control of one of them.*

Nope, Rowan replies. *Only once they turn.*

Percival hands Exozar something that looks like a cross between a syringe and a throwing dart. After the necromancer examines the device, Percival pulls out a heap more of them and they have a brief conversation.

Percival says the vampire blood will make sleep a problem, but that it's mission-critical for Exozar to be dreaming at noon after a night with a full moon, Rowan explains. *Apparently, in those things is a drug that can facilitate this—the only problem being a nightmare side effect.*

Ah, so it's that Koshmar poison again, the one that makes you see a nightmare based on whatever happened right before you got dosed. It was used on me by the late Dr. Cipactli, also known as the High Priest of the Gomorran Icelus cell. Valerian mentioned that Icelus had many uses for it, and here's one. I guess they now have a quick-acting version and utilize it a bit like how I plan to use my newfound power to put people into REM sleep.

Percival shouts something to one of his pre-vamp companions. The guy comes over and lies on the ground. Aiming the gizmo at his face, Percival presses on the top of the device, and an odorless spray escapes with a hiss.

It seems to take effect immediately; the pre-vamp's eyes start to move rapidly behind their lids.

You know, Rowan chimes in, *last night was a full moon, and it's about noon now.*

Puck. If they needed him to sleep for the reason I think—

As though to confirm my concerns, I hear the dreaded music from the *Dance of the Sugar Plum Fairy.*

Instantly and without explanation, I jolt Rowan awake. Then I do the same to myself—and disappear just as the Nutcracker appears smack in the middle of Exozar's dream.

CHAPTER TWENTY-FIVE

WE'RE BACK in Exozar's bedroom.

Looking disoriented, Rowan sits up.

"The Nutcracker. He's in his dreams right now." I point at Exozar's head.

Valerian narrows his eyes. "That hints he's guilty."

"We don't need hints," Rowan says, all signs of sleepiness gone from her face. "We saw him meet with the pre-vamp Icelus group. He's as guilty as—"

"Wait," I say, holding up a hand.

Something's wrong, but I can't figure out what.

Fabian's ears prickle. "I hear shuffling footsteps in the other room."

At the same exact time, I understand what's bugging me.

It's a specific feeling—or lack thereof.

"Exozar's awake," I exclaim, finally putting my finger on it.

Though the necromancer's eyes are still closed, I

can no longer feel him in REM sleep. The Nutcracker must've woken him up with a jolt.

As if waiting for me to say that, a handful of zombies rush into the room, no doubt under Exozar's control.

Stanislav swings a fist at Exozar's face, but the necromancer rolls off the bed, yelps in pain as he hits the floor, and rolls under the bed before anyone can get to him.

Ariel gives the bed frame a hard kick. The wooden structure collapses on top of Exozar, and we hear the necromancer grunt in pain.

"This is not good," Felix says in a frightened voice.

I follow his gaze.

Puck. That's a major understatement.

One of the attacking zombies is strapped with dynamite, and another has just lit the fuse.

Before my life can flash before my eyes, Rowan shoots multicolored energy at the zombie-bomb. The zombie stops in his tracks and swiftly backs away from us. However, a fellow zombie kicks the dynamite carrier's leg, breaking it like a twig, and another zombie breaks the other leg as two more tackle the wounded bomb-zombie to the ground.

"Run!" Rowan bolts for the door.

Fabian grabs Dylan, throws her over his shoulder like a sack, and sprints after Rowan. Stanislav snatches up Felix and Itzel, and Ariel grabs me, whooshing out of the house before I can so much as think "holy uber."

As soon as we're outside, she puts me on my feet and shouts for me to run.

I instinctively launch into a sprint, then stop and spin around, eyes widening in horror as I register the lack of a tall, broad-shouldered figure behind me.

Valerian.

He's not here.

He's still inside that house—and there can't be much length left on that fuse.

CHAPTER TWENTY-SIX

I LUNGE TOWARD THE HOUSE, but strong arms grasp my shoulders, yanking me to a stop.

"Let me go!" I yell, struggling with Ariel.

She doesn't listen.

After what feels like the longest second of my life, Valerian flies out of the house.

Boom.

The blast sends him flying.

I twist out of Ariel's grasp and sprint toward him. But before I can get to him, he sits up, brushing the dirt and gravel off his clothes.

"You okay?" I pant, crouching next to him.

He nods and gets to his feet. "I got lucky." He looks at the house on fire and curses under his breath. "There goes our chance to question Exozar."

Exozar, right. Rising to my feet, I try to get my frantic heartbeat under control. Valerian is fine. He made it. We all did. Still, my hand is unsteady as I push back my hair and readjust my mask. That second when I thought he wasn't going to make it—

Nope, not going there. Got to focus on the situation at hand. Exozar must've done this on purpose, sacrificing himself for the Icelus cause—or to avoid getting tortured for information.

"Maybe we can question his corpse?" I ask Rowan when she runs up to us. Whew. My voice is finally steady.

She shakes her head. "I need something left of him to resurrect."

A necromancer dressed in red rushes past us in the direction of the house. Behind him is a group of about twenty zombies, also wearing red.

"The fire brigade," Rowan says, and indeed, the zombies are already tossing buckets of water and bags of sand at the burning house.

Once the fire is out, we go over to assess the damage.

There are no discernable pieces left of Exozar, nor can we locate the flask with the vampire blood, or Koshmar sprayers, or any other evidence.

Rowan kicks a charred and mangled soup pot. "I guess we have to hope the Parliament takes our word on this."

Stanislav clutches his chest. When he notices me staring, he jerks the hand away.

Puck.

"Are you having heart palpitations?" I ask cautiously.

"Isn't everyone?" he replies gruffly. "We were nearly blown to pieces."

Dylan eyes him worriedly but lets it slide.

"Let's go back to the Parliament," Valerian says. "The sooner we explain what happened, the sooner we can go back."

Assuming we *can* go back. I don't say it, though, because it's clear from everyone's grim faces that they're thinking the same thing.

———

AS WE WALK to the Parliament building, I tell everyone what Rowan and I discovered.

"I'm not surprised Icelus pre-vamps are behind the spread of the virus," Valerian says. "Vampires and pre-vamps hate necromancers, so they have an extra motive to want to destroy this particular world."

"Let's hope the hatred is mutual," Ariel says. "It might increase the odds that the Parliament goes after Icelus for us, even though we can't provide any evidence."

"Oh, it is mutual," Rowan says. "But can I ask a dumb question? What is Icelus, exactly?"

Valerian tells her about Collywobbles and how Icelus are an organization that worship him, while the Overtaken are people who were taken over by him while they dreamed a very specific nightmare. He then warns her about letting people share their dreams with her.

"We should spread that advice through as many Otherlands as we can," Felix says. "Talking about nightmares might become as impolite as showing off your toenail fungus at the dinner table."

Dylan chuckles. "I'll mention this to Maxwell the next time I see him in my dreams. Assuming he's not reached the same conclusion independently."

We enter Decagon Square and march into the Parliament building.

"Take the helper masks and clothes off," Rowan says. "They might not like the disguises."

We comply, leaving everything in the corridor before entering the meeting chamber.

Rowan strolls into the center of the room and confidently gives her spiel.

Immediately, Keyser begins shouting, while Shegan speaks in a calmer voice. The rest of the Parliament fall somewhere in the middle. When the most vocal Parliament members settle down, Rowan speaks some more, and the reactions repeat.

"My husband-to-be clearly hasn't taken his afternoon nap yet," Rowan says to us when the Parliament quiets again. "He's pricklier than a hedgehog cactus."

Dylan rolls her eyes. "What she's trying to say is he doesn't believe us, nor her for that matter."

"Shegan does, though," Rowan says. "Some of the others might also."

I don't like where this is heading.

"Why would we lie?" Ariel asks, exasperated. "More importantly, why concoct such a story?"

"Don't forget the blown-up house," Felix says.

Rowan sighs. "I raised all those points. Let's hope that helps us when they vote."

I knew it.

Another vote.

Shoot me now.

CHAPTER TWENTY-SEVEN

KEYSER STANDS up from his chair.

I grit my teeth.

A long second passes.

Keyser looks around in confusion.

Not a single other Parliament member stands up.

Rowan grins from ear to ear and says something in Necronian.

Keyser's giant collapses back into his throne and monologues for a couple of seconds. Then his limbs hang lifelessly, as if a puppeteer had given up control of a marionette.

Rowan rolls her eyes and addresses the other giants.

Shegan gives her a curt reply, and they go back and forth for a few minutes.

"Let's go," Rowan says to us and strides for the door.

"We're not getting killed, right?" Itzel asks.

Rowan waits until we're in the corridor. "Not only

are we not getting killed," she says proudly, "but after Keyser had his tantrum and left, I got a chance to negotiate on your behalf."

"She got them to make Icelus their top priority." Dylan looks approvingly at Rowan. "She then gave them some sensible quarantine procedures to follow while they wait for the cure, and she even got us access to the Parliament's own personal supplies for our trip."

Rowan has her zombies hold the doors for us, and after we exit, she says, "I assume we want to travel to the hub without stopping?"

Dylan cuts her eyes toward Stanislav. "Time is not our friend."

Nodding, Rowan leads us to a storage facility, where she recruits particularly strong-looking zombies and gets us a raft-like platform twice the size of the one Nulen used to bring us to Necropolis.

Laying the platform down in a nearby yard, she asks us about food preferences. To my relief, she doesn't bat an eye at my request for copious amounts of the banana-like fruit and distilled water.

"Also, can you get us real beds instead of the usual zombie contortions that pass for furniture on the road?" Valerian asks. "Or at least one real bed, for Bailey."

Great. I'm beginning to sound like a prima donna.

Rowan is totally fine with this request as well, and thanks to the zombie labor force, getting the beds and chairs only delays us an extra couple of minutes.

In the end, we have everything, even a leather canopy for the zombies to hold over our heads in case of rain.

Rowan gives us a speaking glance. "If you don't like going into a chamber pot held by a helper, use the facilities now and do your best not to drink too much."

"She's talking to you," Felix whispers, winking at me conspiratorially.

I pinch his side, eliciting a loud yelp, but I do take advantage of the nearby restroom facilities, as advised.

Everyone settles into their chairs, and we head out.

As we navigate the streets of Necropolis, necromancers follow us with curious eyes. After a few minutes, we spot a dead bird by the side of the road, the kind that had brought zombie reinforcements for Nulen when we first arrived on Necronia.

"Poor thing," Rowan says and shoots the dead creature with multicolored energy.

The bird flies up and perches on the platform by Rowan's side, right next to Frank.

I have to admit, her power is rather useful.

"You did a great job back there," Valerian tells Rowan when we go through the Necropolis gates and start making our way through the zombie wall that surrounds the city.

She smiles. "Thanks. I have to admit, I've been trying to get on your good side before asking for a favor."

We all look at her with varying degrees of wariness.

"You've all met Keyser." She leaps out of her chair and begins to pace the wooden platform.

I wrinkle my nose. "We've had the displeasure of making his acquaintance, yes."

"Well, not marrying him isn't an option for me," she says. "Nor is moving to another world with necromancers. They're all friendly with Necronia and would locate me for a big shot like Keyser." She stops pacing and looks at me pleadingly. "I was hoping you could put in a good word for me with the authorities on Earth, so I'd be allowed to immigrate."

Huh, okay. I look at Valerian. "If anyone could make that happen, it would be you."

He frowns at Rowan. "That's an enormous ask. Why didn't you negotiate freedom from Keyser when you had the Parliament by the shorthairs back there?"

She examines the wood at her feet. "It's not just about the marriage. I got spoiled when I lived on Earth. I could bore you for hours talking about all the freedoms I wish I had, but if I'm honest, I just as much want to move because I love everything about Earth— its human cultures, the internet, music, movies, video games…"

"Not a single necromancer has ever been allowed to do what you're talking about," Valerian says. "Vampires are a powerful voice among the Earth Cognizant. And they live such long lives, some of them have grievances with your kind from personal experience."

She sighs. "I knew it was a long shot."

I make a mental note to talk to Valerian some more

on Rowan's behalf. I like her, and her request doesn't seem so unreasonable to me—except for the part where she wants Earth, instead of a more civilized world, like Gomorrah.

Rowan sits back down, and we ride on the nice road for a while without talking. I must zone out for a bit because when I refocus on the path ahead, I see a group of people in the distance.

I jump up from my chair and approach Rowan. "What do you think that's about?" I ask, nodding at the crowd.

Our zombie bird takes flight and swoops down to take a look at the newcomers—and as it does, Rowan's forehead creases with a frown.

"It's Keyser," she says. "He's waiting there with a warrior-helper contingent. We could try going around, but it might be wiser to hear what he's got to say."

Valerian's already on his feet, peering intently at the obstacle. "Do you think the Parliament have changed their minds?"

"I doubt it." Rowan has the zombie bird land by her feet. "This might just be about me—in which case, I'll go with him willingly, then urge the Parliament to assign you another necromancer guide posthaste."

I don't want to give her back to that pet-killing brute, but on the flip side, a delay might cost Stanislav his life.

Judging by my friends' expressions, they're having similar thoughts.

We continue toward Keyser and his helpers, and it's

only when we're right next to them that I realize he isn't here for Rowan at all.

I also realize we're in big pucking trouble.

It's Keyser's eyes.

They have that telltale magma in them—like those of the rest of the Overtaken.

CHAPTER TWENTY-EIGHT

PUCK. He must've taken that nap Rowan briefly mentioned and never properly woken up from it. Exozar—or one of the Icelus—must've shared the viral nightmare with him, and here we are.

"Maybe he can't use his powers in that state?" Felix says, his voice shaking.

No such luck. His warrior zombies—big, beefy individuals—mobilize and rush toward us.

Valerian steps forward, shielding me with his body. "My illusions aren't working," he says tensely. "He's seeing through zombie eyes, like a regular necromancer."

Rowan's zombies lower our riding platform to the ground and rush at Keyser's troops.

It soon becomes clear that we have a twofold problem with this form of defense: We have fewer zombies to start with, and each of Keyser's beefier specimens is worth two, if not three, of ours.

Zombie arms are ripped from sockets, and zombie heads are bashed with them. The sounds of tearing flesh and breaking bone are nauseating, as is the sight of all the gore.

Dylan raises her voice to be heard above the clamor. "Knocking out Keyser is our only option."

Rowan grimaces, muttering, "Mrs. State-the-Obvious nails it again." But she makes her dead bird take flight and swoop at Keyser's head.

I watch with bated breath. If this works, we win.

Unfortunately, Keyser shoots the bird with his necromantic mojo, and the thing flies back at us. Rowan shoots the bird again, taking it over. Keyser wrestles control back—and they keep going back and forth.

"We need to distract him," Dylan says.

Fabian strips off his pants before turning into a huge wolf. His shirt rips to pieces in the process, but he's already leaping into the zombie melee with graceful wolfu-powered moves.

The beefy zombies swarm around him—and pay dearly.

"He'll take too long to get through," I say. "Itzel, can you do your thing?"

A lightning ball forms inside Itzel's palms and flies at Keyser.

A beefy zombie throws himself in front of his master, taking the projectile in the chest.

Itzel hurls another lightning ball.

Another zombie sacrifices himself.

In the distance, a crowd gathers. Judging by their clothing, they're human, so I doubt they'd help us even if they wanted to. In fact, seeing how our enemy is on the Parliament, there's a higher chance they'd help *him* if they could.

Itzel shoots futilely again.

Fabian's claws tear through Keyser's zombies like recycled tissue paper, but there's only one of him and scores of them.

"Are you able to fight?" Valerian asks Stanislav.

With a string of Russian curses, the chort rushes forward. He doesn't do nearly as much damage as the werewolf, but whenever a zombie takes a swipe at him, they find incorporeality where flesh should be.

"Can you take care of the Mordamned bird?" Rowan shouts at Ariel.

Ariel grimly nods.

Rowan stops the necromantic push-pull of the bird and aims her fingers at a particularly muscled zombie near Keyser.

Her plan is clear: She's going to try to have Keyser's own zombie knock him out.

The bird dives at Rowan.

Ariel leaps into the air with uber speed and strength, catching the bird by the tail.

Pucking puck. The feathers rip out of the bird's tail and stay in Ariel's hand while the bird's beak smashes into Rowan's forehead.

Ariel curses bitterly as Rowan's eyes roll into the back of her head and she collapses.

Dylan sprints over and kneels next to the necromancer. Frank, Rowan's zombie pet, hisses at Dylan but lets her get close to his mistress.

Keyser has the bird fly up again, but Ariel leaps up and grabs it again, this time by the sides. Unable to flap its wings, the bird stays put. The reprieve only lasts a second. Keyser shoots at our zombies one by one, and they start to switch sides.

"Give that thing to me," Valerian barks at Ariel, and she does—but the bird is so big and strong I have to help Valerian keep it immobilized. Panting, I wrestle with its clawing feet while he constrains its wings, preventing it from taking flight.

In the meantime, Itzel launches another lightning ball that a zombie takes for his master. Itzel herself collapses, having overused her power.

Ariel leaps off the platform into the fight, but as more and more of our zombies switch sides, she, Fabian, and Stanislav have a harder time keeping them at bay.

Ten zombies jump onto our platform.

Felix rushes at them, fists raised, and is knocked out immediately.

Exchanging a grim look, Valerian and I let go of the stupid bird and take fighting stances.

The bird takes flight in the direction of Keyser. A zombie closes the distance between us and swipes at my head. I duck and deliver a flawless uppercut at my opponent's jaw. My knuckles sting, but the zombie shows no sign of having felt the blow.

Another zombie joins the already-hopeless fight. I sidestep her punch and sweep the legs of the first zombie. He jumps over my sweep and grabs my right hand. His friend does the same with my left.

Not good.

A third zombie lunges at me and rips off my mask. I gulp in a breath, only to realize the mask has been greatly dampening the stench of the battle. Gagging, I try not to hyperventilate as the zombie throws down my mask and stomps on it until it's all but useless.

I flail and kick at my captors. Two zombies dive for my legs, grasping them and holding them in place. To my left, Valerian is bashing a zombie on the head with an arm he must've ripped off from another attacker. An armless zombie—presumably the owner of Valerian's makeshift club—takes a swing at Valerian with its remaining hand.

A dozen more zombies gang up on Valerian, and I lose sight of him for a few terrifying seconds. All I hear are thuds of flesh beating flesh. I struggle harder. For some reason, the thought of him perishing is infinitely worse than the thought of myself dying in this putrid mess.

Some of the zombies shift aside, and I catch sight of him—bruised and battered but alive. My breath escapes in relief. Two zombies are holding his left arm and three his right, with each of his legs also meriting a couple of zombies.

For a guy with no supernatural speed or strength, he's certainly holding his own.

The zombie who destroyed my mask lunges at Valerian and gives his mask the same treatment. Puck. This mask-stealing is deliberate.

There's a flurry of movement from where Dylan stands over Rowan, but before I can make out what's happening there, a shadow blots the sky, stealing my attention.

I look up as far as I can, nearly dislocating something in my neck.

It's the bird, and it's holding Keyser in its talons.

Puck. He's found a way to bypass Fabian, Stanislav, and Ariel.

The bird deposits Keyser in front of me, and we lock eyes.

My heartbeat skyrockets.

His eyes aren't just fiery. They're rimmed with bloody tears.

Whoever made him the Overtaken also made sure he was infected with the virus.

I rip at the zombie hands holding me with renewed vigor, but I might as well try to move a concrete wall.

Keyser closes what little distance was between us, makes a disgusting hawking sound in his throat, and spits a large wad of mucus straight into my face.

I reflexively cringe, closing my eyes, and feel viscous liquid cover every inch of my face. My stomach heaves and my skin prickles as though it wants to crawl away from my body. This is worse than the dive into the moat sewer where I nearly got eaten. I'm so grossed out I think I might go into shock of the type people get when they lose a limb.

I crack open my lids in time to see Keyser spit at me again. It lands on my chin and drips down, sending a surge of bile up my throat.

"An agonizing end for you, child of Soma," Keyser says in a gloating voice, killing what little hope I had that the splatter of blood under his eyes wasn't the symptom of the virus.

CHAPTER TWENTY-NINE

BEFORE I CAN RECOVER from the gross assault or process his words, Keyser turns to face Valerian, who's putting up a solid fight with the zombies trying to pin him down. As I realize Keyser's intention, all blood drains from my face.

"No!" I yell—just as Keyser makes the same awful hawking noise and spits in Valerian's unprotected face.

"I haven't forgotten you either," the necromancer says gloatingly.

My heartbeat is nearing lightspeed, and my vision is red from anger. I strain against the zombie hands holding me in place, but to no avail.

If I were free, I would rip Keyser into little pieces with my bare hands. I really would.

Through the haze of fury, I catch another sign of movement near Dylan.

It's Rowan. She's sitting up and looking around, her gaze unfocused.

Spotting Keyser, she shoots multicolored energy at one of the zombies holding Valerian's right arm. That zombie releases Valerian and smashes a fist into Keyser's face.

The bird takes flight and dives for Rowan. She shoots necromantic energy at it, while her zombie punches Keyser in the stomach. Air audibly whooshes out of Keyser's lungs.

In the meantime, Valerian yanks on his partially freed right arm and twists it out of the other zombies' grip. With a murderous look in his eyes, he punches Keyser in the temple.

The bird swoops, snatches Keyser with its claws, and takes flight. When they're some twenty feet off the ground, Keyser shoots the bird with his energy. As an Overtaken, he seems oblivious to pain, which allows him to recover impossibly fast.

Rowan shoots the bird also, wrenching the control away long enough to force the bird to open its claws. Keyser plummets. With a desperate twist in the air, he takes over the bird and makes it swoop after him, but Rowan steals the bird back and makes it fly up.

They ping-pong like that until Keyser lands on his back with a loud splat, his arms and legs splayed in unnatural positions.

Shockingly, he's somehow still alive and in control of his zombies.

Leaving Rowan's side for the first time since the battle began, Frank scurries over to Keyser and covers the necromancer's face with his furry body. Keyser's arms must be too broken to move because he just lies there as the opossum-like creature slowly smothers him into oblivion.

With Keyser unable to interfere, Rowan takes over the zombies around us. She starts with the ones holding Valerian. As soon as he's free, he rushes to my side and pries away the hands of the zombies holding me.

"Thank you," I say, panting, when the last zombie is off me.

"Here." Valerian rips off his sleeve, wipes the gross spit off my face, and holds the hygieia device over it for triple the required time.

In the periphery of my vision, I see Rowan taking over the zombies that our friends are fighting. My full attention is on Valerian, though. He cleans himself in the same fashion, then pulls me to him and holds me tight, his strong hands stroking my back as if I were his pet cat.

I'm grateful for the kindness. Though I'm mostly numb, I can feel the horror gradually creeping in, and I wrap my arms around Valerian's waist, pressing harder against him.

A flash captures my attention, and I turn around in Valerian's embrace to see Fabian back in his human form—and completely naked. Casually, he locates his pants on the platform and struts over to check on the rest of us.

I step out of Valerian's embrace and start toward Felix, but Ariel is already checking on him.

"He's fine," she says, seeing my concerned face.

"So is she," Stanislav reports, kneeling over still-unconscious Itzel.

Ariel, Fabian, and Stanislav appear uninjured also, apart from some minor cuts and bruises.

Fabian peers into the distance with a frown. "We'd better go. The spectators are moving in."

Sure enough, the humans who were watching the battle from afar are starting to draw nearer.

Rowan, who's having a zombie help her get to her feet, eyes the approaching mob with a gloomy expression. "Frank," she calls out. "Enough!"

Unpeeling himself from Keyser's face, her pet skitters over to Rowan's side with what seems to be a smug expression on his furry face.

"Is he dead?" Ariel asks, looking at Keyser.

In lieu of a reply, Rowan shoots Keyser with her necromantic energy and his eyes reopen.

The fiery glow is gone.

"Oh, good," Ariel says. "It would suck if a corpse stayed Overtaken even after becoming a zombie."

Rowan looks to be straining, but Zombie Keyser can't seem to stand up.

"Too broken," she says through her teeth, then has a couple zombies pick up Keyser's corpse and place it on the platform where we're all gathered. The rest of her helpers lift our platform and launch into a run, leaving the mob of humans behind us.

After a few minutes, Itzel comes to, as does Felix, and Ariel and Dylan render what first aid they can.

As I take all of this in, Valerian stands by my side, stroking my back—which might be the only reason I'm keeping it together.

"I don't understand something," Ariel says, looking from Keyser to Frank. "Why didn't he take over your pet to save himself?"

Looking uncomfortable, Rowan nevertheless shares the secret about Frank—how she broke the most sacred taboo of her kind and created an atypical zombie with free will.

"Oh, I get it now," Felix says with a faint smile. "Frank is short for Frankenstein, isn't it?"

"That would imply that I fear and hate my creation," Rowan says. "But I love my fuzzy-wuzzy."

"Please keep this a secret," I tell everyone. "If the rest of the necromancers find out, Rowan is screwed."

"Oh, it's too late for that anyway," Rowan says. "I killed my betrothed. A member of the Parliament. In front of witnesses. I'm already beyond screwed."

"You got his body." Ariel nods at the reanimated Keyser corpse. "No body, no crime."

"No, I'm as good as dead," Rowan says, then walks over to her chair and collapses into it.

"I don't mean to add to your distress, but you'd better stay away from Bailey and Valerian," Dylan says to Rowan in a low voice. "They may be infected."

May be infected. My heart skips a beat, and my legs begin to shake as I gulp in shallow breaths. I've been desperately trying not to think about the implications of my mask being gone and that glob of spittle landing on my face, but I can't ignore it any longer.

"Shh, don't panic." Valerian pulls me to him, but my shaking only intensifies, and after a moment, he picks me up and carries me to the bed farthest away from Rowan's.

I curl into a ball on my side.

"It's going to be okay," Valerian's voice states in my ears. He must be using his power to make it sound as though it's coming through headphones.

If I could summon the will to speak, I'd tell him it pucking isn't going to be okay.

He may be infected.

I may be infected.

Those two thoughts buzz around my head like angry bees.

Valerian murmurs more reassuring words that I ignore. At some point, he must tire of talking and lies next to me, wrapping his arms around me.

Eventually, I pull myself together enough to get up and force myself to eat a couple of pieces of fruit. I think I'm still numb, and I hope to stay that way.

As I trudge back to my chair, I see Stanislav. Clutching his stomach, he tosses a piece of dried meat off the platform.

"What's wrong?" I ask.

He shrugs. "Necromancer food not good for my digestion."

Before I can press further, he turns his back to me and stomps over to the other side of the platform.

I let him go, though I don't buy what he said. Not after I saw him clutching his chest before. The virus symptoms in order are tears of blood, heart palpitations, upset stomach, and purplish-red skin.

He seems to have had three out of the four.

In fact, is it my imagination or is his skin already a smidge purple?

I hurry over to Valerian. "Can you use your powers to give us privacy?"

"Sit in your chair," he says, and I oblige.

He tells Itzel to stay far away from us, then plops in his own chair. Suddenly, our surroundings change. I find myself in the same chair but in the middle of a gorgeous garden filled with plants from both Gomorrah and Earth.

"Now the others can't hear us," he says. "Not unless you want me to pull someone in, that is."

I take in a calming breath. "Does Stanislav look purplish-red to you?"

Valerian peers in the direction of the cherry blossom tree, his forehead creasing. "Maybe."

"Can you pull in Dylan?" I bend down and pick up a daffodil. The flower has the texture and scent of the real thing. Sometimes I forget how impressive Valerian's power really is. If I were to make this flower in a dream, I'm not sure I'd be able to give it as much detail.

A second later, Dylan appears in the garden with us, her chair right next to me even though in the real world, it's about twelve feet away.

I tell Dylan about my observations of Stanislav, and she looks progressively gloomier as I list all the symptoms I've observed.

"I'm afraid you're right," she says. "His infection seems to have progressed."

Valerian's hands squeeze the arms of his chair. "How long does he have?"

"Depends on the chort immune system in general and his in particular," she says. "I'm sure the exertion of our recent fight didn't help."

"Are we talking hours, days, or weeks?" Valerian presses.

Dylan fiddles with her mask. "I don't think he'll make it to Gomorrah. My hope is that the cure is simple to make, so I can do it on the world where we met Maxwell. The hospital next to the hub there has a rudimentary lab."

Pom's fur is pitch black on my wrist as I pet him in order to self-soothe. "I thought the cure hasn't been developed yet," I say quietly, trying not to give in to the panic beating in my chest.

She sighs. "They've made progress. The best minds are on it. Hopefully they'll have it by the time we need it."

That's a lot of life-critical outcomes riding on mere hope.

Though on some level I'd rather not know, my mouth forms the words. "What about us?"

Valerian glances at me sharply. "You sure you want to talk about it?"

"I'd rather know," I lie.

"Then tell it to us straight," Valerian says to Dylan. "I saw the look on your face when you told Rowan we may be infected. Your poker face is crap."

Dylan flushes. "I'm sorry. I just didn't want anyone to panic. The sad truth is that you received a massive viral load. Unless your immune system is like that of a pre-vamp, you're going to show symptoms soon."

I cover my face with my hands as my carefully nourished numbness gives way to unbridled existential dread.

I'm not ready to die.

And I'm even less ready for Valerian to die.

"Thanks, Dylan," he says, his voice coming as if from a distance. "Go to sleep now, okay? We don't want to miss the moment when Maxwell tries to dreamwalk in you."

"On it," she replies, and when I lower my hands, Dylan is gone and Valerian is standing next to me with an unreadable expression on his face.

Anger, sharp and irrational, surges through me. "How are you so okay?" I demand, jumping up. "Why aren't you freaking out?"

He gives me a crooked grin. "I'm obviously freaking out too. Having the power of illusion helps when you're trying to look cool, though." As if to highlight his words, stylish sunglasses appear on his face, and his nondescript traveling outfit transforms into a skintight bodysuit.

A reluctant smile tugs at my lips. "That outfit is more sexy than cool, you know."

He grins back at me. "As long as it's distracting you from germ worries, who cares?"

To my surprise, it *is* distracting me. His face has been covered by the mask for so long, I'd forgotten the effect it has on me. Now it's all coming back with a vengeance.

Wait, what am I thinking? Is my body going into some kind of "procreation before death" mode? Clearly, being as sex deprived as I am is throwing my priorities out of whack.

"There's more we can do to distract you," he says, as if reading my mind.

I stare at his lips, then slowly lick mine.

His gaze darkens, and he clasps my hand, pulling me closer.

Gazing up at him, I trace my finger over his sensuous lips. "Is this the real you?"

"An illusion," he says hoarsely. "Despite what Dylan said, there's always a small chance I'm sick and you're not. I'd never forgive myself if I infected you."

I'm perversely disappointed.

He leans down and kisses me. Hard.

All my troubling thoughts evaporate as I return the kiss, my core turning into a geothermal spring as his tongue brushes over my lips.

Panting, I make my tongue dance with his.

Or do I?

I pull away. "You're not really feeling this, are you?"

His sexy lips curve. "It's fun to make *you* feel things. Besides, if I got to *really* taste you, my ability to maintain the illusion might be compromised."

Is that a compliment? It sure feels like one.

"Why don't we take this into the dream world?" I bite my lower lip. "I want you to feel things too."

His nostrils flare. "Does this mean you've forgiven me?"

I freeze, having forgotten all about the grudge until now.

Have I forgiven him? I guess I have. It seems petty to hold on to anger given the danger our lives are in right now—and everything he's done to keep me safe. Actually, if I'm honest, I probably forgave him the very first time he used that hygieia device on my behalf.

Another thought occurs to me. Have I been using my grudge to avoid thinking about my feelings for him? And what exactly are those feelings?

No, I'm too overwhelmed to think about *that* pesky question.

Realizing he's waiting for my answer, I say quietly, "I think I have forgiven you." Seeing his cocky smile, I quickly add, "But I still want to learn about Soma, especially given—"

"That child of Soma bit Keyser spouted?" His face is serious now. "I've been pondering that too."

"And did you figure it out?" I ask, not bothering to hide the eagerness in my voice.

"I was allowed to keep very few of my memories." He

looks like it pains him to utter every word. "Everything to do with Soma is secret, so if one wishes to leave it and go to the Otherlands, the way I did, the price is the very memory of Soma. Only a powerful dreamwalker can break a black window, and the most powerful of your kind live on Soma, making this a perfect security system." He pauses, looking at me. "Well, almost."

"So one of the windows is all your memories of Soma?" I ask, aghast. "As in, your whole childhood?"

"Young adulthood too," he says with a wince. "But think about how effective the system is. Even if tortured, I wouldn't be able to reveal anything about my home—not that I would. I'm allowed to remember how much I loved it… and how much I want to keep it safe."

He looks like he's in pain, so I squeeze his hand— that is, until I realize he can't feel that either.

"I saw two black windows," I say softly. "If one is Soma, what about the other?"

He pulls his hand away. "I don't know. Obviously, it's an important secret, but I wasn't left any hints as to what it is."

"Maybe you'd know more if you got your Soma memories back?"

"Possibly. I genuinely have no clue."

I touch him—or his illusionary form—again. "How about you remove the illusion, and I touch you for real, putting you in REM sleep?"

He sighs. "You need to rest. So why don't we agree

to this: I go to sleep, and you do as well. Then, when you dream naturally, we break the Soma window."

"I don't know if I'll be able to fall asleep with everything that's happened," I say.

He smiles ruefully. "Which is why I wanted to properly motivate you to rest."

"Evil. Where's my bed?"

"There."

The bed materializes in the middle of a flower meadow, surrounded by forty-two different species of dahlias. I tiptoe over the flowers as though I could actually break them. When I lie down on the bed and close my eyes, the sound of a gentle ocean surf caresses my ears.

"What if the Nutcracker comes and kills me this time?" I ask without opening my eyes.

"I already spoke to Fabian," the wind replies in Valerian's voice. "He'll subdue you if necessary."

Fine. I do my best to even out my breathing. The scent of salty ocean air conspires with the sweet aroma of flowers to calm me.

It takes an hour or so, but eventually, I drift off.

CHAPTER THIRTY

ARMS OUTSTRETCHED, I'm flying in the skies on Gomorrah, dodging skyscrapers in my way.

Wait a second. When did I learn to fly? This must be a dream.

I check my wrist. Yep. Pom is missing.

I halt my flight and take myself to my dream palace.

Pom is here, his fur a happy purple.

"Hey, bud," I say. "How are you?"

I don't tell him our lives are in danger, but there's a chance he knows via an unauthorized snooping inside my mind.

"I just finished some exposure therapy." His fur turns brown. "It goes better and better each time."

Whew. He hasn't yet picked up on the danger. "Excellent. How about you work on it some more while I take a trip into Valerian's dreams?"

"You want privacy?" he asks, the tips of his ears turning a jealous green.

"It's not what you think," I say, though I hope that we do find time for what Pom is alluding to. "I'm trying to learn a secret from Valerian, and if he sees you, he might get skittish."

His fur takes on a light orange hue. "You'll tell me the secret though, won't you?"

"I will," I say solemnly.

"Unless it's gross or scary," he amends.

"Sure. I doubt this one will be, though."

He nods, ears flopping, and I teleport into the tower of sleepers, right into Valerian's nook.

He's here. It's now or never.

I place my lips on his to make contact and dive in.

———

VALERIAN IS MAKING out with a dream version of me. She's really into it, and so is he. We're in his bedroom, and both of the windows are black—which is what I'm here for.

"Great job with the dream," I say after I've watched my fill. "They say when you practice something while sleeping, you get better at it in the real world."

He looks at me—a second version of me from his perspective—and recovers from surprise with record speed. "You think I need to get better at this?"

"No. You're a sex god," his dream version of me says in a sultry voice.

Though feeling jealous in this case doesn't make

sense for multiple reasons, I still take perverse pleasure in making her disappear.

Valerian looks vaguely disappointed. Heaving a sigh, he points at the black window nearest us. "That's the one with Soma memories. It's one of the few things I know."

I head toward the window in question.

"Wait," he says. "We want to break it so that I get the memories back when you're done."

"I have no idea how to do that."

"I do." He comes up to me and takes my hand, his touch giving me warm tingles even in the dream world. "Just bring me with you when you go."

Oh. I can do that. I think.

I make us both fly into the window, and he squeezes my hand tighter as I make contact with the black glass.

———

I PLUNGE into icy black water.

Two problems are apparent right away.

First is that a rope is wrapped around my waist. It attaches me to a rickety boat, inside which is an unconscious Valerian. This must be the side effect of dragging him with me.

What's more worrying is the size of the body of water around us. It's either a sea or a small ocean—I can't see a shore in any direction. The last time I tried to swim through something like this, I drowned, and that time, I didn't have to drag a boat with Valerian along.

Then again, I'm supposed to be more powerful now. Maybe that could give me an edge?

I try to use my powers, willing myself to become lighter than water so I can float. This didn't work before and doesn't now. I will the boat to fly like a balloon, but it doesn't.

All right. I'll swim the old-fashioned way.

I swim for what feels like an hour with a freestyle stroke, then switch to breaststroke and swim some more. Still can't even see the shore. The rope makes it awkward to do a backstroke, so I switch to butterfly and swim that way for a while.

After what feels like a day, my every muscle aches and the irritation from the rope burns messes with my concentration.

I keep on swimming. It becomes a meditation, with my movements as the mantra. One arm after another. I think only about swimming. And swimming. And swimming. My breathing grows more labored, yet the shore is still nowhere in sight.

A part of me wants to give up and sink, but I can't. If I do, I'll be kicked out of the dream world with my powers depleted. More importantly, I want to learn about Soma and give Valerian his missing years back.

At some point, the exhaustion and pain grow unbearable, but then, to my surprise, I get a second wind.

Is it my newfound powers kicking in? Maybe I've

manipulated the balance of oxygen in my body to somehow counteract the buildup of lactic acid in my muscles. Or maybe I've just figured out a way to boost the endorphin production in my brain. Whatever it is, I'm not complaining.

I swim and swim and swim, and finally, I spot a distant shore.

Gulping in air, I kick harder, ignoring the fact that the distance I have left is greater than any I've tried to swim in prior black windows.

Just as I did before, I remind myself of a simple truth: My muscles are not really tearing into bits. It's not oxygen I lack. There's no lactic acid in my muscles, and the rope cutting into my waist isn't real. This is just a dream construct that makes it difficult for weaker dreamwalkers to access the locked memories.

That last bit helps perk me up. Surely I'm not weak with the boost I got.

The second wind lasts halfway through my desperate sprint to the shore. The pain returns, infinitely worse, and my strength flags. Still, I refuse to give up. I just swim as though my life depends on it.

As though if I drown, that is it.

Something shifts then. My arms and legs move without my conscious control. I begin slicing through the water like a shark, and keep this up all the way to the shore.

My feet brush the sand, and the ocean around me disappears.

———

I FIND myself in a familiar clearing in the woods populated by alien trees, some resembling coral reefs, others baobabs. The surreal, forest-filled sky is familiar as well and implies that this planet—or spaceship—is a pretzel shape instead of a sphere. Or, as Itzel put it, it's a structure made of two counter-rotating cylinders known as the O'Neill colony.

This clearing is also the very place where Mom killed Asha.

If I had any doubts that I was born on Soma, they're gone now.

Setting that aside, there are two Valerians here, and one of them looks noticeably younger than mine. The young Valerian is shirtless—a great look on him—and is fighting with a tall, striking stranger, while the regular Valerian is standing right by me, looking awestruck by the scene.

"I can't believe I forgot this," he mutters. "I know that's how black windows work, but now that I'm here, it's hard to believe I couldn't remember this."

"Why are you fighting this guy?" I ask.

"I'd never fight Kojo," he says with a faint smile. "We're just sparring."

Kojo. Where have I heard that name? I don't get a chance to ask because the memory changes.

———

THIS TIME, Valerian and Kojo are young teens, both climbing a baobab-like tree.

Aha. Just like in Mom's black window, the memories are coming at us out of order. What's different is that this memory plays out fast, like a slightly sped-up video. Or maybe the boys are just fast climbers?

"Isn't it dangerous to climb that quickly?" I say to grown-up Valerian, who's next to me again. "Or is something else going on here?"

"The memories will speed up as my presence compromises the black window's integrity," he says. "What I want to know is, how do I remember this factoid already? I don't think I knew this before we started."

"Integrity?" I ask as Kojo and Teen Valerian reach the top and sit on a thick branch.

"At some point, the black window will shatter," my Valerian says. "After that, we'll get kicked out, and I'll have the memories back."

I start to reply, but the memory changes again.

———

VALERIAN LOOKS to be two or three, and is as adorable as a toddler can be. His ocean-blue eyes are twice their current size, and his cherubic face already shows a hint of adult Valerian's striking features.

A woman is holding the toddler, and it doesn't take

a rocket scientist to figure out it's his mom. Her loving expression and their resemblance make that clear.

"This is my earliest memory of her," my Valerian whispers reverently. "I think she's about to sing."

She does, and even sped up, the song is beautiful and serene. Soon, toddler Valerian's eyelids begin to droop, and the memory flips again.

———

WE'RE in an achingly familiar room.

Grown Valerian gapes at the people here, and so do I.

The young Valerian is about six, and so is Kojo. To my shock, I recognize both of them at this age. I've seen them in another black window—my mom's.

But what stuns me most is the sight of the two girls playing with the boys.

Two identical twins.

Bailey and Asha.

Little me and my dead sister.

CHAPTER THIRTY-ONE

MY PARENTS ARE THERE TOO. In fact, I think I saw Mom's memory of this exact event. Young Valerian was there; I just didn't yet know that's who he was. At that point, I just thought the boy looked familiar.

My breath catches in my chest.

Valerian and I knew each other as kids. In Mom's memories, I played with him a lot.

I suppose I should've anticipated that this could be the case. He's from Soma. I've been suspecting that I'm from Soma. The possibility of us knowing each other in the past was there.

I turn to the grown Valerian, who's staring at the scene openmouthed. "The first time we met, I thought you looked familiar."

He nods, still looking stunned. "I felt the same. I even told you, remember?" He shifts his gaze to the little me. "I must've recognized you even with the black window blocking the memories."

I also look at our younger selves.

Why can't *I* remember this?

I glance at my mom for answers, but that's useless. Like in her version of this event, she's just holding my father's hand.

I turn my attention to the other adults in the room. One man looks particularly familiar, just as he did when I first saw this in Mom's window.

Now I understand why that is.

"That's your father, isn't it?" I point at the man. "Davu?"

Valerian nods, his jaw tight. "That's him."

"I'm sorry, Davu. I don't think there's a choice," my father is saying as I tune in to the adults' conversation. "The prophecy—"

"Was vague," Davu says dismissively. "If—"

Little Valerian pulls on his sleeve. "Dad, can Bailey and I go to the garden?"

Davu nods, and little me and the boy race out of the room, ending the memory.

———

THIS NEW MEMORY is of a birthday party.

Valerian, Kojo, my twin, and I are playing together with another dozen children.

I'm barely following the events, in part because I'm still reeling from what I've just learned, and in part because the memory is replaying even faster.

"I thought you were older than me," I say to grown

Valerian as a new memory starts, one where he loses his front tooth and puts it in a little box, like treasure.

"Time runs faster on Soma than on Gomorrah," he says. "Since I stayed there longer than you, I've lived longer."

Yet another memory starts, now with everyone moving comically fast. In it, Kojo, Valerian, Asha, and I are playing hide-and-seek and yelling in sped-up, chipmunky voices.

Then a memory of a funeral whizzes by. "My parents," Valerian explains when I look at him questioningly. "The only thing I was allowed to remember about my family was the name of the group responsible for their deaths." His voice roughens. "Icelus."

The next memory passes in an eyeblink, showing Kojo, Valerian, Asha, and me running barefoot outside.

"The window is about to break," Valerian says, and two memories flash by in the time it takes him to finish that sentence. In one, his father is chastising him for something, and in the other, he and Kojo are playing a sport the rules of which are impossible to figure out at this speed.

The next dozen memories go by so quickly I only make out snapshots. In one, he kisses my five-year-old self on the cheek; in another, he's holding her hand.

No wonder I react to him as I do. He was probably my first crush—

The world explodes around us, jolting me awake.

I OPEN my eyes in the real world. I must've slept for a while. It was still daytime when I fell asleep, but it's sunrise now.

Recalling what I've just discovered, I leap to my feet.

Valerian is already coming toward me, hair disheveled and eyes wild. "I remember everything."

Something about his eyes stops me dead in my tracks.

He's got droplets of red moisture near his tear ducts.

Blood tears.

I want to scream, but no sound comes out of my lips.

Valerian's face goes ashen.

Can he see the terrible news on my face?

But no. He points at my eyes, and I know what he's looking at without him saying anything.

I rub at the moisture gathering in the corners and look at my trembling hand.

There's blood on my fingers. Like Valerian, I have bloody tears.

The scream that I'm suppressing grows louder.

Valerian pivots to face the other side of the platform. "Dylan!"

She rushes over, then notices our eyes and freezes. "The massive viral load," she whispers. "I was hoping I was wrong about the implications."

"The cure," Valerian barks. "Do you know how to make it?"

She cringes. "Maxwell says they're close but not yet."

"Go back to sleep and tell him to have a vampire meet us at the nearby world," Valerian orders. "That or a person with a jar of vampire blood."

Dylan bites her lip. "I think I know where you're going with that, and I have bad news. The experts on Gomorrah have done a lot of testing on animals infected with Maxwell's virus. When given vampire blood before any symptoms, the symptom onset is delayed. But if taken after the symptoms show up, vampire blood actually accelerates the progression of the disease. There's a reason they have extremely expensive healers keeping Maxwell alive."

Valerian's hands turn into fists. "We should've made Isis or another healer join this expedition."

Dylan backs away. "Isis refused, remember?"

"I could've dragged her by force," he growls. Taking a deep breath, he says in a calmer tone, "Do you have any tips for slowing down the progression of the disease?"

Dylan looks uncertain. "One thing that might help is to take it easy. As we saw with Stanislav, exerting oneself lowers your body's defenses."

"Right," he says, sounding even calmer now. "When will you be able to go to sleep again?"

"I just woke up," she says. At the narrowing of his

eyes, she quickly adds, "Bailey can use her powers to put me into REM sleep at any time, though."

"Bailey is going to take it easy," Valerian says firmly. "How about you do some exercises to tire yourself out, then eat a heavy meal and attempt a siesta?"

"Sure, I can do that," Dylan says. "I warned Maxwell to—"

"I'm sorry to interrupt," Felix says, approaching with a grave expression. "There's something you need to see."

He motions toward Stanislav's bed.

I look at it—and immediately wish I hadn't.

Stanislav's skin is a deep purple with just a touch of red. Eyes closed, he's thrashing like a man possessed by a demon with ADHD. Under his breath, he's mumbling something in Russian, but the only word I recognize is Murzik, the name of his kitten.

"How long has he been like this?" Valerian asks, his voice roughening as he walks over to the unfortunate chort.

On leaden legs, I follow.

"Don't know," Felix replies, joining us. "I just noticed it."

Rowan, Ariel, Fabian, and Itzel rush over as well, and deny knowing anything when Valerian barks the same question at them.

Stanislav's thrashing slows, and he begins whimpering something in Russian.

"It hurts," Felix translates, his voice pained. "He can't hold on anymore."

Ariel grabs Stanislav's wrist. "Fight it. You're a chort. What's a measly virus to you?"

"Can she get sick from touching him?" I whisper into Dylan's ear.

"Not according to Gomorran experts," Dylan whispers back. "Her mask will keep her safe."

Stanislav stops thrashing. In a few seconds, he stops whimpering also.

"I'm sorry," Rowan says, her expression solemn. "It's over. I can feel it."

Ariel doesn't seem to accept that. She checks Stanislav's pulse—only his dead body turns ghostly and disappears in her grasp, leaving behind nothing, not even the clothes.

She draws back, startled, and Felix puts a hand on her shoulder, squeezing lightly. "Chorts phase one last time when they pass."

CHAPTER THIRTY-TWO

VALERIAN WHIRLS ON DYLAN, his face a mask of fury. "It happened overnight. You said he'd make it to that nearby world!"

Dylan staggers back. "I hoped. I'm sorry."

Fabian steps between Valerian and Dylan, his expression grim. "We're all upset," he growls. "Let's remember it's Icelus we're upset with."

Valerian unclenches his fists. "I didn't mean… This is a lot to process."

You can say that again. During our travels, I'd grown to like Stanislav quite a bit. He wasn't at all how I'd expected the infamous chorts to be like—in a good way.

"Felix," I say unsteadily, thinking back to when I dreamwalked in Stanislav. "You have to tell his girlfriend."

"Of course," Felix murmurs.

A droplet of something slides down my cheek—

probably blood—but I don't check. "Make sure to tell her to take care of the kitten. She'll understand what that means."

Felix nods somberly.

"She'll be taken care of," Valerian says. "Both of them will be."

Ariel looks around. "Does anyone want to say anything?"

Fabian turns to the now-empty bed. "I'll start. I've known Stanislav for…" And as he goes on, reality presses on me from all sides.

This is a eulogy.

Stanislav is gone.

My heart squeezes painfully in my chest, my emotions in turmoil. Grief is there, for sure, but also a good dose of guilt. There's a selfish part of me that grieves Stanislav's passing for the wrong reasons: Now we see how precarious Valerian's situation is. And mine.

"You should rest," Valerian's voice intrudes into my mental fog.

He takes me by my elbow and leads me away from the makeshift funeral. As soon as my rear hovers over the edge of the bed, my knees give out. I end up hunched over in an awkward position, but I don't care.

Valerian sits by me and gives me a bear hug.

His scent and warmth provide a tiny bit of relief—that is, until I allow myself to really assess my situation.

Despite a lifetime of obsessively using hygieia and hand sanitizer, of sacrificing touching, kissing, and even hugging, I got sick. And not just sick. Infected with a deadly virus for which there's no cure yet.

Phobetor truly is the god of nightmares. He found a way to make my worst one a reality.

And what a nightmare it is. I can almost feel the virus releasing its unholy genetic instructions inside my cells, can sense my cells getting overpowered and starting to work for the enemy, creating enzymes that help the intruder make more copies of its disgusting self. I can picture new copies of the virus ripping out of the cells like nightmarish creatures from the *Alien* movie. Even as I'm thinking this, more cells are falling victim. And more. Until—

"Look at me," Valerian demands.

I obediently shift my gaze to his face.

"You're going to be fine." The words sound more like an order than reassurance.

I swallow the thick lump in my throat. "How could we possibly be fine?"

"Dylan will get the recipe for the cure in her next dream," he says confidently. "It will be easy to make. We'll rush to the nearby world, and she'll make the cure there, no problem."

I stare into his ocean-colored eyes. "If you're trying to pass for a seer, your fortune-telling needs to be more oblique."

He puts a finger to his temple and with mock concentration says, "I see you in a different bed. There's moaning. A pond is nearby."

I smile weakly. "That vision isn't all that mysterious. There's a pond in your apartment on Gomorrah."

He leans in, eyes gleaming. "It doesn't change the fact that there's moaning in your future." And closing the remaining distance, he presses his lips to mine.

Holy puck. I'm kissing in the real world—and it's magic. Amazingly, bacteria and viruses couldn't be further from my mind. Instead, all my senses are focused on him, on the way his lips feel, how his breath is warm and faintly sweet... how anxious butterflies in my stomach are now flapping their wings in a mating dance.

Deepening the kiss, I grab his hand and slide it under my shirt.

He stiffens and pulls away.

I eye him in hurt confusion.

"We can't," he says raggedly.

"You can give us privacy with your powers," I protest.

"It's not that. You need rest, and taking this further would be just the opposite."

Taking this further.

Is that what I want?

Incredibly, yes. All the way yes.

"Why don't you lie down," he says. "I'm going to go see if Rowan can speed up her zombies some more."

"But—"

He's already on his feet, striding away.

Ugh. Stupid Dylan and her "take it easy" advice. If

the virus kills me, I'll be really pissed I didn't seize the moment just then.

My heart is still fluttering like a leaf in a tornado, and I take a few calming breaths—though what I actually need is a cold shower.

My pulse continues racing despite the relaxation attempt.

Wait a second. Aren't heart palpitations a symptom?

No. No way. Too soon. Besides, that way lies another freak-out.

I'd better distract myself—and I know just the thing.

Stretching out on the bed, I touch Pom's fur and go into the dream world.

―――――

AS SOON AS I appear in my dream palace, I leave my body, even out my heart rate, and jump back in.

Pom appears in front of me, his expression subdued.

I came here to level with him, but he might already know something.

"Is everything okay?" he asks instead of his usually cheerful hello.

"It's not," I say and tell him about the virus situation.

As I talk, his fur turns black.

"I'm sorry," I say when I finish. "In hindsight, I'm a terrible host."

The tips of Pom's ears redden. "That's stupid. Even

with the virus in mind, I wouldn't want to be anyone else's symbiont."

"Thanks." I grab him off the floor and press him against my chest. "On the bright side, this virus has shown me what a true parasite is like. I never should've called you anything but a symbiont."

Pom wiggles his ears. "I've been trying to teach you."

"You have," I say. "And now I'm telling you how I really feel."

He wriggles out of my grasp and lands gracefully on the floor. "How about Valerian? Did you tell *him* how you feel?"

I hesitate, then shake my head. "I'm sure he knows."

"How? I don't think even you know."

I heave an exasperated sigh. "What does it matter if we're both going to—"

"You can be so stupid sometimes." His fur is deep red now. "Sometimes I worry I use too much of your brain."

I narrow my eyes. "What do you mean, *use my brain?*"

His angry red hue morphs into a guilty beet. "Well, yeah. I don't exactly have my own head in the real world, do I?"

"You don't, but—"

"As part of our symbiotic bond with the moofts, we loofts borrow some brain cells to be able to expand our consciousness. Later, we stimulate neurogenesis to compensate for the—"

"You know what, I don't think I want to know." I fold my arms across my chest. "Just tell me one thing… When I talk to you, am I talking to myself?"

"My neurons have very limited interaction with your own." His fur is a kaleidoscope of colors. "I'm a separate entity, just one that happens to share things with you."

"Yeah," I say sarcastically. "Things like my blood, and as it turns out, my brain as well."

"I thought you knew. How did you think I was able to use your powers? Or pick up your thoughts?"

I pinch the bridge of my nose. "You must've stolen the part of my brain that was responsible for asking those very questions."

"Like I said, neurogenesis—"

"And like I said, I'd rather not know the details. How about we play a game instead?"

When I see how quickly he turns a happy purple, I feel a pang of guilt that I haven't offered this to him more often.

Better late than never.

We play every game I've ever heard of, then invent some of our own and play those.

"I'm tired," he says after I beat him thrice at our latest invention: tic-tac-toe but on a three-dimensional array of cells, using kittens and puppies instead of naughts and crosses.

"How about you rest?" I say. "I was thinking I'd give a free therapy session to all my clients."

"Smart," Pom says sagely. "They say helping others can make you feel better."

"Nice. So altruism is selfish."

He grins and does his Cheshire cat disappearance.

"I could use feeling better, that's for sure," I mutter and teleport to the tower of sleepers.

Of course. Just as I'm in a giving mood, not a single one of my patients is asleep.

Fine.

I go to the memory gallery and recreate my first kiss in every juicy detail. If I do survive the virus, this is an experience I'll want to enjoy again and again.

Since I'm here, I replay some of my other favorite memories—especially those with Mom.

Poor Mom. Bad luck has a sense of irony. Just as I've hopefully gotten the power to bring her out of her comatose state, a virus is going to stop me from doing so.

Nope, not going there. Dwelling on bad outcomes isn't part of "taking things easy."

For Mom's sake, I create the most soothing environment around myself that I can muster, then meditate for what feels like days. Eventually, I grow very, very bored of taking things easy. At least the dream-world kind of easy.

In any case, I should check on how Valerian is doing.

To that end, I jolt myself awake.

———

BEFORE I EVEN OPEN MY eyes, I realize this was a bad idea.

Out here, in the real world, my heart is hammering irregularly in my chest.

There's no doubt now.

It's a symptom of the virus.

Opening my eyes, I see Valerian stretched out on his bed. Someone dragged it over to be next to mine.

Valerian notices me looking and sits up with a grunt.

I look at his chest area. "Is your heart—"

"Yours too?" he asks worriedly.

I nod. "Also, I think I'm starving."

His face darkens further. "Are you sure it's hunger?"

I examine the gnawing sensation in my belly.

Puck. It might well be the third symptom. If so, purple skin will be next, and after that is the end.

"There's good news," Valerian says, gesturing in the direction we're moving toward. "We're almost there."

I sit up.

Yep. I recognize the mountain ridge in the far distance.

Still, given how quickly the virus has been progressing with that insane viral load we got, we might not make it to the gates. And even if we did make it, last I checked, Dylan doesn't have the cure.

Speak of the devil. Dylan walks over, an excited expression on her face. "I just woke up. Maxwell explained how to make the cure. It's simple. I can do it at that lab at the hospital on the nearby world."

Okay. Now we have a chance. A small one but still.

"What do you think are the odds we'll last that long?" Valerian asks, echoing my concerns.

"It's hard to say for sure," Dylan says. "My hope is that you make it."

She also hoped Stanislav would make it, and that didn't turn out so well.

"I want more than hope," Valerian says. "Rowan," he yells. "Can you come here?"

Rowan hurries over, a curious expression on her face.

"Is there any way we can speed up this ride some more?" Valerian asks.

"I've stolen all the helpers from the fields we've passed," Rowan says. "Short of helping them carry this thing myself, I'm not sure what else I could do."

"Shouldn't there be some zombies by the gate?" I ask.

Rowan rubs her forehead. "Sleeping beauty has a point. Let me check."

The dead bird Rowan found earlier takes flight and zooms ahead of us.

As I wait, I carefully examine Valerian's skin.

There's the slightest tinge of purple there—though it could be the stress playing tricks with my vision.

Looking at the back of my hand yields the same result. I think my hue is a little purple, but I'm not certain.

Rowan frowns, her gaze distant.

"What's wrong?" Dylan asks.

Rowan's tone is grim. "Let me make the bird dive down to be sure."

She concentrates for the next minute, then turns a pained gaze on us. "It's Icelus. They're blocking our way to the hub."

CHAPTER THIRTY-THREE

WE START PEPPERING her with questions, but she winces and exclaims something in Necronian.

"Mor blast them," she growls in English. "Apparently, pre-vamps are expert jumpers. The helper bird was caught."

"Back up," Valerian says. "Are you sure this is Icelus we're talking about?"

"It's the pre-vamp Percival who did the jumping," Rowan says. "The others are also from Exozar's dream. I've never been surer."

"And they got your bird?" I ask, feeling sick. Aside from the danger posed by Icelus, the delay doesn't bode well for Valerian and me. "As in, they know we're coming?"

"They might not know the bird was a helper," Rowan says without much confidence. "As soon as they caught it, I withdrew my control, so they might think it croaked from the fright of being caught."

"Everyone," Valerian shouts. "We need to talk!"

Fabian, Ariel, Felix, and Itzel rush over, and Rowan tells them what she just discovered.

Some of the same questions as earlier get asked all at once.

"Guys, shut up," I say sternly. "We need a plan, not a game of twenty questions—and I think I have one. Felix, what's the reach of your powers?"

He looks like a lightbulb has just lit up above his head. "I'm on it," he says and shoots an arc of magenta energy into the distance.

Soon metal glints in that direction, proving Felix and I are on the same page.

Rowan cocks her head. "Is being coy part of the plan?"

"Felix is about to reunite with his robot suit," I explain. "Inside the suit are our weapons, including poison grenades. My plan is inspired by what Exozar did to us. You send in a zombie with a grenade and—"

"When pre-vamps die, they turn into vampires," Ariel says with distaste. "We'll just be facing more powerful enemies."

"But we have a necromancer." I nod at Rowan. "She can take over vampires and make them do her bidding. Can't you?"

"It's a good plan," Rowan says. "Unless the wind blows the poison toward us, that is."

"The masks block poison," Itzel chimes in.

"That's great for those with masks," Rowan says.

"What about me, sleeping beauty"—she looks at me —"and her beau?"

My beau?

"We have spare masks that were meant for members of the team that didn't make it," Itzel says. "Those masks might not fit the three of you well enough to wear for long, but if you hold one tightly against your face, you'll block the poison."

"Why would we get close enough to Icelus to be in danger of the poison in the first place?" Felix asks.

Rowan scratches the bleached side of her head. "I've only taken over a vampire once. It was in self-defense when I was on Earth. I'm pretty sure I need to be nearby to do that."

"It doesn't matter," Valerian says. "Pre-vamps or vampires—I can make us invisible to their eyes."

Rowan looks skeptical, but Valerian must show her a quick demonstration of his power because her eyes widen and she gives an impressed whistle.

"I like this plan," Fabian says. "Especially if Rowan can make one or more of the Icelus come with us to Gomorrah for questioning."

"Seems feasible," Rowan says. "At least in theory."

"I also like the plan," Valerian says, darting me an approving glance.

Something flutters in my belly in response, almost making the virus-driven stomach upset recede.

"That doesn't look like Earth technology," Rowan says, looking at the four limbs of the approaching robot.

"I helped Felix build that," Itzel says proudly. "A lot of the parts are from Gomorrah."

"Please," Felix says. "I could've built it on Earth if—"

"Open the thing and let's get to business," Valerian says sternly.

Looking sheepish, Felix stops the robot and has it open its shell.

Ariel rushes over and reverently grabs the handle of the gate sword Chester gave her. She then examines the guns and throws them in the backpack, muttering about the lack of ammo.

Fabian pulls out a Gomorran gun and Stanislav's saber, and hands both to Dylan. When their fingers touch, Dylan blushes.

Valerian repossesses his sai, and I get my katana and Gomorran gun.

"You shouldn't have gotten up," Valerian says as I secure my weapons. "Take it easy."

I lift my chin. "You got up, so I got up."

He shakes his head, walks over to his chair, and demonstratively plops into it.

I mime his actions, and as soon as I do, I realize how weak the virus has already made me.

Sitting is a relief.

Felix removes the backpack from the robot and sets it on the ground before letting the suit envelop him.

Itzel rummages in the backpack until she locates three masks that look to be about the size required, along with a set of tools.

When we try the masks on, not a single one fits.

"That's what the tools are for," Itzel says, unperturbed, and starts messing with the masks.

Meanwhile, Fabian takes out a poison grenade from the backpack and hands it to Rowan, who gives it to a zombie with particularly muscular legs.

"Here," Itzel says, handing me just the front of a mask. "Hold it tight against your face."

I do, and the ad-hoc scents of the mountain air go away.

Nodding approvingly, Itzel gives the hacked masks to Valerian and Rowan as well. Like me, they press the masks against their faces and hold them there, their muscles tense.

Fabian strips but doesn't turn into his wolf form, creating a distraction for the female part of the team, especially Dylan.

The rest of the way to the canyon, we ride in tense silence. Eventually, we arrive at the entrance where Felix left the robot before.

"Icelus are just through there," Rowan whispers, pointing toward the smaller canyon.

"Is this close enough for you to take them over?" Valerian asks in a low voice.

"Should be," she replies. "Can you make us invisible from here?"

"No," he says. "But I don't think we should get any closer."

Rowan nods, and the grenade-carrying zombie rushes into the canyon. The rest of the zombies put down our platform, and we get our weapons ready, just in case.

Rowan's brows furrow. "Percival is missing, but the rest of them are there."

We survey the canyon we're in. It's big enough for someone to hide behind the rocks.

Our zombies scatter.

"I'm going to have them look for him," Rowan explains.

"Don't forget to throw the grenade," Valerian says. "If you take over the newly formed vampires, you'll have more resources to search for the missing Percival."

"Already done," she says. "They're choking to death as we speak."

A few minutes later, a squadron of vampires rushes out of the canyon—clearly under her control.

A shadow blots the sky for a second.

I look up sharply, expecting another bird, but it's a person plummeting toward us.

"Percival!" I shout, pointing at him.

All heads tip back, following my gaze. They must be wondering the same thing I am: Where did he come from? Did he jump from the cliff above us? Or leap from behind a rock forty feet away?

In either case, Rowan wasn't kidding.

These pre-vamps can jump.

I aim my gun and shoot.

I must've missed. Percival lands, his legs miraculously unbroken, and before anyone can so much as blink, he hurls something at Valerian and Rowan.

Rowan collapses, the mask in her hand rolling to the side.

The vampires she was controlling are blinking and shaking their heads in confusion.

Not good.

Valerian also hits the ground, his mask rolling away.

Puck!

I aim my gun just as Fabian shifts into his werewolf form. Swiftly, I change the setting to nonlethal; if I kill Percival, I'll make yet another vampire for us to deal with.

I shoot.

I must miss again.

Percival hurls something at me just as Fabian's claws swipe at his neck.

I feel a sharp prick in my neck, then blackness.

CHAPTER THIRTY-FOUR

I COME to my senses just as Fabian's claws miss Percival's neck. Either their fight has gotten repetitive, or whatever Percival used on me hasn't taken effect.

I don't have time to dwell on it long, though, because the newly made vampires are here and beginning their attack.

Four jump at me, and I swing my katana in wide circles to keep them at bay. One vampire from the core group leaps at Itzel but gets a lightning ball in his chest.

Two attack Ariel. She punches one, but that gives the second one a window—and he sinks his fangs into Ariel's neck.

Puck, no.

Ariel drops to her knees, her skin paling with each pint of blood the vampire steals.

I slice at one of the vampires attacking me, and in the periphery, I spot a vampire ripping off an arm from Felix's suit.

Felix's shriek chills my blood. That metal arm must've contained his actual arm—no other way to explain the fountain of blood that gushes out of the broken suit.

This can't be happening.

But it is. Another vampire punches a hole through Dylan's chest, rips out her heart, and sucks it dry of blood.

The vampires attacking me get bolder, and I slash ever wider circles with my katana in a frantic effort to keep them away. My arms are tiring, though, and I don't know how long I can keep this up.

Then I notice another horror in my periphery. Valerian is thrashing around, just like Stanislav did at the end. His skin is a deep purple with just a touch of red.

No. Please no. Anything but this.

I redouble my efforts against the vampires, even though my strength is waning with each second. I can't let Valerian die. I refuse to. He has to live. He has to make it, even if I don't. He can't die so horribly, so—

A pitch-black Pom shows up between me and the vampire nearest me.

"You wanted me to interfere if there's a nightmare," he says, ears flopping. "Here I am. This is a bad one."

I look at my wrist.

Pom's not there.

But how?

Then it hits me. The thing that pricked my neck was an injector dart with that Koshmar drug. Of course. I saw Percival give a heap of these to Exozar. He obviously kept some for his own use.

In the heat of the battle, I didn't recognize the cursed injectors for what they were.

A breath of relief whooshes out of my chest. Ariel and Dylan were not killed. Valerian didn't go into the last stages of the virus, and Felix didn't lose his arm—that was all a nightmare.

Then again, who knows what's happening in the outside world. It's feasible that they *are* dead, just in a different way from what the drug made me see.

"Shouldn't you wake yourself up?" Pom asks, echoing my thoughts.

"Not yet," I say and teleport to the tower of sleepers. "I need to wake up Rowan and Valerian. He can make us invisible to the vampires, and she can take them over completely."

Whew. Rowan and Valerian are here. For a second, I was worried they got hit with something other than Koshmar—or worse, were killed while I dreamed.

"What's that?" Pom asks, his ears pricking. "Are you making that music?"

Pucking puck!

It's the *Dance of the Sugar Plum Fairy* again.

"The Nutcracker," I say through gritted teeth.

MOTHERPUCKER. The enemy dreamwalker couldn't have attacked at a worse time—and that's probably the point.

Since going to a random locale on Earth seemed to help me battle him the last time, I do so again, teleporting to the entrance of the insectoid-looking Opera House in Sydney, Australia.

At the same time, I try to jolt myself awake.

It doesn't work, and the reason why is clear. The Nutcracker appears in front of me, his clown-like painted mouth twisted in a sneer.

Puck. He's still able to prevent me from waking up.

When we faced each other the first time, I was pre-boost, and we were evenly matched. Then, when we fought after I'd gotten the boost, things stayed the same. At that point, I thought that maybe I just hadn't internalized the boost. Now there's been enough time for that, and I have to consider a theory I dismissed the last time: that he's somehow gotten a boost that matches mine.

A bazooka appears in his hands.

I fiddle with the gunpowder.

He must've planned for this somehow, because when he squeezes the trigger, a rocket whooshes out.

I dodge.

The rocket hits the Opera House, and a huge explosion levels the place.

Pom, who's managed to stay with me until now, disappears without so much as saying the word *scary*.

I take flight toward the Sydney Harbour Bridge. An orca jumps out of the water below. There's no way something that big can jump so high, so I normalize the gravity below the orca just enough so that its teeth miss me by a nanometer.

Reaching the bridge, I alter the gravity and turn the soles of my shoes into magnets, so I can run on the side of the bridge, parallel to the water.

None of my shenanigans slow the Nutcracker. He's either practiced dream fighting for ages or has a background conducive to it, like me with video game design.

"The more time you waste, the higher the odds that Percival will kill you in the real world," the Nutcracker says in his creepily melodic voice. "After he's done with all your friends, that is."

I turn and manifest a massive anvil right above his head, as if we were in a roadrunner cartoon. "I'm pretty sure Fabian and his wolfu have made mincemeat out of that pre-vamp already."

He dodges the anvil and throws a cloud of spiders at me. "A pre-vamp? In your dreams. Percival is one of the most ancient vampires. Your werewolf is as good as dead."

Oh, puck. That explains that superpowered jump. With a shudder, I recall what Edith, another ancient vampire, was able to do. If Percival is as powerful, Fabian is indeed in trouble.

All of us are.

If the Nutcracker's goal was to throw me off my game with this revelation, it works spectacularly. I miss my chance to destroy the spider horde, and now they're creepy-crawling all over me—and biting.

Acting purely on instinct, I dive into the water below, turning my body into metal on the way. The Nutcracker knows what I look like and can turn me back, but hopefully not before I get rid of his arachnid friends.

With a loud splash, I hit the water and sink like the chunk of metal that I am.

The spiders drown, as I hoped, but my reprieve is short. The Nutcracker shows up, incongruently standing on the ocean floor despite his wooden body.

With a flick of his hand, he returns my body to its flesh-and-blood form.

I begin to resurface, so I quickly adjust the density of the water around me, allowing me to stay put.

With a smirk, the Nutcracker creates a giant bubble

of air around us, then manifests a saber in his hand and lunges at me.

My katana shows up in my hand just in time to parry.

This isn't good. Our sword fighting didn't go so well the last time. At least not until I played my secret weapon—the multiple body technique.

In a blink of an eye, I exit my body, create a duplicate of myself, and leap into both. The two of me raise our katanas—and are blocked with two sabers in the hands of two Nutcrackers.

"Fool me once, shame on you," the Nucrackers say in unison. "Fool me twice…"

I don't listen to the rest. I let one of me parry the thrusts of the two Nutcrackers, while another me exits her body and creates a third copy of me.

It works—but the Nutcracker does the same, and there are now three of him fighting three of me.

Desperate, I create a fourth copy.

He does as well.

Fine.

Each version of me teleports to a different location on Earth—one to Big Ben, one to the Eiffel Tower, a third to the Leaning Tower of Pisa, and the fourth to the Brandenburg Gate.

The Nutcracker joins us in each location, his saber clashing with our katanas in a furious assault.

Each me has the same problem: Our slices don't hurt his wooden body as much as his injure our regular flesh.

Still, we battle on.

That is, until the Big Ben Nutcracker says, "Screw this." He turns himself into a nuke and kabooms with a mushroom cloud over all of London.

Puck.

The Big Ben version of me is gone now.

The rest of us fight harder, but the Nutcracker likes his nuke strategy, so he blows up his Eiffel Tower and Leaning Tower of Pisa selves in the same exact way.

We're down to one on one again.

If he commits suicide one more time, we're both going to be insane in the real world. Maybe it wouldn't be that big of a change for him, but I don't like that option.

Calling on my last remaining strength, I speed up my attack. The plan is to keep him too busy to turn himself into a bomb.

His saber nicks my wrist. Blood spurts out, but I'm fighting too hard to leave my body and heal the wound. Lunging forward, I slice his right shoulder, but my blade doesn't hurt the cursed wood.

If I don't figure out who he is, I'm going to lose. Soon.

He's not Maxwell, but he *is* someone who knows me. Maybe someone I don't think of as a dreamwalker. Someone who might've boosted his power recently and—

The puzzle pieces crash into place.

Parrying a saber slice, I allow myself a moment of

distraction, willing my opponent to take the form I've just guessed to be his real one.

To my shock, it works.

The nightmarish face turns attractive, with symmetrical masculine features and strong dark eyebrows. Only the eyes stay the same.

I should have recognized those eyes the first time we met.

The Nutcracker is Ratridevi Bhairava, Valerian's head of development.

Or as he likes to be called, Rattie.

CHAPTER THIRTY-SIX

"WHAT GAVE ME AWAY?" Rattie asks in his own voice, skillfully parrying my next attack.

"I should've seen it sooner." I keep talking in the hopes I'll distract him enough to pierce his flesh. "Your development team teased you for overusing spiders and clowns, and the Nutcracker's face is very clown-like. Not to mention, I've lost count of how many spiders you've thrown my way."

As I speak, I parry and slice, but he's too fast.

"Now that I think about it," I continue, "an important character in the Nutcracker story is called the Rat King—not a far cry from Rattie."

I block his counterthrust and cut his wrist, which bleeds in a mirror of my own injury.

Score. Talking works.

Encouraged, I go on. "The power boost is what *really* gave you away." I glide out of his attack like a Kendo master. "You like to make the villains in your games look like you, and the big bad in the *Lucid Dreamer* project—who's also called the Rat King—had your face in the demo that I tried."

I see him slowing down from his wound, so I ignore my own blood loss and attack with renewed vigor. "You pretended to make yourself a playable character in the game 'for replayability,' but really, it was to get as much power as me."

I don't remind him about the other clue—how his video game design background makes him so formidable in the dream world. Why boost his ego? Instead, I execute a truly awe-inspiring set of moves that end with the tip of my katana pressed against his throat. "The problem for you is that I'm better than you."

"Are you?" he sneers, and I realize his saber is in the same position against my neck.

Puck.

When I press the tip of my blade deeper into his neck, he does the same to me.

We're back to the mutual suicide scenario—and I see determination in his eyes.

He might actually be willing to go insane together.

CHAPTER THIRTY-SEVEN

DEADLY TENSION BUILDING, we stare at each other like two gunslingers.

Suddenly, Pom appears behind Rattie and sinks his teeth into the dreamwalker's ear.

Wow. I guess all those bravery practice sessions haven't gone to waste.

Rattie's eyes widen and his head whips around, but Pom is already gone. There's brave and there's suicidal, and my little symbiont knows the difference.

It doesn't matter, though. You snooze, you lose.

With deep satisfaction, I bury my katana in Rattie's neck.

He makes a gargling sound.

I don't bother trying to figure out what he's attempting to say. Ripping the katana out, I slice his head clean off.

As life leaves Rattie's body, a shockwave hits me, like the aftermath of a massive explosion. It's raw dream manipulation energy—and it twists everything around me, threatening to tear apart the very fabric of this world.

Only it doesn't.

Instead, it forces me awake.

CHAPTER THIRTY-EIGHT

I WAKE up to a gnawing pain in my stomach and an irregular heartbeat in my chest.

Puck. The virus is progressing.

Then again, there's great news. Thanks to my newfound REM detection sense, I can feel that both Rowan and Valerian are still alive and asleep, no doubt dealing with Koshmar-induced nightmares.

Gathering my strength, I open my eyes, sit up, and take in as much information as possible in the span of a few eyeblinks.

Despite Rattie's dire predictions, Percival hasn't defeated Fabian. At least not yet. They're fighting so preternaturally fast it's hard to follow what's happening. The vampire moves with a savage brutality, while the wolf is graceful, with copious hopping from paw to paw in the dance that is his martial art.

Felix and Ariel are back to back. He's beating up a vampire with his suit's four arms, while she's slashing a different vampire with the gate sword. Judging by the pile of severed vampire body parts near them, things are going well there.

Itzel and Dylan, likewise back to back just a leap away from me, are also holding their own.

Itzel throws a ball of lightning at a vampire who tries to grab her. Her attacker flies back almost to where I sit, lands on his head, and doesn't get up. Great result, but I can see Itzel is weakened by the use of that power.

At the same time, Dylan is waving Stanislav's saber wildly, and without any technique. The freshly made vampires attacking her don't seem to realize that the saber isn't all that dangerous in Dylan's hands and are keeping out of the thing's reach. At least, for now.

My gaze falls on Valerian and Rowan's unmoving bodies.

I need to wake them, starting with Rowan. If she takes over the vampires again, our problems will be—

A vampire leaps at Itzel again. She shoots a ball of lightning at him. The vampire flies back, landing next to me. His leg is clearly broken, with bone sticking out, but he doesn't pass out like the guy who landed on his head. Instead, he locks eyes with me—and I see the thirst gleaming in his bloodshot orbs.

Puck.

I frantically pat the ground for my katana.

The vampire crawls toward me, fangs out.

My hand lands on the hilt. I grab it, leap to my feet, and swing.

My attacker's head separates from his body, and the world spins around me as if it were my head rolling on the ground.

Must be weakness from the pucking virus.

Another vampire lunges at Itzel. She gets this one smack in the face with the lightning ball—only to fall to the ground herself, unconscious from power overuse.

The vampire she blasted flies toward me.

I sidestep and slice with my katana, beheading him mid-flight.

The vampire is no more, but my wooziness worsens.

I pull myself together as best I can. With Itzel on the floor, Dylan's back is exposed, and she doesn't seem to realize this.

"Dylan, behind you!" I yell hoarsely.

But my warning is too late. A female vampire grabs Dylan's saber hand from behind and twists, causing the blade to fall. She then covers Dylan's nose and mouth with her hand, blocking her airflow.

Staring at us with wild eyes, the vampire hisses, "If you don't put down your weapons, she's dead."

CHAPTER THIRTY-NINE

NEITHER ARIEL nor Felix put their weapons down, and Fabian doesn't stop fighting Percival—not that he's got weapons besides his claws.

The vampires who were circling around Dylan spin around and leap at me.

I tighten my grip on the katana. If I put it down as the hostage taker demanded, we'll all get killed anyway. As is, Dylan should have a minute or two before she suffocates. I need to dispatch the group of vampires rushing at me and wake up Rowan before that happens.

I don't let myself dwell on the alternative. Because if Dylan doesn't survive, any chance of getting the cure in time is out the window. Even if we beat the vampires, Valerian and I will perish from the virus.

The first vampire lunges at me but stays out of the reach of my katana.

"Coward," I mouth and go on the offensive.

The gash I slice across his torso would fell a man,

but this is a freaking vampire, so he keeps on coming—and is joined by two others moments later.

Being outnumbered generates enough adrenaline to make my wooziness subside, and I cleave the wrist of the next vampire who tries to get me, then behead the next.

"Jump on the katana!" I hear Percival yell from a distance.

No one is going to obey that. Unless... are these vampires sire-bonded to Percival? That happens if a pre-vamp drinks the blood of a vampire before they turn.

That must be the case here. The vampire without the hand leaps forward and shish-kebabs himself on my sword.

Puck.

He lets his body go limp and drops to the floor, taking the katana with him. Before I can so much as take a fighting stance, the vampire right behind the sword-jumper grabs my throat.

"Now!" he bellows triumphantly. "If you don't put down your weapons, this one will suffocate too."

CHAPTER FORTY

MY LUNGS ARE on fire and my head feels like someone took a bat to it.

All my instincts scream for me to thrash and fight, but I go limp instead. Let my attacker think he's won. I have only seconds of oxygen in my system, and I intend to make them count.

First, I attempt remote-entering Rowan's dreams.

Nope. That technique is too novel for me to execute in this state.

Hoping the vampire doesn't notice or care, I touch Pom's fur—and because I've done this a million times, I catch a whiff of ozone and plummet into the trance even while being choked.

———

I APPEAR in the dream palace lobby and realize I have a problem.

Lack of air is pulling me out of the dream world.

I strain my powers to stay in, the reverse of jolting awake. It seems to work, so I teleport right into Rowan's room in the tower of sleepers.

Pom shows up, but I ignore him. Slapping my palm on Rowan's forehead, I leap into her dream.

———

NOT SURPRISINGLY GIVEN the Koshmar dart, Rowan's dream is taking place in the canyon battlefield that would be our waking world.

Every single one of us is already dead here, clearly of hideous causes.

"This is too weird and scary," Pom says when he sees what's happening to Rowan, and promptly disappears.

I can't blame him. Covered in blood and gore, Rowan is lying among our body parts, the top of her skull opened as if in the middle of a neurosurgery. Frank is here, and he's eating Rowan's brain as she convulses from time to time—I guess when he chomps on the parts responsible for movement.

That's gross and disturbing. Then again, I've recently learned that my own pet had done something like this to me for real—stealing some neurons instead of eating them, but still.

I make Frank disappear, heal Rowan's brain and skull, and remove all the gore from our surroundings.

"This is a dream," I tell her. "You need to wake up and save everyone, starting with me and Dylan."

She looks at me with bulging eyes.

"This. Is. A. Dream," I enunciate. "Save me and Dylan first. Got it?"

She gives me the smallest nod but doesn't speak, a bad sign.

I have to trust she understood what I said. There's no time to waste.

I jolt her awake.

Now Valerian.

I teleport to the tower of sleepers again, but before I can touch him, the lack of oxygen yanks me out of the dream world.

CHAPTER FORTY-ONE

FOR A SECOND, everything is black, and my lungs feel like they're bursting.

Then the hands around my neck let go, and as I greedily gulp in air, I'm gently lowered into a sitting position.

Rowan's clearly come through.

Remaining in a sitting position is a struggle, but I force myself to stay upright and survey the battlefield.

The vampire suffocating Dylan has already let her go as well, and she's lying on the ground, hopefully just resting.

Felix and Ariel dispatch the vampires they were fighting without realizing it's no longer needed. Then they gape at the rest of their opponents—who are standing unnaturally still, ready to follow Rowan's commands.

But not all of them are subdued.

Percival is still fighting Fabian, and Fabian is clearly getting tired.

"I can't take over Percival!" Rowan shouts. "I've been trying."

Right. Edith was immune to necromancer powers as well.

"Help Fabian!" is what I try to yell back, but nothing comes out.

Percival must realize the direness of his situation—and tries a desperate maneuver. He allows Fabian's claw to enter his shoulder, then smashes a fist into the werewolf's jaw.

Fabian flies up and lands in an unmoving heap.

Percival's wound would kill anyone else, but he's not even paying attention to it. What's worse, the wound is healing. Rowan sends her vampires toward their sire, and in the distance, I see her zombies. She's bringing them back from their search for Percival.

The first Rowan-controlled vampire reaches Percival and is ripped into pieces in an eyeblink. The second one gets the same treatment. The third one gets his neck snapped.

All this happens insanely fast—that or my brain is slowing.

Rowan makes the rest of the vampires and the newly arrived zombies attack Percival en masse. At first, it seems like an easy win, but vampire blood and zombie limbs are flying all around Percival, and he's no worse for the wear.

Moving preternaturally fast, he rushes at Felix and Ariel.

Puck. He'll rip them apart. I need to do something.

I concentrate like I've never done before. I picture myself touching Valerian in every detail possible—and because it's him, my imagination has no trouble with this at all.

Percival smashes a fist into Felix's chest just as I connect with Valerian and fall into his nightmare.

———

VALERIAN IS KNEELING in a puddle of blood and gore, holding my lifeless body in his hands. Bloody tears stream down his cheeks, and the expression of sorrow on his face wrenches at my insides.

I evaporate my corpse and loudly clear my throat.

Valerian looks up at me, wild hope flashing in his eyes.

"This is a dream?" He looks around. "That drug?"

"Time is of the essence," I say quickly. "As soon as you wake up, help Felix and Ariel with Percival."

He leaps to his feet.

I jolt him awake and leave the dream world.

———

PUCK.

A lot must've happened in the brief time it took me to wake Valerian.

Felix is lying a few feet away, a huge dent in the chest of the robot suit.

Ariel is in trouble too. Percival's fangs are in her neck, and he's draining her at the same time as he's trying to rip the gate sword from her grasp.

Amazingly, Ariel is not letting go of the weapon.

I look for my katana. Maybe if I could—

Valerian sits up.

Normally, when he uses his power, it's invisible. But this time, an arc of pulsing red energy streams from his fingers into Percival's head.

Belatedly, I realize that making Ariel invisible isn't going to help her.

But that doesn't seem to be what Valerian is doing.

Releasing Ariel, Percival whirls around with a war cry.

Whatever Valerian has made him see must be frightening indeed, because the ancient vampire is trembling as he faces it.

Ariel comes to her senses and swings the gate sword.

"Wait!" Valerian yells.

He must want the leader of this Icelus group for questioning—and the sort of questioning Valerian has in mind is exactly what Percival deserves.

Ariel doesn't hear or care if she does. Her sword slices through the vampire's neck as though it were made of vapor. Percival's headless body collapses, the head rolling to the side.

Valerian curses up a storm.

Ariel faces him unapologetically. "You're too sick to safely contain him and you know it."

Valerian glares at her, but the cursing stops.

She's right, I realize with a sinking feeling. Valerian's color is a deadly shade of purple.

I glance at my hands.

So is mine.

Rowan rushes to check on Itzel while Ariel begins peeling Felix out of his ruined suit.

"The gnome is okay," Rowan says to my relief.

"So is Felix," Ariel says, lifting another weight off my shoulders.

Rowan checks on Fabian next while Ariel approaches Dylan.

"The werewolf's heartbeat is strong," Rowan says— and just to confirm her words, Fabian morphs into his naked human form, jumps to his feet, and scans his surroundings with an impressively alert gaze.

Rowan glances mournfully at Ariel.

She must already know what Ariel is about to say. After all, she can feel corpses.

My breath seizes in my lungs.

Ariel looks up, subdued.

"I'm sorry," she says gravely. "Dylan didn't make it."

CHAPTER FORTY-TWO

VALERIAN'S GAZE homes in on Rowan. "I want you to resurrect her." He jabs a finger at Frank. "Do to her what you did for your pet."

Rowan backs away. "Impossible."

"You've done it before, so it's clearly possible," Fabian growls.

Rowan darts Frank a quick glance. "That was a crime of passion. I shouldn't have done it."

"But you did, and he's back." Fabian's face twists as he looks at Dylan's body. "How could that be a crime?"

"You don't understand what you're asking," Rowan says. "This is my people's biggest taboo for a reason. Dylan wouldn't want this."

Fabian advances on her. "Dylan took a big risk helping us with this mission. She deserves to be brought back."

Rowan backs farther away.

Fighting a bout of nausea, I drag in a deep breath.

"Please, Rowan. If you don't want to do it for Dylan, do it for me and Valerian. She's our only chance of surviving the virus."

Rowan looks at Valerian, then at me, no doubt noticing our skin coloring and the fact that we're barely able to remain sitting. "Why don't I bring her back as a regular zombie? She could then talk you through making the cure."

Fabian glares at her. "We don't just need a chemical formula. We need a scientist. Dylan has multiple PhDs. She's a virologist. None of us can do what she can, especially not by playing a game of Simon Says with a zombie. By not bringing her back, you're signing Valerian and Bailey's death warrants."

Rowan's face tightens as she glances at her pet. "Frank's not the same person after what I did."

"He wasn't a person to start with," Ariel says. "He's an opossum or whatever."

"You know what I mean," Rowan says. "His personality—"

"Is his memory intact?" Ariel cuts in.

"I guess." Rowan grimaces. "But there were other side effects that—"

Valerian's hands begin trembling. Catching us looking, he balls them into fists. "We don't have time for this. You said you're no longer welcome on this world and want asylum on Earth. Do this, and I'll see to it personally that you get it. I'm on the New York Council and have favors I can cash there. You know how much vampires despise your kind. I'm your only chance."

Rowan lets out a defeated sigh and gingerly approaches Dylan's body. "This can go apocalyptically bad. That's a lot to have on my conscience."

Valerian's eyes glint coldly. "How about I help you deal with your conscience. Tell yourself you have no choice—because if you don't do this willingly, I'll be forced to use my power to make sure you do it." He must show her a taste of what he means because she pales to a nearly translucent hue.

"Don't do that again, please," she says unsteadily. "And promise me this: If Dylan asks afterward, you tell her I didn't have a choice. Also, whatever she does, it's on you."

"Done," Valerian says, his tone gentling.

Rowan kneels next to Dylan's body, and a blinding energy beam shoots out of her fingertips, just like when she did it to Frank in her dream memory.

I desperately need to lie down, but hope and curiosity keep me in a sitting position.

Dylan stirs. Rowan soothingly strokes Dylan's hair as she opens her eyes. Her gaze is unfocused, but she's clearly not dead anymore.

Beaming, Fabian rushes over to her. "Dylan. Are you okay?"

Dylan looks at the naked werewolf uncomprehendingly. "I… am Dylan."

"Do you remember the cure?" Valerian asks her. "The virus?"

A hint of recognition sparks in Dylan's eyes, and she rattles out a chemical formula, as well as what must be Earth-specific scientific words that don't ring a bell for me, like Erlenmeyer flask.

"Can you walk?" Rowan asks her.

Dylan slowly stands up and makes a circle around the necromancer in halting, awkward steps.

Fabian looks at Ariel. "Can you carry Bailey? I can grab Valerian and the gnome, and Dylan can drag Felix."

Felix sits up. "I don't think I need to be dragged."

"Me neither," Itzel says, but without sitting up.

I ignore the rest of the logistical chatter and allow myself to lie down.

It's a mistake. The mother of all post-adrenaline crashes allies with the weakness from the virus to make me woozier than a drunk hippopotamus on ice. My consciousness cuts in and out. At one point, I open my eyes long enough to see Ariel carrying me into the gate. The next time I have the strength to peek at the outside world, we're in the hospital near the hub, the one that has a lab where Dylan can make the cure.

Assuming the resurrected Dylan can do it. She's not exactly her usual self.

The next time I come to, my limbs are trembling, and no matter how much I want to know Valerian's status, I don't have enough strength to roll over and check on him.

Sometime later, someone gives me a gentle shake.

With a monumental effort of will, I open my eyes.

It's Ariel. She's got a beaker in her hand.

"Drink this," she croons, placing it against my lips. "Dylan came through with the cure."

"Valerian," is what I try to say, but only a gasp comes out.

She must know what I mean because a smile touches the corners of her eyes. "Felix is giving Valerian his dose as we speak. Now drink."

I painfully swallow the bitter substance she pours into my mouth.

"There's something in there that should help you sleep," Ariel says from a long distance away.

Whatever substance she meant was probably overkill.

As soon I close my eyes, I'm out.

———

I AND A DELEGATION OF DWARVES, elves, and other Cognizant from Gomorrah come through the gate and take in the world of Necronia. We're all carrying jars labeled "The Cure," but written in English for some reason.

That's odd. Shouldn't that have been written in Necronian? Also, shouldn't we be wearing masks? Also, why—

I glance at my wrist.

Pom is missing.

Of course. This is just a dream.

I'm probably in a hospital bed right now, the cure

hopefully eradicating the virus in my system. That is, if Dylan didn't accidentally make a laxative drug instead. She did seem pretty loopy after her resurrection.

Still, in this dream I feel great, a positive sign.

When I teleport to the tower of sleepers, a multicolored Pom is already in Valerian's nook.

"I knew you'd come here," he says, ears flopping.

I pick him up and squeeze him in a hug. "How are you feeling? Do you think we're getting cured?"

His voice is muffled against my chest. "I hope so. Hard to say."

I set him back down. "As you so insightfully predicted, I'd like to talk to Valerian now. Want to join?"

"Nah. I'm going to invent a game that we can play. Something that I can always win."

"Good luck with that." Grabbing Valerian's wrist, I dive into his dream.

———

LITTLE ME AND little Valerian are sitting in a dark closet. He has a mischievous expression on his face, and I'm giggling.

This is an actual memory. Must be from the batch that flashed too fast for me to register.

Before I can let my presence be known, the kids clasp hands and run out of the closet into a room where one of the windows is black.

"Ah," I say out loud. "More unexplored secrets."

Little Valerian halts, looks intently at me, and morphs into a grown version of himself.

"I'm sleeping?" he asks, his tone dreamy.

I point at the black window. "Ready for total recall?"

He nods, and before he can come to his senses enough to change his mind, I grab his hand like the child version of me did, and launch us into the black glass.

————

I'M BACK in the black ocean, and Valerian is in a boat, like before.

The swim is just as hard, only it doesn't bother me as much this time around. After everything I've been through recently, a swim, no matter how difficult and long, is a vacation in comparison.

After what feels like a day of swimming, I touch the shore, and the flood of memories begins.

————

VALERIAN AND I show up in a large meeting room.

A dozen adults are sitting in a circle, Valerian's and my parents among them. In the middle of the circle is a person I did not expect to see in the context of Soma.

It's Nostradamus, the seer, with his werewolf lying at his feet like a dog.

Kid Valerian is here too, standing to the side where nobody seems to pay him any attention.

"Oh, right," my Valerian says. "I remember this now. I snuck in and used my powers to make it so that the others couldn't see me."

Nostradamus begins to speak. "If Phobetor isn't stopped, he'll destroy everyone, not just your little world."

"We know this," my father says. "Tell us something we don't."

"There's one thing that will give you a chance at victory," Nostradamus says. "A minuscule chance."

Mom looks at the seer skeptically. "What is it?"

"Only Two working as One can defeat the god of nightmares," Nostradamus says. "Remember, only Two working as One."

Everyone, including me and grown Valerian, gazes at him in confusion.

"That's much too vague," my mom says. "Who are the Two? How do you work as One?"

Nostradamus stands up. "I might've already said too much."

Everybody starts shouting questions, but the werewolf growls at them and leads the seer out of the room.

With that, the memory ends, and a new one begins.

———

VALERIAN'S PARENTS are standing next to a glass door that leads into a padded room. My mom is in there, with the signature fiery eyes of the Overtaken.

She's yelling obscenities and literally climbing the walls.

Is the memory speeding up already, or is Mom just acting crazy?

Young Valerian is here again, spying.

"Clearly, they weren't the Two," Valerian's mother says. "Else Phobetor wouldn't have been able to take them over, would he?"

"I think it's clear who the Two are," Davu replies. "Why else is Phobetor trying to have their parents murder them so desperately?"

"Poor twins." Valerian's mom shakes her head. "To have—"

She stops and narrows her eyes directly at where little Valerian is standing.

"You forgot to control my sense of smell," she says sternly. "What have I told you about—"

The memory cuts off.

———

DOZENS OF PEOPLE are gathering in a large room. Young Valerian isn't the only child this time—a bunch of them are here, looking bored.

Since nothing interesting is happening in the memory, I spin around, facing grown Valerian. "Does any of this make any sense to you?"

"Some," he says. "I was young when this went down. As you saw, what little I do know was via spying."

"The twins your father meant are me and Asha?" I

look around to see if they're here at the gathering. They're not. "Phobetor took over my parents and murdered my sister because he thinks we might bring about his downfall?"

"Call him Collywobbles," Valerian reminds me. "And I have no idea what he thinks, but your parents did try to kill the two of you while under his control. That's why they were locked in padded rooms."

I rub my eyebrows. "How did they get Overtaken? Did someone describe that viral nightmare to them?"

"I don't know."

"And what the puck did Nostradamus mean by Two as One?"

"I don't know that either," Valerian says. "Though in that case, I doubt anyone does."

Before I can pepper him with more questions, his mother addresses the gathering. "Dear illusionists, we gather here with heavy hearts to discuss the fates of Bailey and Asha."

Everyone falls silent, giving her their full attention.

"I propose a simple plan," she continues. "Phobetor wants their parents to kill them, so we must do what we do best. We must create an illusion that will make them—and the one controlling them—think they succeeded. After that, we'll send them into exile and raise the girls in secret."

I look at Valerian, my eyes widening.

Before I can say anything, the memory terminates.

———

THIS NEW MEMORY runs much faster, but I'm still able to follow.

Valerian's parents are standing next to another glass door that leads into a padded room. Only it's my father inside this time, and he's not thrashing around.

He's hugging his knees, catatonic.

"I don't know how Lidia escaped," Davu says. "And it was pure bad luck that she saw Bailey on the way out."

Valerian's mother is frowning. "Any idea where she went?"

"No clue," he says.

"Well, all we can do is pray she's banished Phobetor for good," she says. "Else the next time she goes to sleep, he'll learn of our deception and have her kill Bailey for real."

Again, the memory terminates too fast for me to say something.

———

A FAMILIAR SCENE BEGINS, set in the fateful clearing on Soma. In the version I saw in Mom's memory, Asha and I were about seven, and we were running and screaming in terror.

But my sister and I aren't here.

It's just my parents chasing nothingness with machetes, their eyes those of the Overtaken.

The crowd that was chasing after my parents in Mom's memories is here too. In the front, I spot my grandmother, Davu with his wife, little Valerian, and Kojo and his parents.

"Stop!" Davu screams at my parents.

They don't respond, just keep chasing what they must think are the twins.

I have to use my recollection of Mom's memories to fill in the details.

Illusory Asha trips over a root.

The illusion of young me keeps running for a few moments, then looks back, panting. "Asha, no!" she gasps and rushes to her.

At least that's what my parents must be seeing—and so must Phobetor through their eyes.

This is the moment illusory Asha started crying, and I tried to lift her.

Our parents close in.

Our father faces the crowd while Mom raises her machete.

This is when the illusory me screamed, "Mommy, no!" in Mom's memory.

Mom slashes with the machete through empty air—though of course, she thinks she's just beheaded Asha.

Numbly, I watch as Mom's strange eyes gaze at another spot. One where the illusion of me must be sobbing uncontrollably.

Just like in her own memory, Mom's body tenses, her face twisting with alternating expressions of blankness and horror. Her eyes flicker between magma-like fire and their normal brown hue, and her left hand grabs her right, as if trying to steal the machete from it. Finally, her eyes stay brown, and horror eclipses all else on her face.

Wow. This is what Davu had meant in that out-of-order memory that preceded this one.

Somehow, Mom has banished Phobetor from her mind, reversing her Overtaken status.

She looks at the bloody machete in her hands, then at where the headless Asha would be if she were real. With a raw, guttural moan, she spins around—just as my father smashes a fist into her temple.

Having knocked Mom out, my father sprints over to where the illusory version of me would be and slashes at the empty air with his machete.

The memory terminates.

———

IN THE NEXT MEMORY, Valerian's parents are speaking too fast for me to comprehend their words, but I think they're explaining the need to forget the incident at the clearing and the associated memories via a black window.

I'm only half listening anyway, as I'm desperately trying to make sense of what I've just learned.

Mom didn't actually kill my sister, just like my father didn't kill me.

They were made to think that they did this by the Soma illusionists.

But that means—

The world explodes around us, instantly jolting me awake.

———

BACK IN THE REAL WORLD, I open my eyes.

The room is too dark to see anything.

I sit up.

Someone turns on the light.

It's Valerian. His skin isn't purple anymore.

I look at my own hands and see they aren't purple either.

My eyes fly up to his face. "My sister is alive?"

He comes toward me. "First, how are you feeling?"

"Peachy," I snap, and it's the truth. No sign of earlier weakness or stomach pains. "My heart is beating fast, but that's normal given what I've just learned."

Looking relieved, he reaches over and clasps my hand in his large palm. "Bailey—"

I glare up at him. "Answer me. My sister—"

Smiling warmly, he squeezes my hand. "She's alive."

"And you had no idea?"

"Not the slightest. They left not a single clue."

"But wasn't she in your memories of Soma? Your parents said we'd be raised there."

"She wasn't. I suspect that after your mom's escape and before making everyone forget, my parents took Asha to the part of Soma that's separate from the rest. That's what I'd have done in their shoes."

Holy puck. I stare at him, my heart skipping around

as if the virus were back. My mind races furiously, flipping through all the memories I've seen.

My sister is alive.

Mom didn't kill her.

I have a living sister, a twin.

And there's apparently a prophecy about us… and Phobetor.

The implications of it all are overwhelming, and as I stare into Valerian's eyes, the words tumble out of their own accord. "I need to speak to Mom about this. If my powers aren't able to snap her out of her coma, this news—"

"I'll take you to her," Valerian says softly, and leaning down, he presses his lips to mine.

SNEAK PEEKS

Thank you for reading! I hope you're loving Bailey's story! Her adventures conclude in *Dream Ender (The Bailey Spade Series: Book 4)*.

Not only is Phobetor real, he's about to destroy life on every world with sentient beings. You could say he's becoming a bit of a problem.

Unless I'm somehow the hero of an ancient prophecy—and let's face it, I'm not—everyone I care about is in major trouble.

My name is Bailey Spade, and this is how my story ends.

Do you want to be notified of my new releases? Sign up for my email list at www.dimazales.com!

Love audiobooks? This series, and all of my other books, are available in audio.

Want to read my other books? You can check out:

- *The Sasha Urban Series* - the fantastical urban fantasy series set in the same universe as Bailey Spade, where Felix and Ariel first appear
- *Mind Dimensions* - the action-packed urban fantasy adventures of Darren, who can stop time and read minds
- *Upgrade* - the thrilling sci-fi tale of Mike Cohen, whose new technology will transform our brains *and* the world
- *The Last Humans* - the futuristic sci-fi/dystopian story of Theo, who lives in a world where nothing is as it seems
- *The Sorcery Code* - the epic fantasy adventures of sorcerer Blaise and his creation, the beautiful and powerful Gala

And now, please turn the page for a sneak peek at Chapter 1 of *Dream Ender* and an excerpt from *Upgrade*.

I'm kissing Valerian.

This is my second time kissing in the real world, and it's glorious. The hospital room around me spins on its axis. My fingers are buried in his thick, silky hair, and his lips are soft and smooth, his tongue skillfully—

Someone rudely clears his throat.

I stiffen. Before that moment, the thought of bacteria and viruses couldn't have been further from my mind, but now, images of post-nasal drip invade my consciousness, ruining the mood.

Valerian draws back from me and glares at the intruder—a bashful-looking Felix, who looks extra thin without his robot suit.

"I'm sorry." Felix backs out of the room. "I—that is, the others… If you're up, we should head back."

Head back. To Gomorrah. Right.

As much as I hate to have been interrupted from

what Valerian and I were doing, going back is an excellent idea. Between the boost to my dreamwalker powers and the revelation about my not-so-dead twin, getting to Mom is at the top of my priority list.

"We're on a post-apocalyptic world ravaged by a deadly virus," Felix says, still sounding defensive. "It's not exactly a place to Netflix and chill."

Valerian must show Felix something with his powers because he pales, turns on his heel, and sprints away.

"We should go," I say reluctantly, my eyes on Valerian's sensuous lips.

"To be continued," he murmurs into my ear and strides out of the room.

With a sigh, I follow.

When I was brought to this hospital from Necronia, I was barely conscious. Now that I'm walking through the white corridors with my awareness intact, I wish someone would knock me out again so I wouldn't see all the dead bodies sprawled around.

The virus Icelus had planned to unleash on Necronia had made its way here first, with deadly results.

The dreariness follows me all the way outside, where our team is waiting inside a circle of corpses that are standing upright. That's thanks to Rowan, the necromancer who left Necronia with us.

As we approach, she pushes her signature steampunk-style goggles higher up on her head to combat a few unruly strands of her strangely colored hair—half of her head is bleached white, the other half is jet black. Behind her is Fabian in his musclebound man form, dressed for once. Next to him is Dylan, her long brown hair uncharacteristically disheveled and her blank eyes lacking the razor-sharp intelligence that always made them so lively. Itzel, our gnome friend, and Ariel, Felix's uber roommate, are with them also.

Spotting me, Ariel flashes a radiant smile that shows off her uber-perfect teeth.

"Finally. Sleeping Beauty awakens," Rowan says to me. "I bet there was a kiss involved." She winks at Valerian.

Felix reddens and Valerian shakes his head, while Itzel just huffs into her breathing mask.

"Newly made zombies?" I ask Rowan, glancing at the upright corpses.

She nods. "I gathered some *helpers* for our trip." She emphasizes the preferred Necronian term.

Ariel looks worriedly down the street. "It's a good thing she did. The Overtaken attacked us twice while you were out."

I scan the zombie herd, but of course, in death, the Overtaken look identical to other corpses. "Twice? I didn't realize there were enough people left alive on this world to Overtake."

"There are," Felix says. "In fact, while you were out, I was able to locate a computer in the hospital and use my powers to get into this world's equivalent of the internet. I spread the formula for the cure as widely as I could. Should give the survivors a chance."

Ariel smacks Felix approvingly on the shoulder. "I wonder if the Councils could leave some ready-made cure here when they bring it to Necronia."

"I'll tell them to do so," Valerian says. "Now we should head out before more Overtaken attack. We have no cure for *that* problem."

Fabian pushes the zombies aside and hands me and Valerian our Gomorran guns. Once we have those stashed, he also gives me my katana and Valerian his sai.

Dylan is still standing there, her gaze unfocused.

"Dylan," I say formally. "I wanted to thank you. If you hadn't come through with the cure, Valerian and I would be part of Rowan's zombie herd."

At the mention of her name, Dylan looks in my general direction but doesn't meet my gaze. Nor does she acknowledge the thanks.

Weird.

She hadn't acted like this before.

Is this one of the side effects of Rowan bringing her from the dead? With a pang of guilt, I recall Rowan saying Dylan wouldn't be the same, yet Valerian, Fabian, and I pressured her to perform the special resurrection anyway.

Then something else catches my attention. With the exception of Itzel, no one is wearing masks anymore—despite the fact that we're on a virus-infected world.

When I ask about it, Dylan seems to perk up a little. "The cure isn't just a cure," she says with a hint of her usual professorial tone. "It works prophylactically as well."

Ah, so they all drank it. Smart.

Rowan runs a hand through the bleached side of her hair. "Let's go."

She and Fabian cross the street, with zombies and the rest of us close behind.

We enter the train station again, and thanks to Rowan, the purplish corpses lying around join our herd of zombies.

Due to sheer numbers, our procession takes a while to navigate the maze of corridors into the hub, where I watch Rowan do something strange: She grabs the nearest zombie by the hand, that zombie grabs the hand of another, and so on. They daisy-chain like that until everyone is holding hands, like a bunch of macabre kindergarteners.

"It's the only way I can get them through the gate," Rowan explains. "This way, they register as my possessions."

I dart a guilty glance at Dylan.

Rowan bends over and places Frank, her resurrected opossum-like pet, in a sack hanging crosswise over her body. "Dylan is still Cognizant. I think she'll be able to get through without me. Hopefully."

Fabian extends his hand to Dylan. "How about we don't take any chances."

If I were Dylan, I'd make sure to point out that I'm

not Fabian's possession, but she just meekly grabs his hand while avoiding the werewolf's eyes.

Puck. I really hope this odd behavior is temporary.

Valerian looks at Rowan. "Where's the body of your betrothed?"

"We questioned him while you were out," she says. "Keyser didn't know much. The ancient vampire had glamoured him to thwart anyone who mentions the word 'Icelus.' That was also when he'd gotten infected and was told about the nightmare that made him into an Overtaken."

"What about all the vampires we killed on Necronia?" Valerian asks. "Could you bring them back for questioning?"

"I tried," Rowan says. "I guess it doesn't work with dead vampires—which kind of makes sense, seeing how it's their second death and all."

Valerian curses under his breath. "We desperately need intelligence on our enemy."

I put a hand on his shoulder. "Maybe Maxwell will have something for us when we get to Gomorrah." I look at Dylan. "Did he tell you anything on that topic in your dreams?"

Dylan doesn't respond.

"Dylan," Fabian says soothingly. "Did you sleep?"

She shakes her head.

Rowan pats the sack where she's stashed her pet. "Frank doesn't sleep either."

Neither do vampires—another type of the undead— but it wouldn't be courteous to mention that.

"Let's go," Rowan says, and before anyone can object, she leads her zombie train into the pink plasma gate.

We step out on a hub located in a lush forest meadow where we'd camped on the way to Necronia.

"This time, let everyone else go first," Valerian says to Rowan as we approach the next gate. "That way, if there's an attack, we can cover your arrival."

With a barely perceptible eye roll, Rowan gestures for everyone to go ahead, like a doorman.

Ariel, Fabian, and Dylan take the lead, Itzel and Felix step in next, and Valerian goes right before me.

When I come out on the other side, it's to the sound of battle.

———

Visit www.dimazales.com to learn more!

SNEAK PEEK AT UPGRADE

A successful venture capitalist with billions in the bank, Mike Cohen has it all figured out. That is, until the life-changing new technology he's developing lands him in the middle of a global conspiracy, and the only way to save himself, his loved ones, and his tech is to embed the highly experimental Brainocytes in his own brain.

Brainocytes transform the human experience, making you smarter, faster, and more powerful. With enemies at every turn, Mike must use his newly enhanced capabilities to save his family, his friends, and ultimately, the world.

———

"A cure for dementia and Alzheimer's?" Uncle Abe's gray eyes pulse with excitement, the way Mom's often do.

"It's not exactly a cure," I say at the same time as Ada says, "It's mostly a treatment for the symptoms."

"How cute," Uncle Abe says in Russian. "Your chick is already finishing your sentences."

As though she understood the Russian words, Ada's face lights up with an impish grin.

"We're not a couple," I tell Uncle Abe in Russian.

"Yet?" He gives me a knowing wink.

"It's not polite to speak in Russian in front of Ada," I say in English.

"I'm okay," Ada says. Only the shadow of a smile lurks in the corners of her eyes now, making her look like a punky version of the Mona Lisa.

"Still, I'm sorry," Uncle Abe tells her, his accent softening the *t* and the second *r*.

As we stroll through the hospital corridor, Ada takes the lead. She's a typical New Yorker, always twitchy and multitasking. I surreptitiously look her up and down, my eyes lingering on one of my favorite assets of hers—that special spot between the soles of her Doc Martens boots and the tips of her spiky hair.

Ada glances over her shoulder, her amber eyes meeting mine for a second. Did she feel me gawking at her just now? Before I can feel embarrassed, she stops in front of a green door and says, "This is the room."

The three of us walk in.

Unlike my dream, this isn't an operating room. It's

spacious, with big windows and cheerfully blooming plants on the windowsills. At a glance, it's reminiscent of my stylish Brooklyn loft—if a mad scientist's wet dream was used as inspiration for the interior design.

Staff members from Techno, my portfolio company that designed the treatment, are already in the back. Mom is sitting on an operating chair in a white hospital gown, with a plethora of cables attaching her to a myriad of cutting-edge monitoring tools. Completing her getup is a headset—something straight out of the old *Total Recall* movie. It must be the "latest in portable neural scan technology" that JC, Techno's CEO, mentioned to me. I make a mental note to define *portable* to him.

I hear a "hi" from the farthest corner of the room. The person who spoke must be hidden behind the wall of servers and giant monitors. The other Techno employees keep working silently, though it isn't clear whether they didn't hear me come in, or if they're being antisocial.

Many folks at Techno could stand to improve their social skills. A psychiatrist might even label some of them as borderline Asperger's. Personally, I find those types of labels ridiculous. Psychiatry can sometimes be as scientific and helpful as astrology—which I don't believe in, in case that's not clear. A shrink back in high school tried to attach the Asperger's label to me because I had "too few friends." He could've just as easily concluded I had Tourette's based on where I told him to shove his diagnosis. Then again, maybe I'm still sore about psychiatry and neuropsychology because of how little they've done for Mom. Pretty much the only good thing I can say about psychiatry is that at least they're no longer using lobotomy as a treatment.

I look around the room for JC. He's nowhere to be found, so he must be in a similar room with another participant of the study.

Mom turns her head toward us, apparently able to do so despite the headgear.

My heart clenches in dread, as it always does when Mom and I meet after more than a day apart. Because of the accident that damaged Mom's brain, it's feasible that one day she'll look at me and won't recognize who I am.

Today she clearly does, though, because she gives me that dimpled smile we share. "Hi, little fish," she says in Russian. She then looks at her brother. "Abrashkin, bunny, how are you?"

"Mom just used untranslatable Russian pet names for us," I loudly whisper to Ada and wave hello to the still-uninterested staff in the back.

Mom looks at Ada without recognition, and I inwardly sigh. They've met twice before.

"Who's this boy?" Mom asks me in English. "Is he an intern at Techno or something?"

"She's not a boy, and her name is Ada," I respond, trying my best not to sound like I'm talking to someone with a disability, something my mom deeply resents. "She's not an intern, but one of the people who programmed the nanocytes that'll make you feel better."

"Nice to meet you, Nina Davydovna," Ada says as though they haven't done this before.

Mom's eyebrow rises at either the girlish resonance of Ada's bell-like voice or her proper use of the Russian patronymic. She quickly recovers, though, just like the last time, and also like the last time, she says, "Call me Nina."

"I will. Thank you, Nina," Ada says.

I realize Ada addressed my mom so formally on purpose—to lessen Mom's stress—so I give her a grateful nod. Of course, if Ada wanted to go the extra mile, she could've worn different clothing or changed her hairstyle to eliminate Mom's confusion about Ada's gender. Then again, Mom's confusion might be part of her condition, because to me, despite the leather jacket and black hoodie obscuring much of her body, Ada is the epitome of femininity.

"Is she his girlfriend?" Mom asks Uncle Abe conspiratorially in Russian. "Have I met her before?"

"I'm not sure, sis," Uncle Abe says. "From the way he looks at her, I suspect it's just a matter of time before they hook up."

"Oh yeah?" Mom chuckles. "Do you think she's Jewish?"

Blood rushes to my cheeks, and not just because of this "Jewish or not" business. It's something that became important to Mom only after the accident—unless she's always cared but only started voicing it after the brain damage lowered her inhibitions. My grandparents certainly often spoke about this sort of thing, going as far as blaming the situation with my father on him being non-Jewish—something I consider to be reverse anti-Semitism.

It's unfortunate, but their attitude was forged back in the Soviet Union, where being Jewish was considered an ethnicity and used as an excuse for government-level discrimination. Since one's ethnicity was written in the infamous fifth paragraph of one's passport, discrimination was commonplace and inescapable. My mom was turned away from her first choice of universities because they'd hit "their quota of three Jews." She also had a hard time finding a job in the engineering sciences until my father helped her out, only to later sexually harass her and leave her to raise me on her own. Even I was affected by this negativity before we left. When my seventh-grade classmates learned about my heritage from our school journal, they told me that with my blue eyes and blond hair (which darkened to brown as I got older), I looked nothing like a Jew. Though they used the derogatory Russian term, they'd meant it as a big compliment.

What makes the topic extra weird is that in America, where Judaism is more of a religion than an ethnicity, we're suddenly not all that Jewish. I mean, how can we be if I learned about Hanukkah in my mid-teens and when I had a very non-kosher grilled lobster tail wrapped in bacon last night?

Yeah, I also learned what *kosher* means in my mid-teens.

Either way, I couldn't care less about Ada's Jewishness—though, for the record, with a last name like Goldblum, she probably is Jewish. I don't know what that term means to her either, since she's just as secular as I am. I think my biggest issue with Mom's question is that I simply loathe labels applied to entire groups of people, especially labels that come with so much baggage.

"It's hard to say," Uncle Abe says after examining Ada's dainty nose and zooming in on her pierced nostril. "With that hair, she's definitely not Russian."

Here we go, another label. To my grandparents, the term *Russian* was interchangeable with *goy* or *gentile*, but I don't think my uncle is using it in that context. Though in Russia we were Jewish, here in the US we're Russian—as in, the same as every Russian speaker from the former Soviet Union. I'm guessing my uncle is saying that Ada doesn't look like she's from the former Soviet Union, since a certain way of dressing and grooming typically accompanies that, at least for recent immigrants.

I decide to stop this thread of conversation, but before I get a chance to put a word in, Mom says, "When I was young, that kind of haircut was called an explosion at the noodle factory."

They both laugh, and even I can't help chuckling. I know the haircut Mom is referring to, and it's an eighties hairdo that may well be a distant ancestor to what's happening on Ada's head. The bleached, pointy tips make her look like an echidna with a Mohawk—an image reinforced by her prickly wit.

The door to the room opens, and a nurse walks in.

Seeing her scrubs raises my blood pressure, though I'm not sure if it's from the standard white coat syndrome or a flashback to my earlier nightmare. Probably the former. There was no anesthesia in Soviet dentistry when I was growing up, so I developed a conditioned response to anything resembling dentist clothing. Anyone in a white coat gives me a reaction akin to what someone suffering from coulrophobia— the irrational fear of clowns—would experience during a John Wayne Gacy documentary or the movie *It*.

The nurse walks over to Mom and reaches for a big syringe lying stealthily by Mom's chair.

The Techno employees in the back collectively hold their breaths.

The nurse doesn't seem to understand the auspiciousness of the occasion. She looks like she wants to finish here and move on to something more interesting, like watching a filibuster on C-SPAN. Her nametag reads "Olga." That, combined with her circa late-eighties haircut and makeup, plus those Slavic cheekbones, activates my Russian radar—or Rudar for short. It's like gaydar, but for detecting Russian speakers.

I bet Mom is insulted by the hospital assigning this nurse to her. It implies she needs help understanding English. Having earned a Bachelor of Science in

Electrical Engineering after moving to the States in her mid-thirties, Mom takes deserved pride in her skills with the English language—skills the accident didn't affect.

In the silence, I can hear Mom's shallow breathing; her fear of medical professionals is much worse than mine.

Olga grips the syringe and raises her hand.

———

Visit www.dimazales.com to learn more!

ABOUT THE AUTHOR

Dima Zales is a *New York Times* and *USA Today* bestselling author of science fiction and fantasy. Prior to becoming a writer, he worked in the software development industry in New York as both a programmer and an executive. From high-frequency trading software for big banks to mobile apps for popular magazines, Dima has done it all. In 2013, he left the software industry in order to concentrate on his writing career and moved to Palm Coast, Florida, where he currently resides.

Please visit www.dimazales.com to learn more.

www.ingramcontent.com/pod-product-compliance
Lightning Source LLC
Chambersburg PA
CBHW060621100726
47907CB00006B/1713